Praise for

MIDNIGHT CALLER

"Take a walk on the wild side with Rebecca York in a mind-bending tale of sizzling suspense and irresistible romance..."†

SHATTERED LULLABY

"Glick's [York's] prose is smooth, literate and fast-moving; her love scenes are tender yet erotic...what's not to like?"◊

"Chilling excitement...exquisitely tender romance... the very best in romantic suspense."†

NOWHERE MAN

"...a to-die-for hero, chilling suspense and an unforgettable love story."†

"...one of the most heart-wrenching, moving works of romantic suspense in years."*

FATHER AND CHILD

"...great, one-sitting romantic suspense that will keep readers on the edge of their seats from start to finish."*

FOR YOUR EYES ONLY

"Few write suspense like Rebecca York."‡

FACE TO FACE

"Harlequin's first lady of suspense...a marvelous storyteller, Ms. York cleverly develops an intricate plotted romance to challenge our imaginations and warm our hearts."†

PRINCE OF TIME

"Get ready for the time of your life.... Breathtaking excitement and exotic romance...in the most thrilling 43 Light Street adventure yet!"†

◊Michael Dirda, *The Washington Post Book World*
*Harriet Klausner, Amazon.com
†Melinda Helfer, *Romantic Times*
‡Debbie Richardson, *Romantic Times*

Dear Reader,

Harlequin Intrigue has given me the opportunity to write many stories where love triumphs over seemingly impossible odds. With Scott O'Donnell and Mariana Reyes, I had an especially strong challenge.

They met six years ago, when Scott was making a documentary film in San Marcos, the Central American country I created when I wrote *Till Death Us Do Part*. Mariana was from the country's wealthy minority, and her father had chosen a husband for her to ally two powerful families. So when she fell in love with Scott, she knew there could be no future for the two of them. And when government officials told her the only way she could save Scott's life was to help them arrest him, she had a terrible choice to make.

Now it's six years later, and desperate men throw Scott and Mariana together again—to uncover a secret from their past. Yet Mariana has another secret: the daughter she knows Scott won't believe is his.

Scott and Mariana's story brings powerful emotions to the surface, emotions that Scott is hardly prepared to acknowledge. It also brings back several of my favorite characters from previous 43 LIGHT STREET books, chiefly Jed and Marissa (Marci) Prentiss from *Till Death Us Do Part*.

In addition, you'll get to meet the sexy hero of my next 43 LIGHT STREET book, Matthew Forester. He's the new man at Randolph Security, and in *Amanda's Child* you'll get to see both the tough and tender sides of his personality when he comes to the rescue of Amanda Barnwell, a woman who needs his help more than she knows.

Best,

Ruth

Ruth Glick writing as Rebecca York

Rebecca York

NEVER TOO LATE

Ruth Glick writing as Rebecca York

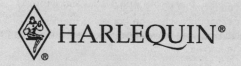

HARLEQUIN®

TORONTO • NEW YORK • LONDON
AMSTERDAM • PARIS • SYDNEY • HAMBURG
STOCKHOLM • ATHENS • TOKYO • MILAN • MADRID
PRAGUE • WARSAW • BUDAPEST • AUCKLAND

ISBN 0-373-22558-X

NEVER TOO LATE

Copyright © 2000 by Ruth Glick

This edition published by arrangement with Harlequin Books S.A.

® and TM are trademarks of the publisher. Trademarks indicated with
® are registered in the United States Patent and Trademark Office, the
Canadian Trade Marks Office and in other countries.

Visit us at www.romance.net

Printed in U.S.A.

Directory
4 3 L I G H T S T R E E T

	Room
ADVENTURES IN TRAVEL	204
ABIGAIL FRANKLIN, Ph.D. KATHRYN KELLEY, Ph.D. Clinical Psychology	509
BIRTH DATA, INC.	322
INNER HARBOR PRODUCTIONS	404
THE LIGHT STREET FOUNDATION	322
KATHRYN MARTIN-McQUADE, M.D. Branch Office, Medizone Labs	515
O'MALLEY & LANCER Detective Agency	518
LAURA ROSWELL, LL.B. Attorney at Law	311
SABRINA'S FANCY	Lobby
STRUCTURAL DESIGN GROUP	407
NOEL ZACHARIAS Paralegal Service	311
L. ROSSINI Superintendent	Lower Level

CAST OF CHARACTERS

Scott O'Donnell — Six years ago, his intentions toward Mariana were honorable. But fate tricked the two of them.

Mariana Reyes — Once she'd been forced to betray Scott. Now she vows she'll never lie to him again.

Alicia Reyes — Mariana's daughter was a pawn in the hands of men playing a dangerous game of politics and betrayal.

Jed Prentiss — He'd help Scott and Mariana if he could, but his options are limited.

Tía Susana — Mariana trusted her with her most precious possession, but was that trust misplaced?

Ed Thompson — Scott trusted him once. Had the shadowy figure from his past switched sides?

Hector Porfirio — To keep his wealth and power, he had to play his cards right.

Pepe Fortunato — Once he'd been Scott's assistant. Now he has his own agenda.

Bernardo Cortez — He'd been engaged to Mariana six years ago.

Pablo Omera — Was he simply an interfering government official throwing his weight around?

Chapter One

"The police are in town—asking questions about you."

Mariana Reyes froze in front of the old porcelain sink where she stood with her hands plunged to the elbows in hot, soapy water. "Are you sure they're police?" she asked, struggling to keep her voice steady.

"They have the uniforms. The guns."

Mariana nodded. Maybe they were police. Maybe they were impostors. But what did it matter? Word had reached her that Benito Lopez and three others were dead. And now the killers were coming for her.

She felt the coldness of fear sink into her bones. It was all starting again: the running, the hiding, the endless terror that was too much for any human being to endure. She didn't know how they'd found her. She only knew it was true.

In this high mountain village far from Santa Isabella where the air was cold and clear, she'd lulled herself into believing she was finally safe. For six months, she'd worked here as a teacher, made a home for herself. Yet all the time, in her soul, she'd waited for this moment to come.

The old woman behind her must have seen the defeated posture. "You have to go," she said. "Quickly. For the *niña*."

Mariana straightened and dragged in a steadying breath. "Yes, for Alicia," she said, knowing that she had to hold on to her sanity—for her daughter. Because the innocent child sleeping in the next room was the only thing that mattered.

Reaching for the coarse towel hanging from a hook beside the sink, she dried her hands. A long time ago, washing her own dishes would have been unthinkable for Mariana Reyes. She'd lived in a huge white house full of servants who'd washed and fetched and carried according to her whims. She'd taken it all for granted, unaware of how lucky she was—until the life she'd known had been snatched away.

She looked down at her rough red hands, wondering if that time had only been a dream.

"Eduardo is talking to them," the old woman said. "He knows what to do. He's sending them in the wrong direction to give you time to get away."

"I don't want him to be in trouble because of me."

The old woman laughed. "He won't. He knows how to act the fool when it's convenient. He's been doing it for years. Remember when your father used to get so angry with him when the oranges disappeared from the trees?"

A smile flickered on Mariana's lips. "Yes," she answered, even as she rounded the dark wooden table and headed for the little bedroom where her daughter slept. Alicia was curled under a bright wool blanket that the women of the village had woven—the kind they had woven for hundreds of years.

From the edge of the bed, she looked down at her child, seeing the long hair so different in color from her own. But the olive tones of their skin were the same, as were their dark lashes and high cheekbones.

Like her hair, Alicia's mouth was her father's—well-shaped, sensual, quick to break into a smile. Incredibly, her eyes were like his too. Not the dark brown of Mariana's own Spanish heritage, but an impossible sea green that grew dark with strong emotion.

For an endless moment she stood very still, fighting the stab of pain that always pierced her heart when she thought of the man she had no right to love. Then she stirred herself and began to move around the room, taking clothing from the shelves that lined the wall, pulling rough wool travel bags from under the bed. Her belongings were meager. Still, she couldn't take them all.

"Mama?"

The quavering voice stilled her hand. She hadn't wanted to wake Alicia. Not yet. Quickly she crossed to the bed and knelt at her daughter's side.

Alicia sat up, looking from the empty shelves to the bags. "Are we leaving in the night? Like the last time?"

"Yes," she whispered, hating the admission, hating the knowledge that her five-year-old daughter already possessed the wisdom of a hardened fugitive. "I've put out clothes. Can you get yourself dressed while I make some arrangements with Tía Susana?"

"I'm a big girl."

"I know." Mariana managed a smile, then returned to the only other room in the cinder-block cottage.

The old woman was waiting. "I've packed some food. You can go in the truck that's taking produce to the market on the other side of the mountain."

"Please, you've done enough."

"No. Not for you." Susana hesitated. "Will you take some advice?"

"Always."

"Write the letter. The one you should have written years ago."

Mariana felt her heart stop, then start again in double time. "I...can't."

"You must. This time, my child, you must swallow your pride."

"I—"

"Don't tell me no. Tell me you want to save your own life and the life of your child."

She gave a tight nod, then whirled away. Before returning

to the bedroom, she dried her clammy palms on her skirt and tried to wipe the look of sick panic off her face.

IN THE 43 LIGHT STREET OFFICES of Inner Harbor Productions, Scott O'Donnell hunched over the video-editing machine, his heart thumping in his chest as he watched the camera pan from low, gnarled trees where finches had built their nests to dark lava rock crusted with sea moss.

In itself, there was nothing threatening about the landscape. It was a desolate, wild scene—the essence of Fernandina Island in the Galápagos. The threat was in his memories.

Stepping out on the deck of the large cabin cruiser that first morning a month ago, he'd smelled the salt tang of the air, listened to the waves pounding on the stark black cliffs and seen the seabirds wheeling in the impossibly blue sky. As he'd stood there, raw, elemental memories of another place—San Marcos—had come flooding back, and he'd wanted to escape.

But he'd signed a contract with Maryland Public Television to film the unique wildlife of the islands, and his personal code demanded that he fulfill his obligations. So he'd prowled the rocky landscape, shooting buff-colored iguanas chomping cactus blossoms and sea lions lounging in the sun—all the while trying to shut out vivid recollections of passion and betrayal.

He'd come back to Baltimore as quickly as possible, knowing in his gut that he hadn't given the assignment his best. And he still wasn't. Because every time he sat down at the editing machine, the old anger and longing came pressing in more closely, making him feel as if he were being sucked into the past, crowded into a space so small that it was impossible to breathe.

Fighting the awful conviction that history was about to repeat itself, he'd flee the Light Street office and prowl the streets of Baltimore. Although the fresh air would sweep away the strangling sensations, it would take hours before he could go back to the cramped confines of the office.

He hadn't told anyone what was happening to him, not even Jessica Adams, who'd founded Inner Harbor Productions and taken him on as a partner after her marriage and motherhood had slowed her career for a few years. He'd been avoiding her for weeks, slipping into the office at night or on weekends when she was at home with her family.

But he knew he couldn't go on like this, knew that something had to change before he went over the edge. So it was with a strange mixture of shock and acceptance that he looked up from the editing machine to find a man he'd hoped never to see again standing in the doorway.

Scott blinked, wondering if he had finally lost it. But the image failed to evaporate in the heat of his fixed gaze.

It was Ed Thompson, with a few more gray hairs and a little more bulk around the middle, but with the same hard muscles and the same dark and cynical eyes. Thompson was a man who could kill as easily as he could down a shot of bourbon. Was that why he'd come here tonight?

They stared at each other in silence, until Scott decided to get it over with. Clearing his throat, he asked, "To what do I owe the pleasure?"

"We're calling in our debt."

Scott kept his gaze steady, suddenly glad that he'd prepared for this moment—at the gym, the firing range, the fencing court, and a dozen other venues where he'd shaped his body and mind into a defensive machine. He could take Thompson. Or at least he had a fighting chance. Although now that the moment had come, he silently acknowledged that beating the man senseless wouldn't solve anything. Because removing Thompson wasn't the issue. Someone else would take his place, and someone else after that.

"You still cleaning up other people's messes?" Scott asked conversationally.

"The pay is good."

Scott eyed the custom-tailored suit. "I'll bet."

"There's someone downstairs in the car who wants to talk to you."

"The Easter Bunny?"

"It's a few months early for that," Thompson answered without missing a beat.

"Yeah." Scott stood, stretched, reached for his coat, then waited to see if Thompson was willing to precede him down the hall to the elevator. A good sign, he thought, as the other man took the lead. At least he wasn't going to get shot in the back.

They didn't stop at the first floor. Instead, his escort ushered him to the basement and out the service door to the alley where a black Lexus with tinted windows waited.

Thompson opened the back door, and Scott slid onto the deeply padded leather seat. Another man sat behind the wheel, his image obscured by the dark glass of an interior window. He was broad-shouldered, probably tall, judging by the distance of his head from the ceiling of the luxury car. There wasn't much more that Scott could catalog, since the driver wore a hat pulled low over his eyes and a scarf that covered the bottom half of his face.

Obviously he didn't want to be recognized. So why had he come?

The question wafted through Scott's mind like a cloud drifting across a winter sky. It wasn't until Thompson climbed into the back seat with him and slammed the door that the claustrophobia kicked in, and he realized that the setup had been deliberate, to put him at as much of a disadvantage as possible. To remind him of the way he'd felt in a tiny San Marcos prison cell six years ago before Thompson had sprung him. He'd been grateful to be rescued. In the years since, he'd had plenty of time to contemplate what payment might be due.

The car jerked away from the curb, telling him that the driver was as off balance as Scott.

Maybe that was good news. Maybe not.

As they turned left onto Light Street, then left again, heading toward the shopping pavilions along the harbor, Scott concentrated on taking slow, deep breaths. By the time they passed the old power plant that had been renovated yet again into a trendy mix of restaurants, shops and virtual-reality amusement arcades, he had conquered the need to roll down the window and thrust his face into the cold wind.

Easing back into the padded upholstery, he glanced toward the rearview mirror and caught sharp eyes assessing him, gauging strengths and weaknesses.

Lifting his chin, Scott returned the scrutiny until the driver flicked his gaze back to the traffic.

Not until they were several blocks from the bright lights of the Inner Harbor did the man speak. But his voice was intentionally distorted by a sound-system broadcasting from the front compartment of the car to the rear.

"We'd like you to handle a delicate situation for us," he said with the casual authority of someone used to having his wishes translated into action. He sounded like a general, or maybe the head of a major corporation.

Scott sat there with his hands clasped loosely in his lap, feeling strangely detached as he waited for more information.

"There's a plane arriving at the Miami airport tomorrow at 8:30 p.m. Flight 231 from Santa Isabella in San Marcos. We'd like you to escort one of the passengers to Washington for a debriefing."

"You've picked the wrong guy," he answered evenly. He'd thought he was prepared for anything when he saw Thompson standing in the doorway, but this request was the last thing he'd expected.

"On the contrary. You're perfect for the job," the man behind the wheel answered. "You know the country. You know the political situation. You've got an excellent command of Spanish."

"My Spanish is a little rusty."

"You used it fluently in the Galápagos last month."

"You were keeping tabs on me?"

The only answer was a small shrug from Thompson.

"Are we talking about a political refugee?" Scott asked, taking another tack.

"It's a national-security issue. I can't tell you."

Scott snorted. "National security. Is this an official request from the U.S. government?"

The driver was silent for a moment, then opened his right hand as if offering an invisible present. "It's not official. That's why we've come to you. The individual arriving tomorrow has some dirt on your friend General Sanchez, the man you'd like to see strung up on a post in front of the President's Palace."

Despite his resolve to remain cool, Scott felt a knot forming in his chest. It was Sanchez who'd ordered him apprehended and thrown into a jail cell six years ago—Sanchez who'd ordered his torture squad to get information out of him that he didn't possess. But that was a lifetime ago.

"As far as I know El Jefe has been in Colorado Province for the past few years, reduced to running a mining operation for the Department of the Interior. People have forgotten about him."

"Things can change rapidly in a republic like San Marcos."

Scott understood the truth of the statement. Like many nations with a great disparity between the rich and poor, San Marcos was a volatile country where political power was as much a matter of calling in favors and eliminating enemies as getting votes.

"Tell me a little more about it," he demanded.

"We're giving you a chance to pay the general back for the inconvenience he caused you. But you can get it from the horse's mouth in Miami. At eight-thirty tomorrow evening."

The window between the front and back seats slid down

several inches, and the driver pushed a folded piece of paper through the opening.

Scott waited a beat, then reached for it. Inside it said:

Room 130
Terminal C
Miami International Airport. 8:50 p.m.

"You're giving me less than a day to make arrangements," Scott said. "I'm in the middle of editing some footage I shot in the Galápagos."

"This won't take more than twenty-four hours of your time. And getting to Miami is no problem. There are plenty of flights."

Scott stared at the man driving the car, at the rigid set of his shoulders, at the way his hands were clamped to the steering wheel. He looked as if a lot was riding on this conversation. Was the man telling the truth about this assignment? The whole truth? Or were there hidden layers to the story—layers he could only uncover by showing up in Miami tomorrow?

MARIANA DELIBERATELY loosened her death grip on the strap of her travel bag as she waited behind the yellow line at the immigration counter. She'd only been to the U.S. once before—with her family. In fact, she'd come through this same airport as a ten-year-old on her way to enjoy the wonders of south Florida and Walt Disney World.

But that was when her rich and powerful father, Constantino Reyes, had walked the earth like the king his name proclaimed him to be. His power to protect her had evaporated six years ago with his untimely death. And perhaps he wouldn't have chosen to aid his only daughter if he were still alive, she thought with a shiver as she remembered the pain and anger in his eyes when she'd told him why she couldn't marry Bernardo Cortez, the man he'd selected as her husband.

Well, all that had happened a long time ago. She'd survived her father's wrath—and a lot more.

Now she waited with the other passengers from Santa Isabella for clearance to enter the United States.

When the man in line ahead of her was passed on to the customs area, she swallowed and stepped up to the counter, surrendering her customs declaration, immigration form and the passport with her picture and the name of a woman named Maria Ramon.

The immigration official studied her picture, flicked his eyes toward her face, then ran his finger down a list of names on a white sheet of paper. When the moving hand stopped, she froze. Yet she tried to look casual, unconcerned.

"Your name is Maria Ramon?" he asked in Spanish, glancing from the sheet to her passport.

"Yes," she answered in English, trying to keep her voice steady and her pronunciation accurate. Her father had sent her to a private school where English lessons were part of the curriculum. And she'd continued the subject at university. But it had been years since she'd needed to use the language, and her skills were rusty.

"You are a native of San Marcos?"

Again she answered in the affirmative, sure that she had already been at the counter longer than anyone else ahead of her in line.

"The purpose of your visit?"

"*Turista,*" she said, realizing that stress had sent her slipping back into her native tongue.

"How long will you be staying in this country?"

"Only a few days," she answered, thinking that was what she'd promised Alicia when she'd left her in the care of Tía Susana.

"Hmm." He rubbed his thumb and finger over his chin, and her eyes followed the movement. "Well, I'm going to ask you to step over there." He pointed toward a door where several uniformed guards stood.

"Why?" she asked, unable to keep a tiny catch out of her voice.

"A random check."

"Oh." A random check. What did that mean, exactly?

Looking over his shoulder, he glanced at one of the guards, who moved forward.

"Please show Ms. Ramon to one of the offices," he said, giving the man her passport.

"I—" She didn't know what she intended to say, but she could see that everybody still waiting to clear immigration was watching the little drama with interest. *Dios,* she'd hoped to slip quietly into the country. She'd been on American soil less than twenty minutes, and it felt as if things were already going terribly wrong. She wanted to make a dash through the door to freedom where the other passengers from flight 231 were rapidly disappearing, but she knew she wouldn't get very far.

"Bring your luggage," the guard ordered.

She didn't remember setting down her travel bag. But now it was on the floor by her feet. Bending stiffly to pick it up, she hoisted the strap over her shoulder again and let the man escort her away from the rest of the group.

The moment the door closed behind her, hiding her from view, she felt a subtle shift in the atmosphere.

"This way," her escort clipped out, leading her down a short corridor and through another door into an office with dull gray walls and a dull gray desk with a messy pile of paper and a small lamp. The carpeting was stained, and a hint of disinfectant reached her nose.

"Sit down."

It wasn't a polite offer; it was an order, and she sank into an uncomfortable chair with a flat seat and metal arms.

The guard stood by the door through which they'd entered,

regarding her with eyes that seemed to pierce her simple navy dress.

He didn't speak, and she forced herself to sit quietly with her hands folded in her lap as she looked around the room. There was another door behind the desk. But no windows, no pictures on the walls, nothing to set the room apart from any other. Yet the very impersonality of the area added to her feeling of dread. This was not a place where pleasant things happened.

The corridor had been air-conditioned. In here, the atmosphere was hot and stuffy, with an oxygen level so low that she couldn't fill her lungs, even when she took a deep breath.

When the man's silence became unbearable, she asked, "Why was I brought in here?"

"We've received information that a major drug shipment is coming into the country from San Marcos. Your description matches that of one of the couriers."

"That's impossible!" she managed to say around the sudden constriction in her throat. "I'd never get involved with something like that."

"Sometimes we make mistakes," he said, his tone implying that he didn't think so this time.

"Please, I haven't done anything wrong."

"Is there anything you want to tell me?" he asked softly, making the subtle suggestion that confession was to her advantage.

She hadn't been to confession in years. And there was nothing she could confide that would do either one of them any good, so she simply shrugged.

He set her travel bag on the desk, riffled through the contents, pulling out clothing and giving each item a good shake as if he expected packets of drugs to come tumbling out. When he turned a pair of panties inside out, she looked down at her hands, refusing to let him see how badly he was frightening her.

She suspected that the effort at composure was wasted.

Probably he knew that she was sitting there with her heart pounding like a drum inside her chest. Probably he was waiting to see how long it would take to make her crack.

When he finished with the contents of the travel bag, he turned the whole thing inside out and examined the lining and the seams. Then he attacked her purse with equal vigor.

When he found nothing, she let out a little sigh, thankful that nobody had planted drugs on her at the airport in San Marcos.

"I told you this was a mistake," she blurted. "I'm not bringing anything illegal into the country."

"I'm afraid we're not finished," he said. "We're going to have to do a strip search."

"No!" She cringed from him, seeing from his eyes that he was enjoying her reaction.

"You don't have much choice. I'll send in a matron to supervise the procedure."

Her mouth went dry. As she moistened her lips to voice a protest, he left the room, locking the door behind him; and she sagged in the chair, blinking back moisture, wondering how everything had gone so terribly wrong. She'd been careful about buying the ticket—and the passport. She'd thought no one had gotten wind of her desperate journey to the U.S. But then why was she being detained like this? Could it really be a terrible coincidence?

The handle on the other door— the one in back of the desk—rattled as if someone was having trouble working the lock. The sound grated in her ears, focused her attention.

The knob turned, and the door swung inward.

Mariana gasped, then rubbed her eyes to clear her vision as she took in the sight of a ghost from her past standing in the doorway.

It couldn't be. It was impossible, she told herself as she stared at his dark red hair that was cut just a little longer than she remembered, at his green eyes that were exactly the same. No, not the same. Six years ago they'd been warm and laughing. Now they were cold and unsmiling.

Like her, he had gone stock-still, the look on his face one of total shock. It was clear he was as dumbstruck as she.

Somehow she got her voice to work. "Scott," she said. "What are you doing here?"

Chapter Two

Scott felt the breath freeze in his lungs. He couldn't speak, couldn't have answered even if he had wanted to. If he could have moved from the place where he stood, he would have backed out the door. But every muscle in his body had gone rigid.

He stood where he was, his eyes focused on the woman in the chair. Mariana Reyes. She appeared the same, yet different.

Six years ago she'd looked so innocent, so trusting. The innocence was gone now, replaced by a tightness around her mouth that spoke of hard times—or fear.

Was she afraid of him? She should be. She should know that this moment would be the most dangerous of her life.

Maybe she did, because she stared at him as if he had dropped from an attack helicopter. Yet she remained facing him. And as he studied her with counterfeit coolness, she sat quietly with her hands in her lap. She'd been like that, he remembered. Prepared for every situation, and too proud for her own good.

She'd pretended the sexual attraction crackling between them didn't exist, and he'd accepted the challenge of breaking through the barrier of rank and status that surrounded her. Back then, he'd been too sure of himself for his own good. He'd gone after her—then given her his heart. And then he would have died defending her honor.

Her head moved, just a fraction, enough to draw his attention to the long hair that fell over her shoulders. It was exactly the same, slightly wavy and so dark that it was almost black. He remembered the feel of it, remembered running his hands possessively through the strands, marveling at the feel of dark silk against his fingers.

His gaze moved naturally from her hair to her face. Her olive skin still had the smoothness of youth. How old was she now? Twenty-five?

Incredible. Even now, she was still so young, but no longer with the innocence of one who drifted through life finding door after door open to her. Now there were dark smudges under her eyes that might come from sleepless nights.

Probably he was making up that last part to satisfy some inner need of his own. He wanted her to be as unsettled as he, as disappointed with the way life had turned out. Had she lived through a series of small disappointments, small shocks to the orderly tenor of her existence? Or were her problems of more consequence?

Something stirred within him—something he didn't want to acknowledge. Compassion had no place in this room, or in his heart.

He needed to feel nothing but anger toward her. Hanging on to the anger was all that allowed him to speak.

"What are *you* doing here?" he asked with a sharpness that told her he was the one in charge.

The question released them both. He found that his muscles would work, after all. And as he rolled his shoulders to ease the tightness, he saw her reach to curl a lock of dark hair around her finger, the old habit betraying her tension.

"I came to meet somebody," she said, shifting slightly in her seat.

Because he spoke to her, he had asked the question in Spanish, and she answered in the same tongue, another link that threatened to swamp him with visions of the past they had shared a lifetime ago in San Marcos.

"Were you expecting me?" he asked brusquely.

"No."

To his astonishment, the denial sent an almost palpable disappointment shuddering through him. Harshly, he pulled himself up short. He had vowed he'd never be in this situation again, yet here he was, making the same mistakes he'd made the first time around.

His fingers dug into the door frame as he held himself in place.

"Scott, I—"

This time, the note of apology in her voice freed him. What was he thinking? That she was sorry about what she'd done to him?

"No. Don't say anything else," he warned her, the edict as much for himself as for her. He didn't know what she was doing in that room, and he didn't want to know the answer to that question, or any other question that pertained to her.

Before he got sucked further into the conversation, he took a step back, carefully pulling the door shut as he escaped into the empty corridor and dragged in a deep breath of chilled air.

It was ten degrees colder in the hallway, and he felt a shiver travel across his skin. Turning, he glanced over his shoulder at the door to room 130, hardly able to believe that his mind wasn't playing tricks. The cold air brought a degree of sanity. Was Mariana Reyes really sitting in an office on the other side of that door?

More important, was *she* the person he'd been sent here to meet?

In his mind he played back the conversation with the man in the car the night before. At the time, his wording hadn't seemed strange. Now Scott wondered if the precise use of language had been intentional. He was to meet someone from San Marcos at this location in the airport. All along he'd assumed it was a man, because the words *she* and *her* had never been used. Deliberately.

The driver of the car had known Scott's attitude toward Mariana Reyes and must have concluded that he would never agree to meet her, even if she did have information about Sanchez. Because when you were dealing with a woman like Mariana, there were no guarantees that what she said had any relationship to reality, even if the look on her face tonight suggested that this time, she was the one in trouble.

It was difficult to think about all that coherently, perhaps because his emotions were on overload. But his instincts were still in perfect working order, and they told him that this whole thing was out of kilter.

Fighting a new sense of uneasiness, he looked up and down the corridor. It was completely empty, not improbable at this hour in the evening when the day staff would have gone home. Yet there was an eerie, hollow quality to the setting, to the echo of his footsteps on the polished tile.

He had taken several steps down the hall, when the sound of a woman's scream stopped him dead.

Mariana.

Despite everything he'd told himself, there was no conscious decision-making process involved. The minute he knew she was in trouble, he spun on his heel, reversed direction and charged back the way he'd come. The door handle stuck again, and he gave it a savage twist.

Beyond the door, an angry male voice demanded, "Where is he?"

"Gone," Mariana wheezed.

Her strangled explanation was followed by a loud male curse and the sound of a palm striking flesh.

Mariana screamed again.

Frantically, Scott twisted the knob. It had been stiff before; now it was locked.

Lifting his foot, he battered the door, kicking repeatedly until the lock gave and the door swung open. It took several seconds for his brain to process the startling scene that confronted him. Mariana was bent backward over the desk, and a large man with a shaved skull and black clothing was looming over her. One of his hands pressed her onto the desk, the other was drawn back to deliver a ringing slap to her face.

Scott saw Mariana's hand scrabbling frantically over the desk. When her fingers found the desk lamp, they curled around the base. Even as she brought the heavy object toward the man's shiny head, Scott was already leaping forward. The lamp connected with flesh and bone seconds before he grabbed the man's shoulders and hoisted him into the air, sending him flying into the wall. He crashed against the wall, slid down and landed in a heap on the floor, his head sagging to one side, a red gash already welling on his skull.

On a sob, Mariana pushed herself up from the desk.

"What the hell is going on here?" Scott demanded, advancing on the man who was doubled over.

Mariana answered. "He came in." She gestured toward the other entrance to the room, sucked in a strangled breath. "He locked the doors. Then…he…grabbed me. I was—"

Before she could finish the answer, the man pushed his back more firmly against the wall. Two paces from him, Scott saw his hand sliding to the black-clad hip, saw the gun in the holster. Acting instinctively, he lashed out with his foot, catching the man's gun hand before the weapon could emerge from the holster. The man screamed, and screamed again as Scott landed a solid wallop to the lantern jaw. This time the guy went down for the count.

Scott stared at him. Where had this thug come from? Was he supposed to be airport security? But since when did airport security dress like ninja assassins?

The knob rattled on the other door—the one that was still locked.

"What's going in there?" a gruff male voice called out.

Scott's eyes shot to Mariana, seeking the same information. She still looked dazed, and under the circumstances, he couldn't blame her.

"Open the door!" the voice demanded.

And then what?

Scott backed away, trying to keep some kind of hold on logical thought. His attempt at rationality was crowded out by images of guards bursting through the door, grabbing him, hustling him into a cell before he could explain that he was only an innocent bystander.

Or was he? He didn't know the answer anymore. All he knew was that the thought of a metal door clanging closed behind him made invisible fingers close around his throat.

It didn't do any good to remind himself that this was different from six years ago in San Marcos. This was the United States of America where prisoners had rights, where you were innocent until proven guilty, where torture was against the law. None of that mattered now. All he could think was that the horror from his past was rising up to grab him by the throat again. Only this time, Mariana was with him. And he couldn't let anybody do to her what they'd done to him.

He whirled, locked his hand with hers. "Come on!"

"Where?" she gasped.

"I don't know. Away."

Behind him someone was heaving a shoulder against the door. Scott charged through the other exit, all but dragging Mariana behind him. They hit the hall, and he started running, forcing her to keep up with him.

"Wait. I—"

"Come on!" he called as he heard what sounded like the office door crashing inward. Seconds later, he heard footsteps pounding after them.

"Stop!"

Any inclination toward obeying were wiped away by the sound of a bullet whistling by his head.

Swearing, he dodged to the side, pulling Mariana around the corner into another long hallway lined with doors. Blocking the center was a bright yellow wooden sawhorse that hadn't been there when he'd come that way a few minutes earlier.

He kicked it aside, then took the chance of sprinting several more yards down the hall before pulling Mariana through one of the doors and locking it behind them. In the dim light, he saw that they were in a large room lined with rows of metal lockers, apparently where employees changed from street clothes into uniforms.

At least the lockers would provide some cover, he thought as he quickly inspected the area. Even better, he spotted another exit at the end of the room.

From the hall he heard a door open and knew the man with the gun was checking every option.

Good. Maybe that would give them a couple of minutes.

As he worked his way down the room, he tried several lockers until he found a blue jacket. A matching cap was sitting on a wooden bench, and he shoved that on his head. Without questioning him, Mariana opened more lockers, finding another jacket, which was several sizes too large.

Behind them the pursuer rattled on the doorknob.

Time to go.

Scott pointed toward the far exit. Mariana followed, and they stepped into another small office.

For a terrible moment, he thought they were trapped, until he focused on the exterior wall and saw a bank of casement windows wet with rain.

Even as he lunged for the nearest window, Mariana was locking the door behind them. By the time she moved to his side, he'd swung the pane open—and broken through the screen with his foot.

Outside, in the cone of illumination from an overhead floodlight, he saw that a sudden tropical downpour was dumping buckets of rain on the airport.

So much the better.

He helped Mariana through the window, and they stood

for a moment under the protection of the roof while he got his bearings.

They were in a broad, paved area where planes taxied to the boarding gates and maintenance crews loaded luggage, refueled, and reprovisioned the passenger sections.

Several domestic jets loomed in the darkness, rain sluicing down their huge metal bodies. A cartful of wet luggage rattled past, followed by a fuel truck.

With Mariana in tow, Scott slipped through the rain, winding his way among the vehicles and circling a jumbo jet. In two minutes he was soaked to the skin, even with the protection of the blue jacket.

"Hey, what are you doing here?" a man dressed in a yellow slicker called, pitching his voice to carry above the downpour.

"Surprise inspection tour," Scott answered without missing a beat. "You guys are gonna get a reprimand on security practices," he added, reaching in his pocket and whipping out his wallet. He flipped it open and flashed it at the guy as if it contained credentials of some sort, then stuffed it back into the pocket and kept weaving his way through the maze of vehicles. Mariana followed.

Hopefully, they were out of sight now. He allowed himself a glance at her. He might have asked himself why he was taking her with him, when escape was more certain on his own. But he dared not frame the question as he ducked around another luggage truck and almost plowed into a blue van. The lights were on, and exhaust wafted from the tailpipe.

He couldn't believe their luck. He opened the door, hoisted Mariana inside and ran around to the driver's side. Glancing into the back, he saw stacks of magazines and newspapers. Too bad. Some passengers were going to miss their *Miami Heralds*.

Throwing the vehicle into reverse, he backed away from the plane, then continued toward the end of the building.

Above the noise of the rain, he thought he heard somebody shouting at him to stop, but he ignored the command.

"Where are we going?" Mariana whispered, pushing wet hair away from her face.

"Montana," he growled as he slammed into first gear and maneuvered around a plane. When he reached the end of the building, he half expected to plow into a police barricade, but the lane was clear.

Decision time came when they reached a driveway that led to the parking area. He could pull into the garage, ditch the van and try to find another vehicle. The idea had merit, since someone might already be looking for their stolen transportation. But the van had no logo or lettering on the side, and chances were, the driver hadn't memorized the license number.

In some part of his mind, he was standing back, watching himself make life-and-death decisions. But he'd known from the moment they'd almost been shot in the back that surrender was not an option, at least not until he figured out what the hell was going on.

So he kept driving along the access road, merging into the flow of vacationers and hotel shuttle buses, moving to the middle lane where he felt less exposed. He let the traffic flow carry him out of the airport, following signs to downtown Miami.

The radio was playing a golden oldie—a slow fifties tune about young love, adding another layer of surrealism to the scene. His eyes flicked to Mariana, symbol of his youthful folly. Fresh as a spray of apple blossoms. At least that was the way she'd looked to him when he was under her spell. Now her luxuriant mass of hair hung limply around her shoulders, her clothing was plastered to her body, and water dripped from her skirt to the floor of the van.

When he raised his gaze to her face, he saw her eyes were huge and dark as they regarded him with something between admiration and shock.

He waited for her to speak, but she only wrapped her arms around her shoulders and hunched forward slightly. They rode in silence for several miles until he decided that she wasn't going to volunteer anything.

"Are you ready to tell me what's going on?" he finally growled as he changed lanes and took the first available exit, trying to dredge up his skimpy knowledge of the Miami area.

Mariana pushed herself up straighter, staring through the window into the darkness. "I don't know."

"You don't know why that guy was slapping you around?"

Gingerly, she raised her hand and touched the red spot that still marred her right cheek.

He watched the movement, noted the way she barely grazed the surface of her skin. "Are you okay?" he asked, hearing the thickness in his own voice.

"Sí." She answered automatically, although he was sure it wasn't true.

Lowering her hand, she twined the fingers in her lap, staring down in another gesture that he remembered very well. She was composing herself, trying to think of what to say. But he wasn't going to give her enough time to make up some cock-and-bull story.

"What did baldy want?" he demanded.

She glanced up again. "He was looking for you. When he didn't find you in the room, he got angry."

"I don't believe that. Nobody knew I was coming to the airport except—"

"Who?"

He didn't owe her an explanation, but he muttered, "I was asked to meet a passenger arriving from San Marcos. Escort the individual to D.C. I wasn't expecting you."

She took a hitching breath. "That makes both of us."

"Okay, let's try another approach. Why are you in Miami?" he asked, determined to get an answer he could trust. Or at least something that made sense.

"I came in on a flight from Santa Isabella."

"Which flight?"

"Two thirty-one."

The plane he was supposed to meet. But how many flights a day could there be from a small Central American country like San Marcos?

"Okay. So you entered the terminal. Then what?" he prompted, dividing his attention between her and the road.

"In Immigration, all of the passengers were moving right through. But they stopped me. They took me to that office and told me they thought I was carrying drugs. I—" She looked at him and pressed her hand to her mouth.

"What?"

"They still have my passport. And everything else." She gave him a panicked look.

He answered with a tight nod. That was a problem, all right. "Then they know who you are."

"No. I was traveling under a…a false name."

"Why?" he pressed, keeping the questions coming.

"Because I didn't want anyone to be able to track me," she murmured.

"Sure. That makes perfect sense." He sighed. "Maybe we'd better start with—was this whole thing a setup? Were you sent here to trap me into something?" His chest tightened as he waited for her to speak, not sure if he was capable of believing anything she said, yet hanging on the answer.

"No. I swear it. I told you, I didn't even know you would be at the airport."

He took his eyes from the road again, studying her intently before turning his attention back to the traffic. If he had to make a judgment call, he'd say she was telling the truth. Yet he knew his judgment had never exactly functioned at peak efficiency when it came to her.

"A lot of things have happened since I saw you last," she said in a barely audible voice.

"Such as?"

She closed her eyes, and he saw her lower lip quiver. Before she could work up the nerve to get out whatever it was she wanted to say, the music on the radio cut off in midsong, replaced by an excited voice.

"We interrupt this program with a late-breaking news bulletin," an announcer said. "According to unidentified sources at the Miami airport, a terrorist attack has been reported there. Details are sketchy, but we have been told that shots were fired and that an unidentified man and woman are reported to have left the airport vicinity in a stolen van. No description of the couple or the vehicle is available at this time. However, the fugitives are armed and considered dangerous."

Chapter Three

Mariana turned huge, dark eyes toward Scott. "They can't be talking about us, can they?" she asked in a strangled voice. "I mean, we didn't do anything besides try to...to keep from getting hurt."

His answer was a sharp, dismissive noise. "Yeah, I think they are talking about us. It fits the pattern."

"What pattern?"

He shrugged. "Call it Alice in Wonderland. Or maybe, Big Brother Is Manipulating You."

"But how can that happen in *los Estados Unidos?*" she asked slowly, trying to understand what he meant.

"If the stakes are high enough, a lot of things can happen."

"We aren't armed. Are we?" she pressed.

He shook his head. "I wish. But tell that to the SWAT team."

She sucked in a stabbing breath. "You mean the men with rifles who...who shoot first and ask questions later?"

"Yeah." He turned from a four-lane highway onto a side street where the houses were fading stucco, the front lawns were patches of dirt, and more pickups than cars were parked at the curb. Not at all the kind of neighborhood she'd expected to see in America.

Pulling under what looked like an acacia tree, he cut the

engine. The rain had stopped, but fat drops of water fell from branches and leaves, plopping onto the windshield, along with a few orange blossoms.

Mariana stared at the trails of water, then murmured, "Nothing's changed."

"What's that supposed to mean?" he challenged.

"I came here from San Marcos because people have been killed. I thought it would be different here."

"Who exactly is getting killed?" he asked sharply.

"People connected with General Sanchez. Benito Lopez. Pepito Hidalgo. Manuel Ruiz. Do those names mean anything to you?"

"No." She saw his hands tighten on the wheel. "Were *you* connected with Sanchez?" he asked, his voice strangely controlled.

She couldn't look at Scott. "I…knew some things about him," she whispered.

He put his hand under her chin, turned her face so that she was forced to meet his angry green eyes. Somehow she knew what was coming, and her whole body tensed.

"Did you know when you planted those military maps in my apartment that I was going to be thrown into jail?" he rasped.

She had lied to him all those years ago. She had told herself that if she ever saw him again, she would tell the truth—no matter what it cost her. Yet it was so hard to force the syllable past her parched lips. *"Sí."*

His hand dropped away, breaking the contact with her flesh. "Why?" he said tightly.

"They told me they wanted you out of the country. They said that if I helped them get you deported, that would be the end of it."

"And who were 'they,' exactly?"

"Men. They said they were from the government," she said, hearing the thinness of her own voice.

So many times, in the dark hours of the night, she had

imagined this confrontation. She'd pictured herself telling him the secrets that weighed on her heart like stones. In her imagination, it had always been the old Scott she had talked to—the man she'd known. The man she'd fallen in love with. But now she understood that man had died long ago—in a San Marcos prison.

The Scott O'Donnell sitting in this stolen van with her was somebody different. Not simply older. Harder. Angry at her for what she'd done to him. He had every right to be angry. Yet she hadn't dared imagine the mask of bitterness that tightened the muscles of his face.

That uncompromising look made her want to close her eyes, or turn away. Somehow she managed to sit there unblinking, hoping she could make him understand how it had been for her when she'd been so young and scared.

"Scott, you don't know what it can be like in San Marcos. People disappear or turn up dead. Even now. It's still happening. Like the men I just told you about. But back then it was worse. The government men told me either they were going to kill you, or they were going to get you out of the country, and I believed them. They *made* me believe.

"A nice story."

"It's the truth."

"Why didn't you come to me, let me protect both of us?"

"I was afraid," she said in a small voice, knowing that she hadn't really made him understand. "And I guess I didn't think you had any more chance against them than I did."

Instead of replying, he turned toward the window and stared into the darkness. When she put her hand on his arm, she felt his muscles tense.

"Scott, what did they do to you...when they had you in custody?"

He kept his face turned away from her. "They wanted information that I didn't have. Which was pretty inconvenient for me," he said in a clipped tone.

He didn't elaborate. But the implications of his words tore

at her heart, at her soul. "Please believe me. I didn't know anything bad would happen. I'm sorry." She swallowed.

He let the apology hang in the air between them, then reached for the door handle and pushed it open. "I'll be back in a few minutes."

She wanted to tell him that she wasn't finished, that she needed to unburden herself of another secret. Instead she let him climb out of the van. He moved down the block, and she lost sight of him as he rounded the corner.

He hadn't told her where he was going or what he was doing. She simply waited for him to return, feeling the seconds tick by, then minutes—or perhaps it was centuries.

He said he'd be back, but was he telling the truth? If he left her here, what would she do? Where would she go?

Her passport was in the hands of the men who had detained her at the airport. Thank the Lord she'd been smart enough to put a few things into the money belt around her waist.

Through her wet dress, she pressed her fingers against the leather pouch and breathed out a little sigh when she felt that it was still in place. Inside were pictures of Alicia, the phone number of the man she was supposed to contact, and some American dollars. Not enough to get her very far in a country where the currency was worth twenty times what the San Marcos peso brought on the world market.

Leaning her head back, she tried to stay calm, tried not to think about what would happen if the police arrested her and charged her with terrorism.

If Scott didn't come back, she'd have to leave, without telling him what had happened after he left San Marcos. *Dios,* she should have gotten to the rest of it while she'd had the chance, although she was sure that if he hadn't any faith in what she'd already revealed, he wouldn't be very receptive to the rest.

Her heart leaped into her throat as a car pulled to a stop in back of the van. Expecting the glare of a police spotlight, she made a small, choking sound when Scott materialized beside her window instead.

"Come on."

Unable to move, she watched him pull open the passenger door.

"We have to leave, before somebody gets curious. Although in this kind of neighborhood, they're probably thinking we're having sex in here," he muttered.

She felt her face grow hot, then flinched when he took her arm and helped her down. As soon as her feet hit the ground, he hustled her toward another vehicle, an older American car, judging from the size and condition. The seat covers were ripped in several places, and the floor was littered with bags from fast-food restaurants and other trash.

"Where did you get this?" she asked as he pulled away from the curb.

"It was sitting in front of a house where the lights were off. Maybe the owner will be grateful I took it off his hands."

"He gave you the keys?" she asked, knowing as soon as she'd voiced the question that it was stupid.

"No. I helped myself."

"You do this often?"

"Not since I was a teenager," he said, his gaze swinging toward her, then back to the road. "But the old skills come back when you need them."

She didn't ask him to elaborate. She knew about his getting into trouble when he was a kid. It was another secret that she'd kept when they'd been together, because she'd understood that he hated anyone to know about his background.

As he drove through the neighborhood at a sedate pace and then onto the highway again, she watched him from the corner of her eye, noting the tight set of his jaw, the narrowed eyes. He'd said he didn't believe her explanations for why she'd gotten him arrested. Yet he could have abandoned her, and she was still with him. Did that mean some of the old feelings for her were buried beneath the flinty exterior he chose to show her?

She inched her hand along the seat, wishing she had the nerve to touch him, craving at least that much physical contact. But she didn't have the courage to breach the gap.

Back on the highway, he drove for several miles, then took an exit where brightly colored neon lights advertised a variety of motel chains, gas stations and restaurants.

After turning in at one of the motel parking lots, he told her to wait and got out of the car, pushing his hair off his forehead and straightening his clothes as best he could. He still looked as if he'd gone for a swim in his clothing.

The lobby and the Latin music blaring from somewhere inside the building swallowed him up. But he was back a few minutes later, sliding behind the wheel without comment and driving around to the back of the motel, where he parked in a dark corner of the lot.

Then he was unlocking the door of a motel room and ushering her inside. A cold blast from the air conditioner hit her as she walked across the threshold into the room. Clasping her hands around her shoulders, she surveyed the furnishings—the dresser, the television set, the double bed.

Then the sound of the door closing and the security chain sliding into place made her throat go dry.

A long time ago in San Marcos, she and Scott had spent almost two days in a hotel room together. A room not so different from this one. And in the endless time since then, she'd secretly imagined being alone with him again, free to do anything she wanted. Now here they were with all the privacy in the world, and there was no freedom at all.

He seemed to tower over her, and she lowered her eyes, taking several steps back, until her knees hit the edge of the bed, and she sucked in a strangled breath.

When she looked up, he was staring at her. "Don't worry, I'm not going to do anything against your rules."

Her rules. She remembered them, but they hadn't done her any good. "I...didn't think you would."

"It's not because I'm still such a gentleman." He gave a harsh laugh. "Lying on a straw mattress in that prison cell gave me plenty of time to think about what a fool I'd been. I'd have to be insane to get involved with you again."

She knew he had intended to hurt her with the caustic observation, and she couldn't blame him. Frantic words of explanation bubbled inside her, but she kept them locked within. She'd already tried to make him understand her thoughts and actions and he hadn't believed her.

She needed to sit, but not on the bed. So she kept standing, staring down at the carpet to keep from seeing the accusing look in his eyes.

"So did Sanchez send you here? Is that what's going on? Is he trying to get back into power?"

"No!" She closed her eyes for a moment, then opened them again. "I mean, he didn't send me. I don't know if he's trying to regain power."

"Look at me," he ordered. "So I'll have a better chance of knowing whether you're lying."

She jerked her head up. "I told you, I haven't had anything to do with Sanchez."

"What are you doing in this country?"

"I needed help. So I wrote a letter—to a man who was a friend of my father. He told me that if I came to the U.S., I could contact someone he knew."

"The contact's name?"

"Jed Prentiss."

Scott took her by the shoulders and turned her to face him squarely. "*You* know Jed Prentiss?"

"No. My father's friend knows him. He...he..." She tried to keep her voice steady, but the touch of Scott's hands on her chilled flesh was too much. She was no longer able to keep her teeth from chattering, to keep her whole body from quivering with a deep response that went beyond anything physical.

His hands dropped away from her shoulders, and she wondered if the contact had been as powerful for him as it had been for her.

He gave her an appraising look. "You need to get warm."

"I...I'm all right."

"Go in the bathroom. Take a hot shower."

She lifted questioning eyes to him.

"Go on, before you catch cold," he ordered, and she sensed that he needed distance as much as she. "We'll talk later."

Whatever the reason, she was grateful for the reprieve as she turned and fled, closing and locking the door behind her. Automatically, she began to pull off her wet clothes, piling them in a heap on the vanity. Finally, she took off the money belt and laid it carefully on top.

When she caught sight of the naked woman in the full-length mirror beside the door, she drew in a sharp breath. Scott was out there, on the other side of the door, and she was in here with no clothes on.

She pivoted and faced herself. It was a long time since she'd had such a mirror, and she took a critical look at her body. It had changed in the years since she'd last seen Scott. She put her hands under her breasts, pushing them upward, noting that they had lost some of their youthful firmness. Her hips were rounder, too.

She dared to lower her eyes to the ugly scar that marred the curve of her abdomen. It wasn't red now, but it was still a shock to see it slicing jaggedly across her flesh.

She closed her eyes against it, remembering instead the scalding touch of Scott's hands on her body and the shock of his lips where she'd never imagined such an intimate touch.

The memory brought a moan welling in her throat. She cut it off by pressing her fist against her mouth.

Stop remembering, she told herself. *Stop feeling anything. He doesn't want you now. He made that very clear. Think about your daughter. She needs you. That's why you made this trip. To save her life. She's the one who's important. Not you. So stop worrying about what you want, and worry about her.*

The frank little talk was what she needed to get her thoughts back on the right track. Fleeing from her image in the mirror, she stepped toward the tub, looking at the unfamiliar shower controls. She'd feel better when she was warm and dry, she told herself. A hot shower was an indulgence she had almost forgotten. She would try to enjoy the luxury while she could.

IN SAN MARCOS, a man glanced at his watch, then at the telephone that sat like a silent accusation on the ornate stand beside his leather easy chair. He slapped his fist against his palm, the sound ringing in the empty room. He should have heard something by now, but no call had come.

He'd been instructed to wait for a coded message. But the waiting had become intolerable. Who did they think he was, some peon content to beg for crumbs at the table of the master? He was a rich and powerful man. And he deserved some common courtesy.

In the drawer of the phone table was a sheet of paper. He pulled it out, studying the list of possible questions. There were only certain things he was allowed to say. He couldn't mention Mariana Reyes or Scott O'Donnell. He had to refer to the woman as "the package." The man was "the delivery boy."

The wording was childish, he thought with a snort as he perused the list. But he understood the reasons for caution. There were satellites in the sky picking up communications from all over the earth and relaying them to government spy agencies. They could eavesdrop on any call. And if the information he was waiting for fell into the wrong hands, it could spell disaster for him, and the American who had insisted on this risky course of action. Really, it would have been so much easier just to make sure Reyes and the American ended up with a bullet in the back. But that wasn't the way things were done in the U.S.

With a grimace he poured himself a glass of expensive brandy and downed a couple of swallows. Feeling more in control, he picked up the phone and dialed a number that would relay his call to Brazil and then to Mexico and finally to a secure number in the United States.

It seemed to take forever for the call to go through. When it did, it was answered at once.

"Yes?"

The deep voice was instantly recognizable.

He cleared his throat, wondering now if he should have been more patient. But he had a right to know what was going on, he told himself. He'd paid for the privilege.

"I wanted to inquire about the package that arrived in Miami."

There was dead silence on the other end of the line.

"Are you there?"

"I told you not to contact me unless it was absolutely necessary."

"I want information," he answered imperiously.

"There was a problem with the delivery," the other speaker snapped. "We are checking."

"What about the delivery boy?"

"We are checking."

Before he could ask for more information, the line went dead, and he was left clutching the receiver, knowing that he had angered the man on the other end of the line. Fear threatened to swamp him. Downing the rest of the brandy, he poured more into the glass and forced himself to sip more slowly.

TRYING TO COPE with yet another shock, Scott stood staring at the closed bathroom door.

Mariana had been sent here to contact Jed Prentiss, of all people. Jed was someone he knew, for Lord's sake. A former secret agent who now worked for Randolph Security, he was married to Marissa Devereaux, one of the owners of Adventures in Travel, downstairs from his own office at 43 Light Street.

It was well known that Jed's specialty was Latin America, yet at the same time he came across as a man with secrets in his past. And Scott had respected his privacy. Now he wished to hell he knew more about Jed.

Whose side was he really on? Or could Mariana be lying about coming to meet him? But how would she have known Jed's name—unless she'd been coached to say her contact was someone Scott was disposed to trust. Yet she'd seemed so genuinely shocked to see him at the airport.

He pressed the heels of his hands against his eyes, trying to think it through. But his brain was too overloaded to deal with puzzles, especially puzzles involving Mariana Reyes. Instead, he found himself listening to the sounds of her moving around, taking off her clothes. Against his will, he imagined her standing naked just a few feet away.

From the other side of the closed door, he heard her make a small sound in her throat, and his whole body went rigid. He had told her he didn't want her. He had wished it were true, but he'd known even as he spoke the words that they were a lie.

He turned away from the door. His own clammy clothes clung to him, making his skin tingle as the air conditioner kicked in again. After a few moments' hesitation he pulled off his shirt, shoes and socks. When he reached for the waistband of his slacks, he stopped, picturing Mariana emerging from the bathroom.

The last thing he needed was to have her come out again and find him stripped for action. On the other hand, there was no point in standing here in the middle of the room feeling uncomfortable. After dimming the lights, he flopped onto the bed still wearing his slacks. He'd been running on adrenaline, and he should try to get some rest while he could.

Instead, he found his eyes straying to the bathroom door, his body tightening in reaction to the thought of her nudity and her nearness.

He closed his eyes. But that didn't help. In the semidarkness, memories he'd tried to hold at bay came slithering past his defenses.

It started with the day he'd first seen Mariana Reyes. He'd been standing in the middle of the aging warehouse he'd rented on the outskirts of Santa Isabella, arguing about the shooting schedule with a guy who came across as an incredibly officious government bureaucrat, Pablo Omera.

He was trying to explain why he needed to film in different provinces, but his Spanish wasn't quite up to the job. Then he'd looked up and lost his train of thought as his eyes focused on a beautiful young woman standing in the doorway, watching the exchange. She was dressed in a navy suit and crisp white blouse, the ensemble set off by navy stockings and high-heeled navy shoes that did wonderful things for her shapely legs.

While he stood there staring, trying to remember what he was saying to Omera, she asked in slightly accented English, "Are you having problems?"

He managed a nod, and she offered to take over the negotiations.

Figuring he had nothing to lose, Scott crossed to the battered desk that had come with the place and handed her a copy of the schedule. After scanning the sheets, she began to speak to Omera in rapid-fire Spanish. Ten minutes later, the guy left, promising to see what he could do.

"Thank you," Scott said, his gratitude genuine.

"I was glad to help," she answered, smoothing back her

long, dark hair. Now that they were alone, she was looking slightly flustered.

"So who are you and what are you doing here?" he asked.

She gave him a tentative smile. "I'm Mariana Reyes. I'm studying English at the University of Santa Isabella. I heard about your project, and I was wondering if I might be able to get a summer internship with you."

He hadn't thought about hiring any summer interns—until that moment. He found himself saying, "Can you use a computer?"

"I am familiar with WordPerfect. And Lotus 1-2-3."

"Good."

"And I've shot some videotapes," she added eagerly. "Nothing professional. But I want to learn from you."

"It sounds like you'd be the perfect addition to our staff," he said, making a decision on the spot. If it didn't work out, he wasn't under any obligations.

Before the conversation progressed any further, a load of boxes balanced on a handcart came through the doorway. When Pepe Fortunato stepped from behind the stack and saw the new staff member, his eyes shot from her to Scott and back again.

"Señorita Reyes," he said stiffly.

She inclined her head in acknowledgment.

He cleared his throat. "What a surprise to see *you* here."

"Señor O'Donnell has hired me as a summer intern."

Pepe snorted.

"You know each other?" Scott asked.

"Only by reputation. She's the daughter of Constantino Reyes," he said, as if that were all the explanation needed. Turning away, he began unloading boxes.

"What was that all about?" Scott asked when Pepe had left the room.

"My father is a well-known businessman with many financial interests. I suppose your employee thinks I'm taking a job away from someone who needs the money."

Scott opened his palms. "Actually, I was about to tell you I couldn't afford to pay you anything."

"Well, what I want is to learn something about making films. I'm not worried about getting paid."

They talked about the hours she could work and what he needed done, and when she'd left, he found himself eagerly looking forward to Monday morning, when she was coming back.

Then Pepe stepped into the room, his dark eyebrows knitted together and his arms hanging stiffly at his sides.

"You don't think she's going to be any help?" Scott asked.

"Look at the way she came here in that fancy outfit, thinking her clothes would impress you. She hasn't worked a day in her life."

It wasn't the outfit that had impressed him, but he said, "She's willing to help us out for free."

"She can afford it. Her father earns enough in a week to support a hundred ordinary families for a year."

"Let's see how she fits in," was all Scott said, sure that there would be no problems. He was right about her work, which was excellent.

And after only a couple of weeks, he wondered how he could have done without her. She was invaluable when he went to towns on market day or to remote Indian villages, because she knew just how to get the people relaxed and natural enough to go about their daily tasks for him to film.

She was just as good with the crowd at the theater and upscale restaurants in Santa Isabella. They were a tight-knit, very private group, suspicious of an outsider with a video camera. But their close ranks opened like magic when they saw she was involved in the filming process.

And her help extended beyond the location shooting. Back in their warehouse editing room she could tell him which scenes were most typical of her compatriots.

They worked together like a long-established team. The

sexual attraction between them was another matter entirely. When they were alone together, there was a charged feeling in the air around them. And he knew that both of them were going to great lengths to keep from accidentally touching, or even standing too close.

He suspected she didn't know how to handle the feelings. She was too young, younger than she looked in her expensive, high-style clothing. Despite the air of sophistication she projected, he was sure she was innocent—which made her off limits, he told himself sternly.

The dynamics between them changed one evening when she'd volunteered to work late, getting out letters to the mayors of six provincial cities where he wanted to film.

Scott was in the back, hunched over the editing machine when he heard her scream.

Rushing toward the partitioned-off computer area, he found a man with a knife advancing on her. Scott attacked from behind, kicked the knife out of the assailant's hand and scored with a barrage of street-smart punches that sent the thug running for his life.

When Scott tried to follow, Mariana grasped his sleeve, held him back, begged him in a high, shaky voice not to leave. The fear in her eyes had breached the invisible barrier between them. Taking her in his arms, he started to comfort her, his hand stroking over her back and shoulders as he murmured that he'd never let anything happen to her.

At first she pressed her face against his chest, sobbing quietly. When she lifted her tearstained eyes to his, lowering his mouth to hers was the most natural thing in the world.

She went stock-still, perhaps as shocked by the kiss as he. He should have stopped. He understood that later. At the time, he'd been too caught up in the taste of her mouth, the softness of her lips, the feel of her body pressed to his.

He had craved the feel of her in his arms for weeks. Still, he didn't push her into anything he knew she didn't want.

Lightly he brushed his lips against hers, giving her every chance to draw back.

Instead she breathed his name and wound her arms around his neck. Accepting the invitation, he angled his head to give himself fuller access to her mouth.

Holding himself in check, he moved his lips against hers, increasing the intimacy by slow degrees so that the pleasure of tasting her blossomed like the heady bouquet of fine wine, where each sip is better than the last.

The kiss deepened, lengthened, took on an erotic tenor that swamped his senses. When he lifted his mouth, she was trembling in his embrace, and he was rock-hard.

"I shouldn't," she breathed, although she made no move to pull away. He took that as a further invitation.

His hands skimmed along the sides of her breasts, drawing a pleading whimper from deep in her throat. And when he slowly stroked inward, finding her hardened nipples, she arched into his caress.

"Ah, Mariana, I knew it would be like this—you and me."

She didn't answer; she only let her head fall to his shoulder, turning her face so that her lips could press against his neck.

She wanted him as much as he wanted her, and the knowledge was like an aphrodisiac. Kissing her deeply, he pulled her close, rocking her body against the aching shaft of his erection.

Instead of remaining pliant in his arms, she made a strangled sound and pushed against his chest. Wrenching away, she stood gasping for breath.

His eyes snapped open, and he stared down into her flushed face, fighting to keep his hands at his sides.

"I shouldn't have let you do that," she said, her note of regret telling him that she didn't necessarily mean what she said.

"It was something we've both been wanting."

"Yes," she acknowledged in a shaky voice. "But I

can't.'' Her eyes were pleading for his understanding—understanding that he wasn't able to give.

Still, he'd never forced himself on a woman, and he wasn't about to start now. Straightening, he ran a hand through his hair. ''All right,'' he said, sounding harsher than he'd intended.

Her hands closed on his forearms. ''Please, you don't understand. I've never met anyone like you. You're so different from the men I know.''

''How?''

''You treat me like an equal, and you haven't tried to take advantage even though…you know I want to—to—'' She stopped and sucked in a breath. ''For weeks, I've dreamed about your kissing me. But I knew I couldn't…let anything happen between us. Then you *were* kissing me, and it felt so wonderful. I didn't want you to stop.''

He nodded, understanding perfectly.

She swallowed. ''I'm not free to pick the man I want. My father has promised me in marriage to Bernardo Cortez. They want a business alliance between his family and ours, so we will become formally engaged at the end of the summer.''

''A business alliance? Is that what you want out of marriage?''

She shuddered. ''No.'' Her voice grew tiny. ''I don't want to marry Bernardo. He frightens me.''

''Then tell that to your father.''

She clasped her hands, then twisted them together. ''You don't understand. You come from a country where people make free choices. I have no choices. My father doesn't care how I feel about it. He only cares that I do as he says. I must let him choose my husband. And I must be…innocent when he takes me to the marriage bed, or I will disgrace myself and my family.''

''That's medieval.''

She managed a little laugh. ''My father prefers to think of himself as traditional. He can trace his family back to the old

Spanish nobility. He has strong opinions about the roles of men and women. My place is to bear my husband's children, run his household."

"Your father let you go to university. He let you come here to work."

"He's letting me have this time as a gift to me, before I must do what is required of me. I won't be able to finish the university course," she said sadly.

Scott stared at her, hardly able to believe what he was hearing. She was so intelligent, so vibrant, and it sounded as if she was going to be shut away from the world, where he would never see her again. Before he thought about the consequences, he reached for her again and pulled her into his arms.

She didn't struggle, yet this time she held herself stiffly.

"I won't hurt you," he said. "I just want to hold you."

"I want that, too. But I shouldn't be here with you," she whispered, even as she laid her head against his chest, sighing deeply.

He could feel her warm breath through his shirt, burning his skin. Unwilling to let her go, he stroked his hands over her back, then over her head, tangled them in the thick, dark hair he'd wanted to touch since he'd first seen her.

"Tell me," he said, trying to make it a request instead of a demand. "I have to know what you're thinking—about us."

She was silent for several seconds, her face hidden, and he thought she wouldn't take the chance. Then she began to speak in a low, shaky voice, her face still close to his chest. "My *dueña* told me that I must never be alone with a man. She says that men have…needs that drive them. That when they get…aroused, they can't stop," she whispered, her voice going high and reedy. "But you stopped."

Barely.

"Because I care about you." He tipped his head to the side, burying his nose and lips in her hair, breathing in the scent of flowers, telling himself it was madness to keep holding her, yet unable to pull away.

"I'm all mixed up. Are the men from your country different than the men from mine?"

He thought about the answer to her question, struggling for honesty. "We have the same desires. But it's a different society. We're taught that we can't just take what we want. We're taught that women are equal partners in any relationship."

"That sounds so..."

"Enlightened," he finished for her.

She nodded gravely. "And are the women different, too?"

He gave a low laugh, wondering how to explain the women's movement in fifty words or less. "In the sixties and seventies, the women fought for equality. They've gained a lot. Some men resent it, but most of us accept the change in the dynamics."

He saw she was hanging on his words. "It sounds like a place I'd like to live."

"Maybe you can."

She shook her head. "No. I think that's impossible. My father would never permit it."

Could he change her mind about that? Was it too dangerous to encourage her to think in radically different terms? Lord, what if he could bring her home with him?

While he was mulling that over, he saw her swallow.

"Susana told me that it's men who can't be trusted. But when you kissed me and touched me, it was myself I couldn't trust."

He made a low sound in his throat, afraid of what he might say, what he might do.

Slowly, she raised her face toward him, her expression so open and vulnerable that he felt his insides clench.

"I like you so much better than Bernardo," she whispered.

"The man you're supposed to marry?" he said.

She nodded gravely. "You make me feel safe. He...he got

me alone. And tried...to do things that weren't proper..."
She let the sentence trail off.

"The bastard," he muttered, forgetting for the moment
that his own intentions hadn't been entirely proper.

"He said we were going to be married, so it didn't matter
when he had me." She shuddered, her expression turning
stark. "It mattered to me!"

"Yes."

"I didn't like it when he touched me..." She took a step
back as her hand came up to cover her mouth. "You've made
me say too much." When she caught the denial in his expression, she went on in a rush, "I mean, it wasn't your fault.
It was the pressure of all the things inside me. All the things
I've wanted to tell you."

Before he could answer, she turned and left the room, left
him standing there, aching with the need to go after her, yet
telling himself that it could only lead to disaster.

Chapter Four

Alicia clung to the doll, smoothing her small fingers over the blue dress that was decorated with pink and yellow flowers. It was such a pretty dress. And the doll had long dark hair, just like Mama.

That was why her name was Maria. Almost like Mama's name. Maria had a wide smile, because she was happy. Alicia was trying to be happy, too. And brave. And a good girl. Mama had told her to try to be all those things while she was away.

A shiver ran over her skin, and she clutched the doll tighter.

Sometimes when she lay in bed, she pretended that Mama had come in and kissed her good-night and put Maria into her arms. Then she pretended that Mama was in the other room washing dishes or sewing, like she did, instead of being far away in the North.

Mama hadn't said where she was going. But Alicia had heard the big people talking about the best way to get to *los Estados Unidos*. A city called Miami. Then somewhere called Baltimore. Those places were a long way from San Marcos. You had to get there on an airplane. With something called a false passport. A false passport was expensive, but Mama had needed one.

Because she had gone for help. Maybe to Daddy.

She had never met her daddy. Mama had explained that he'd had to go away before Alicia was born. She didn't know why, exactly. She only knew that something bad had happened—something Mama didn't like to talk about. But Mama had said that it wasn't Alicia's fault, and that her daddy would love her if he ever got a chance to meet her.

She hoped Mama had gone to him for help. He lived in *los Estados Unidos.* But she hadn't said anything about meeting up with him when she'd left, and Alicia hadn't asked, because when Mama talked about him, she always got a sad look on her face.

She'd looked sad the day she left too, although she was trying to smile. She'd left Alicia in a place called San Rafael del Mar. It was near the water, where sea lions came up on the beach to lie in the sun. They were funny. And some of them had babies. When she was a good girl, Tiá Susana or Tiá Dolores took her down to the beach to see them.

Tiá Susana and her sister Tiá Dolores were taking care of her while Mama was gone. She had come with them across the mountains because her sister lived here, and she said it was a good time to visit.

But Alicia knew they were really hiding. They were always hiding from bad men. Alicia and Mama. Only now Mama had gone to get help. And Alicia had to stay with Tiá Susana.

Mama had promised she'd come back. Sometimes at night, she knew Maria worried about it. But Alicia whispered to her and told her that Mama would never leave them alone. She would come back, for both of them. She had to.

AFTER DRYING HER HAIR with a towel, Mariana realized she had no comb or brush. So she did the best she could with her fingers.

Her clothing was still a soggy heap in the vanity, and the idea of the clammy fabric clinging to her flesh raised goose bumps. So she reached for the white terry robe that was hanging on the back of the bathroom door. It was thick and bulky, and Scott couldn't see anything through it, she told herself.

Still, after putting her hand on the knob, she hesitated, hating to emerge with so little on. But she couldn't hide in here forever. She had to talk to him about Alicia, even though the prospect made her stomach knot.

He had turned off most of the lights, and it took several seconds for her eyes to adjust. Finally, she saw that he was lying on the bed. He'd taken off his wet shoes, socks and shirt but kept on his trousers. His eyes were closed, and he was breathing deeply.

As quietly as possible she moved across the room, expecting his eyes to snap open when she approached. But he really was asleep, she saw as she moved to the side of the bed. Her eyes were drawn to the magnificent expanse of his chest, to the crisp red hair that fanned out from the center and around his nipples.

She remembered the feel of that hair against her fingertips, against her breasts, and she fought to repress the sigh of longing that welled in her throat.

He had been a well-formed man six years ago. Now he must be in his early thirties, and he only looked better to her eye—more masculine, more tempting.

Unable to tear her gaze away, she took a step closer. When she reached the side of the bed, she had to press her hand to her mouth to keep from making a very different exclamation. Up close, she could see that the skin of his chest was crisscrossed with white lines. They were scars that looked as if they'd been made by a lash of some kind, and they extended up his shoulders, where they disappeared from view.

Dios, what had happened to him since she'd seen him last? Her jaw tight from strain, she reached out to touch one of the marks. But her fingers had barely connected with his chest when she found herself jerked off her feet and thrown to the surface of the bed.

In seconds he had rolled on top of her, his body pressing her down even as his hands manacled her wrists and pulled them above her head, effectively preventing her from fighting him.

"Scott," she wheezed, fear rising in her chest as she struggled frantically under him, trying to slip away from his powerful grasp.

He didn't seem to hear. Or he didn't care. Shifting his weight, he lifted his body and brought one large hand down on her neck.

She saw that his eyes were glazed, that he looked like a man caught in the grip of a nightmare.

"Scott," she tried again, bringing her free hand down and pounding her fist against his back, even as she felt her air supply choking off.

The blows to his back seemed to have no effect, so she twisted her fingers in his hair, pulling with all her remaining strength.

Black dots filled her vision and she felt her hands go slack as the supply of oxygen to her brain dwindled. Then, suddenly, the pressure on her windpipe eased, and she sucked in a sobbing breath.

His weight lifted from her, and she lay there with her eyes closed, gasping, hardly aware of the cold air hitting the front of her body.

Beside her, she heard him curse, and she braced for another attack.

He only hovered over her. "What the hell were you doing?" he demanded. "Coming at me like that."

"I...I saw the scars on your chest. I guess I t-touched you," she stammered.

"Never do that!"

"Why did you hurt me?"

"I didn't know it was you." He sighed. "Defending myself has become a kind of reflex action."

She nodded, trying to understand, even as she saw his gaze move from her face to her chest.

The green of his eyes darkened, and she looked down, seeing to her horror that her robe had come open in the struggle, exposing the front of her body to his view. Heat leaped into her face as she focused on her breasts. With a small sound, she snatched at the fabric, trying to pull the two edges together, but the way she'd twisted the material under her made the maneuver difficult.

Scott didn't raise his eyes, in fact he seemed incapable of movement at all. To her dismay, she felt her nipples tighten as he stared down at them.

The only way she could pull the robe closed was to lift her body. Somehow she accomplished the task, feeling her skin heat as she levered herself closer to Scott.

She could hear his breath rasping in his lungs, hear her own accelerated breathing. For heartbeats, she forgot what she was supposed to be doing. Then a measure of sanity returned and she yanked the fabric over her exposed skin, flopping back onto the bed and closing her eyes, grateful at least that the robe hadn't opened all the way and exposed the ugly scar to his view.

She felt the bed shift and sensed that he was sitting up. Letting out the breath she was holding, she rolled in the other direction and pushed herself up, wondering how she was ever going to face him again.

He'd seen her nipples tighten when he'd looked at them, she thought, closing her eyes to shut out the revealing image.

"I'm sorry," he growled, the tone of his voice telling her he felt the same tension as she. Or maybe he was just embarrassed at the blatant show of a bare female body. She could always hope for that.

"I shouldn't have touched you," she whispered. "I'm sorry."

"You didn't know I was going to snap. I'm not so good about people sneaking up on me."

Well, that was certainly true, she thought. When she'd known him in San Marcos, he hadn't been like that. "What happened to you?" she ventured, then added quickly, "I mean, how did you get those scars?"

He gave her a long, reflective look. "From your friends in the government."

"No!"

"You don't believe me? Or you don't *want* to believe me?"

She struggled to keep from looking away. "I thought... they wouldn't do anything like that to you."

"I told you, they were trying to pry information out of me—information I didn't have. Fortunately, I was tough enough to survive."

She had to gasp in a breath before she could speak. "I'm so sorry I was the cause."

"It's too late to change anything now."

Not even the future?

When her hands squeezed into fists, he pushed himself off the bed and walked to the chair where he'd left his shirt, and pulled his arms through the sleeves.

She had come out here ready to tell him about Alicia. At the moment, she felt there was no way to reach him, so she sat with her shoulders hunched, watching him dress. Later. She would tell him later.

His eyes were flat and hard as he asked, "So did you get everything you wanted after selling me out? You don't have a wedding ring. I guess you didn't have to marry your fiancé. What was his name—Bernardo?"

So he'd remembered the name after all these years.

"No," she whispered, knowing that if she had to speak louder, she would begin to weep. "I didn't have to marry him. That was good. But other things happened. My parents were killed a couple months after you left. And I went into hiding. I've been hiding ever since."

He stared at her as if he couldn't believe what she was

saying. "Killed?" he asked carefully. "In an accident or something?"

"Men broke into the house and murdered them. They made it look like a robbery, but...my father had enemies. Business rivals. Men who clashed with him politically. Sanchez." She turned her palms up. "They would have gotten me too, but my father had sent me away from the city. Lucky for me that people who used to work for us were loyal to my family. They've been helping me ever since. But the men who are looking for me started getting close."

His face contorted in shock, and he took a step toward her, then stopped abruptly.

She stayed where she was, her legs tucked under the robe as she played with the belt, pulling it tighter around her waist as a cold hollowness spread through her chest. "It was a long time ago," she finally said, hoping that would make him feel more comfortable.

"Yes."

Before she could say anything else, he turned away, his gaze searching the room for some other point of focus. He looked relieved when he found the television set. With the remote control, he ran through the stations, stopping when he saw a reporter and an anchor discussing the terrorist attack at the airport.

"I'm sorry, Clark, we've been given no further information," the reporter was saying.

When the anchor quizzed the reporter, he got little besides the fact that the fugitives were apparently at large. But nobody had a description. Nobody could confirm the report that shots had been fired.

Scott flipped to another channel and got much the same story.

"That's good. I mean, they don't know who we are," Mariana breathed.

"Not necessarily. When those newshounds can't get information, there's something wrong. I have the feeling that whoever set us up wished they hadn't put out that terrorist story in the first place.''

"Why?"

"They've decided they don't want the police to get us before they do.''

"Who are they?"

"Good question. You said you were supposed to meet Jed Prentiss.''

"Yes.''

"An interesting coincidence, since his wife works in my office building,'' he told her.

She could only stare at him in shock as she struggled to process the new information.

"You didn't know that?'' he demanded.

She spread her hands in a helpless gesture. "Scott, I didn't know that you were going to be involved in this. I swear.''

He nodded, but she still wasn't sure whether he believed her. She wasn't sure she would believe him if she were in his situation.

"I'm going to call him and find out what he knows,'' Scott said. "But not from the room.'' He shifted his weight from one foot to the other. "Will you be okay?''

"Yes.''

"Put the chain on the door when I leave, and don't open it to anyone but me,'' he said evenly.

She tried to keep her voice as steady as his. "How long will you be gone?''

"I'll be back as soon as I can.'' Before he stepped out the door, he turned to her, "You'd better tell me the name of the man who told you to get in touch with Jed.''

"Why?''

"He'll want to know.''

She hesitated. The man had warned her not to trust anyone except Señor Prentiss. Swallowing, she made a decision. "Hector Porfirio.''

"Okay.''

After locking the door and slipping the chain into place, she eyed the chair, but decided she was too wrung-out to sit and wait for him. While he was gone, she might as well lie down. But as soon as she stretched out on the mattress, she caught the scent of his skin. Soap and spicy aftershave, and man. The same as she remembered. Instantly she felt her body responding. She might have scrambled off the bed, instead she reached for the pillow that he'd been using and clasped it in her arms, burying her nose in the casing so that she could breathe in his scent.

Closing her eyes, she was helpless to hold back the memories of the time they'd spent together.

Scott had wanted to do some filming in a village about an hour and a half drive from Santa Isabella. Señor Omera, the government official overseeing the project, had said it was up to the mayor to grant the privilege. Since Scott was worried about getting permission, she'd volunteered to go along and be persuasive.

There was another factor, too. One she hadn't confided to Scott. Her parents were out of town for a few days, she had more freedom than usual, and she was taking advantage of it—despite Susana's disapproval.

So she'd had her family's cook pack a picnic lunch, which she and Scott could eat at a spot she knew in the mountains.

Still, she'd had misgivings as they got into the car. There was a strange stillness to the air and a thick layer of clouds hiding the sun.

The real trouble started about twenty miles from the village, when a black dust started drifting down from the sky, cutting visibility and coating the windshield.

"What the hell is that?" Scott asked.

"Ash. From a volcano. Probably Chipotalli. It must be erupting. We'd better go back to the city—quickly."

He flicked on the windshield wipers, then turned them off as the black powder made a scritching sound against the glass. "Does this happen often?"

"I've seen it a few times," she answered.

Switching on the radio, he turned the dial and picked up an emergency advisory. Mariana had guessed right. Chipotalli, a volcano two hundred miles to the north, was erupting, spewing ash and gases into the sky. Residents were advised to stay indoors because breathing the polluted atmosphere was dangerous.

But with visibility cut to almost nothing, traffic slowed to a crawl. Then they passed a large truck that had skidded in the black powder covering the road, and plunged into a drainage ditch. Not long after that, five cars piled into each other right in front of them, and Scott was barely able to screech to a halt without plowing into the back of the last one.

"It's too dangerous to drive," he said.

"What are we going to do?" she asked, peering into the gloom.

"Wait it out."

"We can't. We have to get back."

He started to say something, then wrenched the wheel to the left as a stalled car materialized in the traffic lane. When he nosed around it, she saw only swirling blackness and knew that they were facing a steep drop.

The tires spun on gravel, and she grabbed the door handle struggling to keep from shaking.

"I'm not going to risk your life trying to make it back to the city," he growled, narrowly avoiding another car that had fishtailed across the lane. Pulling to the side, he inched along their progress dogged by the screech of brakes behind them.

Other drivers apparently had decided to call it quits as well. He stopped at a small hotel, but the rooms were all taken. The same was true at the next place. And every time he got out to open the door, gritty powder drifted into the car, making them both choke.

When he came to a sign advertising another establishment he turned off the road onto a long driveway hemmed in by overhanging trees. The parking lot was packed, and Mariana thought they were going to get the same story—that the inn was full.

"I'm going to call Pepe," Scott said as he reached for the door handle.

Pepe Fortunato. He and Mariana didn't like each other, but they were polite, because they both wanted to keep their jobs.

He climbed out, holding his jacket over his face, and she huddled in the car trying to sort out her emotions. Mariana Reyes—at a hotel with a man. Impossible. Yet they were here, and there wasn't much she could do about it.

When Scott emerged again, he was looking relieved. "I got a room, and I talked to Pepe. He's going to take care of some stuff for me," he said as he shut the door quickly and turned right.

"Scott, we shouldn't be here," she said as he drove past a row of white stucco cottages barely visible through the ash.

"You have a better suggestion?"

He pulled as close to the cottage as he could, so that the hood of the car was sticking onto the porch. "The owner was saving this place for his cousin. But the guy called ten minutes ago and said he's not going to make it—big surprise. I had to pay double the going rate."

Quickly he ushered her inside, then went back for the picnic hamper. By the time he slammed the door for the second time, they were both coughing.

Inside it was almost as dark as night. He switched on a lamp, then stepped into the bathroom and brought her a glass of water.

Taking a sip, she stood in the center of the room. It was small, too small and intimate for what she was feeling. Nervously she looked around at the dark pine furniture and the one double bed.

"Isn't there another room?" she wheezed.

"No. We're damn lucky to get this."

"Scott, I can't stay here with you."

"Why? Are you afraid I'm going to do something out of line?"

She looked at him helplessly. "That's not the point. If anybody finds out, my reputation is ruined."

"Nobody will find out—unless you tell them. I heard another news report when I was checking in. They don't think it will be more than a couple of days."

She nodded, thinking that her parents' absence gave them a chance to pull this off. Yet the prospect held terror, too. She swallowed. "Did you ever hear the saying 'Be careful of what you wish for'?"

He gave a low laugh. "Yeah. I've wished for this. The chance to be alone with you."

"So have I. And now I'm not as brave as I thought I was."

"Do you trust me?" he asked quietly.

"I don't know."

He took her by the shoulders, then carefully folded her into his arms. She didn't pull back; instead she closed her eyes and gave in to the luxury of being with him. They'd hardly touched, not since the night he'd kissed her. But the looks they'd given each other had been as potent as his hands on her body. Coming with him today had been in defiance of every rule she'd ever lived by. Yet she hadn't been able to deny herself the pleasure of simply spending time with him. No, that was a lie. She'd tortured herself so many nights by replaying their kiss in her mind. And she'd planned for them to be alone for a little while. But she'd thought they would be outside, where things couldn't go very far.

When she started to shiver, he stroked her hair and shoulders. "Mariana, I understand exactly what we can't do together. And I promise you, we won't."

"But you're a man. We're alone. You...want me," she managed to say.

He crooked his hand under her chin, and tipped her face up to meet his steady gaze. "Yes, I want to make love with you. Sometimes I can hardly think about anything else. But

I would never do anything to harm you." He cleared his throat, brushed his knuckles gently against her cheek. "Mariana, there are no rigid rules about what men and women do together when they're alone in a bedroom. There are ways that they can make love with each other without…the man's taking the woman's virginity."

"How?" she whispered.

"Just by kissing, and touching each other, if that's all they decide to do together."

"Oh, Scott, is that really true?"

"Yes." His eyes never left hers. "I can show you, if you'll let me."

"I'm afraid," she whispered.

"I know. And I understand." His expression turned regretful as he took a step back. "So maybe I'd better go back to the car and let you have the room to yourself."

He swung away and reached for the doorknob. It seemed to be happening in slow motion, so that the moment stretched into infinity.

Before he could open the door and step into the swirling blackness, she grabbed his arm. "No!"

The thought of being this close to what she wanted and then having it snatched away from her was simply too much. Blindly, she turned him to her and clung to him. Because this was all the time they might have.

He stood very still, waiting.

She couldn't tell him she had fallen in love with him, because she belonged to Bernardo Cortez, and Bernardo was her future. Still she wanted Scott to know how he made her feel. "Susana didn't tell me that when I lay in bed at night and thought about you, my body would get hot and tingly, that I'd feel like my skin was stretched too tight across my breasts…"

He growled low in his throat, gathered her close and angled his mouth so that he could kiss her. Surrendering herself to his care, she opened for him, giving him access to her mouth, to her body, to her heart.

"Mariana, I won't hurt you. Ever."

She still couldn't quite believe him, still feared the power of what she felt, yet she was helpless to turn away.

Moving back, he braced his hips against the wall, splayed his legs and held her in the circle of his arms while he kissed the line of her jaw, the side of her neck, the small triangle of flesh at the opening of her collar.

Her head was spinning—from the sensations he created and from the knowledge that she was taking the biggest risk of her life.

Carefully, he unbuttoned the top button of her blouse, then tenderly kissed the skin he exposed, sending a shiver across her skin.

"Don't be afraid of me."

"I'm not," she told him, willing it to be true.

Slowly, giving her time to absorb what he was doing, stopping to talk to her and kiss her, he unbuttoned the front of her blouse, freed it from her waistband and touched her heated skin and breasts through her satin bra. When he found her swollen nipples with his fingers, she began to tremble.

"Are you all right?"

"I didn't know anything could feel that good."

"We're just getting started." He kissed her lightly, then drew back, "I want you to feel comfortable with me."

Reaching for the hem of his knit shirt, he pulled it off. After a moment of shock, she stared in fascination at his broad chest, at the dark red hair and the small male nipples.

"You've said you've lain in bed thinking about me. I've done the same thing—wanting you with me, thinking about how good your hands would feel on me."

He had asked for her touch, and she gave it, first tentatively and then with more confidence. Closing his eyes, he threw his head back, his breath turning shaky.

The knowledge that she was affecting him as much as he

was affecting her was exquisite. Her fingers quivered as he let her discover ways she could make him tremble or draw in a quick breath.

"In case you can't tell, this is making my knees weak," he growled.

"Mine too."

"Then let me take you to the bed."

His words made her realize that she was playing a very dangerous game, yet she had lost the power to refuse him anything he asked.

When she nodded, he lifted her into his arms and carried her to the bed, bending to pull back the spread and blanket. Then he carefully settled her on the sheet.

She lay there tensely, waiting for him to come down beside her and touch her. Instead he sat on the side of the bed. "How are you?" he asked.

She managed a small laugh. "Nervous."

"You don't have to be. Not with me."

She nodded again, still wary as he shifted toward her. But he only slipped off her sandals and gently massaged the arches of her feet, played with her slender ankles, stroked the curves of her calves. The simple touches stoked the fire burning within her.

He loosened her skirt and pulled it off, leaving her in her silky half slip. Moving higher, he arranged her hair against the pillow, spreading it in a fan around her head as he told her how beautiful she was and how thankful he was to be with her like this.

Each thing he did was slow and deliberate, as if he knew she needed the reassurance that he wasn't going to lose control. Yet the slow touches, the increasing intimacy overwhelmed her senses.

She didn't stop him when he pushed her blouse off her shoulders or when he unsnapped the front catch of her bra. Still, when he stroked the cups out of the way, she found she couldn't breathe, couldn't move.

"I knew you'd be beautiful," he told her, his voice thick and low. "But I couldn't imagine you'd be the most beautiful thing I've ever seen."

He lay down beside her then and gathered her to him, and the mere feel of her breasts against his chest made her whimper. Then the blouse and bra were gone, and he was touching her, kissing her, turning her molten with pleasure.

"That's so good," she gasped.

"Do you want to feel my hands anywhere else?"

She couldn't speak the words. Couldn't tell him what she craved. But he seemed to know. When his hand pressed through her slip and panties at the juncture of her legs, she arched into his touch, then gasped as she realized how brazen that must seem.

With his lips next to her ear, he told her he wanted her to feel all the pleasure her body could give her.

When he pushed her slip around her waist and eased his fingers inside the leg of her panties, she tensed. But he didn't remove any more of her clothing yet. He only stroked her, his fingers gliding through her most intimate flesh, making her feel more than she thought it was possible to feel.

He caressed her breasts at the same time, the sensations reinforcing each other, building so that she teetered on the brink between pleasure and pain. Her body urgently quested toward something she didn't know how to name.

There was no thought of stopping him when he dragged her remaining clothing out of the way, giving him complete access to her quivering body.

"Just let go, Mariana. Just let yourself feel how good it can be," he whispered, holding her close as he guided her into a world where there was only unbearable heat and blinding light.

She thought the power of it might consume her—until he pushed her over the edge into ecstasy. Crying out his name, she clung to him as wave after wave of blinding sensation radiated from the place where his fingers stroked between her legs. It crashed over her, through her, leaving her limp and shaken.

He kissed her forehead, smoothed her damp hair back from her face. And when her eyes blinked open, she found he was smiling at her.

"That was so beautiful," he whispered.

She could only stare at him, marveling at what had happened to her. "I didn't know there was...anything like that."

"I know." He kissed her gently, yet she sensed that his body was still humming with tension—the same tension she had felt before he'd brought her to that vivid peak of satisfaction.

She drew back, her gaze going to the slacks he still wore, finding the rigid shaft of flesh straining behind his fly. Raising her eyes, she searched his face. "You didn't feel what I felt. It was only me."

"It's all right. I planned it that way. I wanted to love you—any way I could."

The next step was overwhelming, but she took it anyway. "Can I...do that for you?"

"You don't have to," he said, kissing her cheek, sifting his fingers through her hair.

"I want to. I want to give you as much pleasure as you gave me—if you'll let me." Pretending more boldness than she felt, she reached between them, pressing her hand over him, moving her palm and fingers, her eyes still on his face.

"Mariana," he gasped, his hips arching toward her.

"Show me how. Show me what feels as good to you as what you did for me."

She sensed that he had lost the will to refuse. Unzipping his pants, he kicked them away, along with his underwear. And she saw his aroused body, saw that the male part of him was large and rigid. Susana had told her that a man in that state was a mindless animal bent on only one thing. With his arrogant behavior, Bernardo had given her the same perception. Yet Scott had proved to her that he was different.

That alone made her reach for his hot flesh, caress him, watch his face and listen to his indrawn breaths as she learned what pleased him. And when he folded her fingers around him and moved his hips against her, she gave herself up to his pleasure.

They had almost two stolen days together. Two days in which she had grown bolder, more confident, more intimate in her loving. Two days in which he taught her wonderful, inventive ways a man and a woman could please each other without taking the ultimate step.

Scott had kept his promise. He hadn't taken her virginity.

But in the end, fate had tricked them, and the consequences had been the same.

Chapter Five

Scott stood with his back to the public telephone, his shoulders hunched against the evening breeze and his hand clenched tightly around the receiver.

"We can't talk over the phone," Jed Prentiss growled on the other end of the line.

"I understand," Scott answered, pulling at the still-damp fabric of his shirt. The wind made the cotton clammy against his skin, although there was definitely another component to the clammy feeling. It didn't take a genius to figure out why the former special agent was reluctant to get involved in the mess in Miami. So his friend's next words shocked him.

"I'll be on a plane down there as soon as I can make arrangements. To be on the safe side, don't call me again." There was a pause on the other end of the line. "We'd better pick a time and a place to meet. Do you remember that party where everybody was admiring Marci's silver necklace?"

Startled by the sudden change of subject, Scott redirected his thoughts.

"It was a couple of weeks ago," Jed prompted. "She was real pleased with it, remember? 'Cause she thinks she got a fantastic deal. Do you remember where she said we were shopping? If you know where I mean, don't name the place!" he cautioned.

Scott pictured the silver necklace Jed's wife, Marissa,

whom everyone called Marci, had brought back from a vacation in Miami. She'd been bragging about her purchases at an outdoor shopping area called Lincoln Road.

"Okay, I've got the location," he said.

"Good. And you remember what time we had that charity board meeting a couple of weeks ago?"

"Yeah." That one was easier. It had been a twelve-thirty meeting with Travis Stone, who had endowed the Light Street Foundation.

"Okay. We'll hook up at that time in that general area. I'll find you."

"Got it," Scott acknowledged. They hung up, and he turned away from the public phone where he'd made the call. Disturbed by the conversation, he swept his eyes over the twilit street as he slipped into his car, which now sported a different set of license plates from a wreck in the back of a downtown parking lot. The vehicle had been covered with a layer of dust and pollen. Hopefully, nobody would take a look at it for another few days.

His thoughts turned back to Jed, who'd stopped him from saying anything important as soon as he'd mentioned General Sanchez and San Marcos. Then he'd instantly volunteered to come down here.

Frustrated, Scott banged his hands against the steering wheel. It was going to be another half a day before he could ask Jed what he knew.

THE COMPUTER CLICKED, and the man in the D.C. suburbs monitoring satellite calls from Miami scowled, then checked the tape he'd made of the transmission.

After placing a quick phone call, he removed the tape from the machine and took it into the next room, to the man sitting in the easy chair staring out the window. The man hadn't moved in hours.

"I've got something for you."

"What?"

"A conversation between Miami and Baltimore. O'Donnell and someone named Jed Prentiss."

"Did you get O'Donnell's location?"

"A pay phone. I have a unit on the way. Unfortunately, nobody's very close."

"Great. Go back to your post."

"Yes, sir."

When the underling had left, the man in the chair put the tape into a portable player and listened once, twice, three times.

The good news was that the system was working. They'd latched on to the call from O'Donnell. The bad news was that Jed Prentiss was a clever bastard.

He was on his way to Florida to meet the fugitives, but only the two of them knew the time and the place. Well, there were ways around that. A twenty-four-hour airport watch, for starters. And a rundown of locations in the Miami area that sold tourist items.

He reached for the red phone, arranged to get a head shot from Prentiss's old CIA files, then made the surveillance arrangements. Finally, he started assessing the manpower it would take to scoop them up. Not just O'Donnell and the woman. Prentiss, too. He'd stuck his nose into it, and he was gonna get it chopped off.

O'Donnell had gotten out of the airport because he'd taken them by surprise. Nobody had expected him to be so quick or so clever. Well, now they knew his capabilities, and it wasn't going to happen again. He was still in Miami, which must mean he was driving around in a rental or a stolen car. So a check of rental agencies and the Miami police computer was high on the list of priorities. Maybe they'd get lucky and bag him and Reyes before their meeting with Prentiss.

WITH ONE EYE on the rearview mirror, Scott headed back toward the motel. The call to Jed had been his second of the evening. His first had been to the emergency number Thompson had given him in case he needed help.

Scott made a snorting sound. Help! All he'd gotten for his troubles was a message that the line had been disconnected.

Now he pictured going back to the motel room where he'd left Mariana and reporting the situation. The prospect didn't generate any enthusiasm.

For starters, being cooped up with her had almost driven him stark raving mad. Even after the stunt she'd pulled six years ago, she still pushed his buttons. God, when her robe had come open, all the blood had drained right out of his brain. Too bad he couldn't turn her over to Jed until twelve-thirty tomorrow.

He wasn't quite sure why he didn't simply cut his losses and leave her twisting in the wind. He'd long since given up the idea that he owed her anything. And the minute he'd hooked up with her again, he'd almost gotten his head blown off.

Six years ago she'd been bad news. Why was this any different?

Remembered pain laced through him—the pain of betrayal and the physical pain of the interrogation he'd endured. After a couple of days of torture, he hadn't been sure how much more he could take. In fact, death had started looking like a reasonable alternative to endless agony when Thompson had finally sprung him from that hellhole.

A few hours later, he'd been on a military flight to the good old U.S. of A. And the best part was that Mariana Reyes hadn't been there to see him barely able to walk up the stairs to the plane.

Lord, what a chump he'd been. He'd thought she was so sweetly innocent. He'd thought the two them could trust each other—after the time they'd spent near Chipotalli. But she'd lied to her parents about that, lied to her fiancé, and he'd been too tied up in fantasies about her to assume she wouldn't lie to him, too.

He was still a chump, he thought as he pulled into the parking lot of a discount department store that was open late. The first thing he'd do when he got back was make it clear that they weren't taking up where they'd left off.

But meanwhile, Mariana needed something to wear tomorrow—something that she wouldn't be caught dead in. Like shorts and a nice, tight, knit top. That wasn't her style. So it would make the perfect disguise, along with a sports shirt and some cutoffs for himself.

THE KNOCK AT THE DOOR made her jump. Then she heard Scott's voice through the door and relaxed a notch. At least it wasn't somebody coming to assault her.

"Mariana?"

"Just a moment," she called, struggling up from the seductive fantasy that her mind had been replaying. Her and Scott, the way they'd been at Chipotalli. Glancing at the clock, she was startled to see it was after midnight. He'd been away a long time, but she hadn't noticed because she'd been too wrapped up in the past.

"Open up."

Scrambling off the bed, she made sure her robe was belted tightly. When she cracked the door, she saw him standing in the hallway, his arms loaded with packages.

As soon as she released the chain, he stepped inside, tossed several bags on the bed and set the rest on the table under the window.

Food smells wafted toward her, and her stomach growled.

"I figured we might as well eat," he said. "It's just burgers and fries."

"That's fine." Crossing to the table, she began to empty the bags, giving herself some focus besides the man standing over her.

Scott. Her lover. Or at least the closest thing she'd ever had to a lover. She'd done everything with him except the one thing that was forbidden to her. But she hadn't thought of it as a compromise. Not when he'd made her feel as if she was soaring to the moon. If anyone had told her she'd had to settle for second best, she would have informed them they were wrong.

Because the hours she'd spent alone with Scott were the sweetest of her life. He'd been so loving with her, so tender. She'd even let herself pretend that the man coming back to this motel room was the same man who'd made love to her.

But it wasn't. That Scott was gone. In his place was a cynical stranger whose eyes narrowed and face hardened when he looked at her.

She kept her own face angled downward, hoping he didn't know what she'd been thinking about while he'd been gone. *Dios,* she should never have let her mind wander down that path. It made things worse—a lot worse.

His hand brushed her shoulder, and she jumped.

"Sorry," he muttered.

She answered with a little nod as she opened the bags. He'd brought soft drinks in large cups filled with ice. She hadn't had ice in a drink in years. Not in the mountains of San Marcos.

The American fast food was also an exotic treat. Alicia would have loved this meal, she thought with a pang, then glanced at Scott from under lowered lashes. She hadn't told him about Alicia yet. She knew she had to do it soon, but not now when he already looked as if he had grim news to impart.

Pulling out one of the chairs, he sat down and squeezed ketchup on the fries.

She took the other seat, and he pushed a box of fries toward her. "Eat them while they're still hot."

Dutifully, she took a bite. "Did you talk to Jed Prentiss?" she asked.

"Yeah. He doesn't like the situation."

"You mean he's not going to help me," she whispered around the suddenly clogged feeling in her throat.

"He wouldn't say much on the phone. But he arranged to meet us at the Lincoln Road Mall."

Her eyes widened in shock. "He's coming here? From Baltimore?"

"Yes. We're meeting him tomorrow at twelve-thirty. Until then, we stay in hiding." He gave her a direct look. "You didn't make any phone calls from the room, did you?"

"No."

"I hope not. I was being cautious when I called Jed. Now I need to find out what he knows and we don't."

He ate in silence for a few minutes, without looking at her, then raised his head and asked, "Did you listen to the news again?"

Guiltily, she shook her head. "I was…lying down."

He stood and switched on the TV. This late at night, there were only reruns of old programs and talk shows.

"I brought you some clothes," he said offhandedly as he turned down the volume. "There's a big T-shirt you can sleep in. And shorts and a shirt for tomorrow, plus sandals."

"Thank you."

"You can put it on the tab."

"What tab?" she asked in a quavery voice, half-afraid that he had some payment in mind.

"Nothing. That was a mild attempt at a joke. I'm not going to make you do anything you don't want to," he said, echoing the assurance he'd given her so long ago. Did he remember every word they'd spoken to each other in that long-ago hotel room—the way she did? Or was the phrasing just an accident?

Her eyes flicked to him, but his head was bent as he chomped on his hamburger.

He ate all of his food. She managed a few bites, then cleaned up the debris before sitting gingerly on the edge of the bed and investigating the bags he'd brought. One seemed to be for him, the other for her. In addition to the items he'd mentioned, there were plain cotton underpants, a stretchy bra that said it fit sizes B and C, a toothbrush and toothpaste.

Turning quickly she brought the packages into the bathroom and pulled on the underpants and bra. They fit. The big T-shirt, with a picture of a teddy bear in the middle, came almost to her knees and halfway down her arms. Still, she pulled on the robe again over top of it.

The casual glance he gave her when she opened the door turned into a more thorough inspection.

"You don't have to cover up with me. I remember what you've got," he said in a conversational voice.

She swallowed. "I guess it's too late to say I feel nervous with you."

"Skip the virgin act."

She had to repress a hysterical laugh. Quickly she crossed the room and lowered herself into the chair, gripping the arms. He was making it harder for her to bring up the subject that she knew they had to discuss.

Before she could work up her nerve to begin, he said. "Fill me in on the guy who told you to contact Jed."

"He was a man who was a business associate of my father's. It was too dangerous for me to even go back for the funeral. But he saw Susana there and gave her a letter for me. It said if I ever needed his help, he'd give it to me."

"So why did you wait six years?"

"He…he…" She stopped, sighed. "I never liked the way he looked at me. I thought there might be…" She fumbled for the idiom. "Strings attached. Then Susana told me I had to write to him because maybe he could get me out of the mess I was in."

"You always listened to your *dueña*."

The tensions—her own and his—were unbearable. "Not always," she snapped. "Or I wouldn't have ended up in that hotel room with you!"

His eyes swept over her. "You want to bring that up *now?*"

"No."

"Then why did you mention it?"

When she could only answer with a tiny shrug, he made a snorting sound. "Believe me, I'm counting the hours until I can turn you over to Jed."

He was doing it again, deliberately saying things he knew would hurt her. She couldn't really blame him, yet she couldn't take any more of it. Not when every nerve in her body felt as though it was being twisted in a vise.

"You trust Susana?" he asked, forcing her to interact with him again.

"Yes."

"Maybe she turned you in."

"No! Somebody else found out," she insisted, unwilling to entertain the notion that Susana could have betrayed her. Not the woman who had promised to take care of Alicia! Yet he'd planted a seed of doubt.

She jumped up, paced to the window and back again, goose bumps gathering on her skin as she felt his gaze on her.

"Have you been in contact with anyone from back then?"

"No. I've been in hiding. Maybe Jed Prentiss can tell us what happened. Maybe there are people involved we don't know about."

"Who?" he challenged again.

"I don't know!" She almost screamed the denial as she paced the confines of the room. Fighting back tears, she struggled for some semblance of calm. "Scott," she whispered, not even sure that she had spoken until she saw his head turn questioningly toward her.

Now that she had his attention, she froze, then gathered her resolve to say, "I'm smarter than I was six years ago. Back then I was so young. And I wasn't very sophisticated. It wasn't so hard to convince me to do something that on the face of it now seems totally wrong."

"So what are you saying? That I tricked you into spending that time with me when Chipotalli erupted?" he growled.

"No! I wasn't trying to say anything like that," she denied quickly, wishing she had used some other phrase. "I was thinking about the men from the government who tricked me."

She saw his hands clench. "Okay, since you're in a confessional mood, do you mind telling me the time frame? Were you already planning to stab me in the back when we…were alone together?"

The hurt and anger came through in his voice, making her cringe. Yet the only thing she had left to give him was honesty. "I never thought I was stabbing you in the back," she answered. "If you're asking if they'd already come around with questions about your film project, the answer is yes."

"Didn't you think I had a right to know somebody was snooping into my business?"

"When you say that now, it makes sense. But back then I was too scared to think that way. They said it was confidential, that I'd get in trouble if I talked to anyone about them. For all I knew they'd talked to Pepe. Or that bureaucrat Omera, who was always pestering you."

His eyes narrowed as he took in that possibility.

"When we came back—after Chipotalli, they were more direct. They told me that you were a danger to the stability of San Marcos."

He made a snorting sound. "The stability of San Marcos! I was making a documentary film about the regions of your country—the customs, the traditions. How the hell was that dangerous to anyone?"

She shrugged. "I don't know. All I know is that San Marcos isn't a free society. You're conditioned to one way of thinking. I was raised differently, and the only thing I knew for sure was that powerful men were worried about what you might find out. Thinking about it now, I can't figure out if they were really from the government, or from some other political faction. I just know that they made me believe that if you didn't get out of the country, you'd be killed.''

"How did they do that?"

"Do you remember the man named Gomez who you hired to drive the equipment truck?" she asked with a catch in her voice.

He nodded.

"Remember when he didn't show up for work, and you were angry? Well, he didn't show up because he ended up under the wheels of a taxicab.''

The awful scene leaped into her mind, and she had to wait several seconds before she could go on. "It was about a block from the office. He was crossing the street, and a car came out of nowhere and hit him—then sped away. He was lying there…''

Her voice hitched, but she forced herself to continue. "His legs were crumpled under him. And there was blood on the pavement. I was going to him, but a man caught my arm and held me back. I thought he was helping me. He pulled me into an alley and started talking to me. He said what I'd seen was a warning—for you."

Shock tightened Scott's features, but he didn't interrupt.

"He said I could save your life by getting you out of San Marcos. All I had to do was slip into your apartment and leave some papers he'd give me. I said I'd never been in your apartment. He laughed and said he didn't believe me— that he knew about us…" She gulped. "Us 'shacking up' at Chipotalli.''

"Shacking up. A nice turn of phrase.'' He considered that for a moment. "So you were frightened he'd expose that and screw up your chances of marrying the guy your father had picked."

"No. Yes." She swallowed, searching for absolute honesty—in her soul and in her words. "I told you I knew I couldn't marry Bernardo. Still, I was terrified of my father's anger." Before he could comment on that, she hurried on.

"But I was more frightened for you." She raised her eyes to his, trying to judge if he believed her. "That's why I didn't come to work. That's why I called you."

He was silent for several seconds, then began to speak in a quiet, unemotional voice. "When you phoned in that morning and said you wouldn't be at work, I was down in the dumps. Then you asked if I'd call and have the *portero* give you the key to my apartment, and I was flying high again, thinking I could convince you not to marry Bernardo."

The casually spoken words stunned her. Was he saying that he'd wanted her to marry him instead? She couldn't ask. All she could do was stand there with her lower lip between her teeth, wishing she could change the past, wishing she had been braver six years ago.

"Of course, you did sound strange on the phone," he went on. "But I thought you were nervous about getting together with me in the city. Then when I came rushing home and found you weren't there, I was worried that something had happened to you."

"Scott, I—"

He plowed ahead. "Imagine my surprise when a couple of clowns from the police barged in and started searching the place. I thought it was amusing at first, because I knew there wasn't anything to find. Then they came up with those military maps shuffled under a pile of newspapers."

She clenched her fists and dug her nails into the palms of her hands. When she was a little more in control, she whispered, "I thought I was doing the right thing. That's all I can say."

"Do you think that confession changes anything?"

She wrapped her arms around her shoulders and tried to fill her lungs with air. "No," she managed to say in a strangled voice. "But I wanted to tell you anyway."

He didn't answer, and she knew there was no place to escape from his gaze, except behind her closed eyelids.

"I'm tired," she murmured, moving toward the bed. After

straightening the covers, she slipped underneath and moved to the far side of the mattress, lying with her eyes closed and her hands stiffly at her sides. She was pretty sure he was looking at her. Probably he was laughing at her for keeping the robe on.

Doing her best to ignore the feel of his gaze on her, she tried to will herself to sleep, tried to ignore the erotic rhythm of the music drifting to her from the lobby.

The exercise was only partially successful. It was easier to block out the music than her awareness of Scott. Every time he shifted his legs or cleared his throat, she felt it. And when he started moving around the room getting ready for bed, she felt her body stiffen. The robe she was wearing was making her body hot and damp. But there was no way she was going to take it off.

Scott eased onto the other side of the mattress, the gap between them wider than the space they each occupied.

She lay poised on the opposite edge, listening to the sound of his breathing, wondering if either one of them would get to sleep. When the music from the lobby surged, she could feel the insistent rhythm pulsing through her body.

The vibration was like counterpoint to the sound of Scott's breathing. Maybe in the darkness, she could tell him the other things she still needed to say.

It might have been a reasonable plan, but she couldn't summon the courage to start another conversation, not with him lying two feet from her.

WHEN SHE WOKE, a shaft of light knifed through the crack in the draperies. But that wasn't what she noticed first. She was more aware of physical sensations. In the night she'd shrugged out of the heavy robe, her nightshirt had ridden up around her waist, and her body had gravitated toward Scott's. They were close to the center of the bed, their bare legs tangled, his body turned toward hers, and his arm across her breasts.

She lay there staring at that bare arm, her fingers itching to stroke the dusting of curly reddish hair, her breasts tingling with the pressure of his flesh on hers.

Slitting her eyes, she dared to turn her head the barest amount. He was sleeping, his breath slow and even. Her mouth was inches from his naked shoulder, and she might have breached the gap to press a kiss to his warm skin. But she didn't chance waking him. Instead she contented herself with taking in all the details of his presence, comparing them to her memories. Even in sleep, his face had lost its boyish innocence. But the new maturity was even more attractive to her.

Casting her eyes downward, she saw that his stomach was still hard and flat. And his body was aroused. Staring at the rigid flesh behind the fabric of his shorts made her insides liquefy.

It didn't help when his arm shifted so that his hand could find her breast, cupping her, rubbing against her tightened nipple so that she had to clamp down on her lips to keep from moaning.

She took a shallow breath and then a deeper one, knowing she should slip away from him, even if it woke him up. Because if she stayed like this, she was going to melt from the heat. But she lacked the will to move. What he was doing felt too wonderful. Being with him like this again was the fulfillment of all the fantasies she'd dared to conjure in the confines of her narrow bed.

Closing her eyes, she tried not to wake him. But there was no way she could control the ragged edge of her breathing. Then, unable to help herself, she turned toward him and pressed her lips against his shoulder, breathing in his scent, opening her mouth so that she could taste his skin.

She knew the moment he woke. For heart-stopping seconds, his hand pressed more firmly against her breast. Then she heard him utter a low curse as he shifted away from her, propelling himself off the bed.

He stood, looking down at her, his chest heaving, his forehead beaded with perspiration.

"Scott…"

He didn't wait for her to finish. Instead, he turned away and snatched up one of the bags that he'd brought in last night. He carried it to the bathroom, stepped inside and slammed the door. When he emerged, he was wearing shorts and a T-shirt.

"I'm going running," he announced.

Then he was gone. She pushed herself to a sitting position, drawing up her knees and clasping them in her arms. For long moments, she rocked back and forth, fighting the cold, choking feeling in her chest, trying not to sob. When she was sure she wasn't going to cry, she heaved herself off the bed and found the other bag, the one with the clothing he'd bought for her.

There was even a hairbrush, she discovered after she'd showered.

The shorts he'd bought made her cringe. The sleeveless knit top was even worse. After she pulled them on, she felt as if she was still walking around half-naked. Maybe six years ago before she'd had a baby the garments might have covered more of her, she thought as she inspected herself in the mirror—then made a decision. It wasn't possible for things to get any worse between them. So as soon as he came back, she'd tell him they needed to talk.

When she heard the brusque knock at the door, she scurried across the room to let Scott in, avoiding his eyes as she took a step back. He was breathing hard and his skin was covered with a fine sheen of perspiration.

"Scott, I need to tell you something," she blurted.

He pulled at the T-shirt clinging damply to his chest. "How about giving me a few minutes?"

Without acknowledging her quick nod, he brushed past her and disappeared into the bathroom.

Rocking on her heels, she listened to the sound of running

water. It was impossible to stand still now. The tension she was feeling translated itself into worry about her child.

What if the people who had tried to kill her and Scott had somehow figured out where to find Alicia? What if someone had paid Susana enough to change sides? She clamped off that thought with a moan. But once the fear took hold, she couldn't shake it from her mind.

Dios. She had to talk to Alicia—and Susana.

She glanced at the bathroom door, thinking that she should have gone and made the phone call while he was out of the room. Now she was going to have to do a lot of explaining.

Before she could cross the room, however, she stopped herself. She wasn't about to tell him about Alicia through a closed bathroom door. And come to think of it, if she told him she wanted to make a phone call to San Marcos, he'd probably order her not to do it.

But he had talked to Jed from a pay phone. Surely that would be all right, especially if she made it a very quick call and got back before he knew she'd even left. She'd be sure they didn't mention any names; and she'd know from the way Susana sounded if everything was really all right.

Once she'd decided to take the initiative, she felt a vast sense of relief. Slipping out of the room, she walked through the hallway to the front lobby, where she asked the clerk to convert some of her U.S. bills into change. Then she asked where she could find a nearby phone.

TíA SUSANA HAD TOLD Alicia to stay in the house. But the house was dark and quiet. Nobody would be up for hours. So she had gotten dressed—all by herself. In the bathroom, she looked at herself in the mirror. Tía Susana had put this stuff on her hair to make it black, to make her harder to notice. But every time she saw her reflection, she was startled, like the girl in the mirror was someone else.

Turning away, she tiptoed into the kitchen for a piece of

flat bread. She washed it down with some of the milk in the refrigerator, then stepped into the yard.

Sometimes Chachi, the cat who lived down the street, came to their yard to play with her.

"Here, kitty. Here, kitty," she called. But Chachi wasn't there. So she opened the gate and made her way down the narrow street toward the little yellow house where the cat lived.

Before she got to Chachi's house, she saw the boy who lived at the corner. He was named Jamie, and he was her friend. Sometimes he even took her down to the beach to look at the sea lions and all the birds. There were little ones who ran along the edge of the water and bigger ones who swooped down to catch fish. She liked the pelicans best, the ones with the big beaks.

"*Hola,* Alicia," the boy called. "You wanna play ball?"

"Sure."

He kicked his old soccer ball toward her, and she kicked it back. "I didn't tell on you," he said after a little while.

"Tell on me? What did I do?"

He shrugged. "I don't know. But there was this guy hanging around, you know, asking questions. He said he was looking for a little girl named Alicia."

Her eyes widened. "What man?"

Jamie shrugged again. "Some guy. But I told him I didn't know anybody named Alicia. So are you gonna tell me what you did?"

"Nothing." She shook her head vigorously. "I have to go home. To my aunt."

"Hey, aren't you gonna stay and play?"

Without answering, she turned and sprinted toward Tiá Susana's house, her eyes on the lookout for strangers as she ran.

TRYING TO LOOK CONFIDENT, Mariana stepped out of the lobby and into the gathering heat of the morning. The clerk had told her that if she didn't want to use the phone in the motel, she could go to the ice-cream shop at the end of the block.

She found the shop with no trouble. Although it wouldn't be open until after lunch, there was a phone near the entrance. After a moment of hesitation, she started to pick up the receiver, just as she heard the sound of footsteps coming rapidly behind her along the sidewalk.

Her heart was in her throat as she started to dodge away. But a hand clamped onto her arm and held her fast.

"What the hell do you think you're doing?" an angry voice growled.

Chapter Six

Scott spun her around, his eyes boring into hers. He'd heard the motel-room door open, seen her leave and jumped into his clothes. Lucky for him the clerk at the front desk could tell him where she'd gone.

His hair was still dripping from the shower and he hadn't shaved. But at least he caught her before any damage was done. At least he hoped to God that was true.

"What are you doing?" he demanded again.

"Making a...a phone call." Her eyes were large and guilty-looking. Her fingers tangled in the hem of the sexy little knit top he'd bought her. Under any other circumstances, he would have watched the way she was pulling the fabric even tighter across her breasts. Instead, he dragged his eyes back to her face.

"Yeah, I can see you headed straight for a phone the minute you thought you could get away with it. Who are you supposed to contact?" He gave her shoulders a hard shake. "Are they waiting for your signal to come and get me? Now that you know I can't give you any information from Jed."

Her lower lip trembled, and she shook her head. "It's nothing like that."

He felt his lips curl into a sneer. He'd been stupid enough to fall for her innocent act all over again. Well, he was through being played for a chump. This time she was going

to come clean with him before he ended up in prison again—
or dead.

"I guess I never learn my lesson," he said wearily.
"Come on, let's go back so you can feed me some more of
whatever story you've been scripted with."

"Scott, I know what you're thinking. I know why you're
thinking it. But I swear, this phone call has nothing to do
with you."

Her eyes told him that she was lying. "Sure."

"I...mean—" She stopped, gulped. "I mean, I was worried about someone in San Marcos. I was trying to call her."

He was about to ask who when a flash of movement over
her right shoulder caught his attention. Looking up, he saw
two muscular men in suits coming down the sidewalk, heading straight for them. He glanced around the sunlit street
lined with stores, searching for an escape route and seeing
none. No alley to duck into. Nowhere to run that wouldn't
give the advancing men a clear shot.

"Two big guys are coming this way. Did you call for
reinforcements?" he demanded.

"No!"

"They're pretty interested in us," he growled, his mind
racing, his words coming rapidly as he scrambled for a way
out. "Maybe they think I'm threatening you. Maybe they're
from the airport. Either way, we throw them off balance. So
take my hand, pull me away from the phone booth and into
the doorway. Hurry up!"

For a moment she didn't move. Then she reached for his
hand and led him into the recessed alcove between the two
front windows of the ice-cream parlor.

Turning to give himself a clear view of the approaching
men, he drew Mariana close and lowered his mouth so that
it was only a fraction of an inch from hers. "Put your arms
around my neck. Move in closer," he hissed, then couldn't
keep himself from adding, "Act like you love me. Like we
were having a lovers' spat and you're desperate to make up."

She went stock-still, her eyes wide.

He felt as if he were drowning in their depths. But there was no safe harbor for his gaze. When he focused on her parted lips less than an inch from his, he was suddenly caught in a trap he'd made for himself. On purpose, apparently.

But his brain was still functioning enough to register that the men had stopped in front of the doorway.

"*Señorita,* are you okay?" one of them asked, speaking in Spanish.

Mariana made a throaty sound and half turned. "Yes. I'm fine," she answered in the same language.

There were several tense seconds of silence before the men moved on. But Scott was hardly aware of them because Mariana gave a greedy sigh and brought her lips up to his.

Lost in the taste of her, the feel of her mouth on his, he forgot about the men, forgot about the phone call. There was only the reality of the warm, pliant woman in his arms. Maybe he had been secretly searching for a way to get her in his clutches, without having to acknowledge that was what he wanted.

Whatever the reason, now that she was here, she filled every corner of his senses. Feelings he thought had died years ago sprang back to life.

He felt his heart slamming against the inside of his chest as his arms came up to imprison her, and his head angled to take her mouth in a hot, demanding kiss.

She could have pulled away. Part of him was still expecting her to slip out of his arms now that any pretense of danger was past. Instead, she made a small whimpering sound in her throat and opened her lips for him, begging him to deepen the contact.

His hands slid to her hips, pulling her against him, letting her feel the insistent pressure of his erection.

Whimpering again, she moved against him, her hands sliding up and down his back, over his shoulders.

They were standing in the doorway of a shop in broad

daylight on a Miami street. They might as well have been in the privacy of their motel room for all he cared about propriety.

With a growl of satisfaction, he tugged up her knit top and caught the wonderful weight of her breasts in his hands. They were just as responsive as he remembered. When he stroked her nipples through the thin fabric of her bra, she cried out and arched into his caress as if begging for more. They were both breathing hard, swaying on their feet, her fevered responses telling him she was just as hot as he was. Well, he knew what to do about that.

He was thinking about how to get them horizontal when a throat-clearing noise made his head jerk up. Standing three feet in back of Mariana, holding a key, was a young woman dressed in a uniform with a frilly blouse and a pink apron. As she stared at the couple in the doorway, her cheeks grew red.

"Were you waiting in line for ice cream?" she asked, her voice dripping with sarcasm.

Mariana shook her head and pulled down her top. Scott managed a curt "no" as he stepped away from the door, trying to keep from swaying on his feet.

Without speaking, he took Mariana's arm, as much to steady himself as her. As they started back to the motel, he silently cursed himself, then tried to figure out exactly what had been in his mind when he'd asked her to pull him into the doorway. For the life of him, he couldn't reproduce the logic. All he knew was that he'd snatched at an excuse to kiss her—more than kiss her—and the experience had left him witless.

Anger at his idiotic behavior quickened his steps so that Mariana was practically running by the time they reached the motel room. He could hear her breathing hard as he led her up the steps to their hallway.

Shutting the door, he snapped the chain into place, aware that they now had all the privacy they'd forgotten they didn't have a few minutes ago. Only now he didn't want it.

He must have been insane for coming up with that idea. And even more insane for thinking with his crotch instead of his head. He slid a glance at Mariana. She looked as shell-shocked as he, as she stood there dragging in air. More to the point, the right side of her jaw looked red and prickly. From his beard, he realized with chagrin. He dragged his eyes away from the place where he'd marked her, sure that the one thing they weren't going to talk about was the kiss.

"Okay, let's get back to that phone call," he snapped, and she tried to straighten her shoulders. She looked like a prisoner on the way to her execution.

"What are you so desperate to hide?" he asked, his voice dangerously even.

"Nothing!" When she reached to twist a lock of dark hair around her finger, he watched the nervous gesture as if it were an admission of guilt.

"Don't lie to me."

"It's not what you're thinking. I wasn't going to turn you in to anyone. I was calling my…my family."

"Uh-huh. Funny, you told me yesterday that your family is dead. Are you having trouble keeping your stories straight?"

"My parents are dead." She swung away from him. "I need a glass of water." Without waiting for permission, she crossed to the bathroom and turned on the tap. He heard her gulping noisily, like someone who'd been stranded in the desert. Then through the open bathroom door, he could see her leaning against the sink, taking deep breaths.

She was more off balance than he was, he thought with a measure of satisfaction. Maybe if he pressed her hard, he could get her to tell him the truth.

"Come out here! I want to see your face when I'm talking to you," he ordered.

Several seconds passed, and he wondered if she was going to comply. Then she slipped from the bathroom and dropped into one of the chairs at the table. Putting himself on her level, he took the other chair.

"Let's start with—why did you sneak out of the room? Why didn't you to tell me you were leaving?"

"You called Jed from a pay phone. I was doing the same thing. And I didn't want you to tell me it was a bad idea. If I'd really wanted to sneak out, I could have done it while you were gone."

The logical answer only made him more edgy. "Quit stalling. I want to know whom you were calling."

"My daughter," she said in a small voice, her hands clenched tightly in her lap. "Well, not her, exactly. I was going to make sure she's all right."

"You have a daughter?" he asked, thunderstruck. It was the last thing he'd expected her to say.

"Her name is Alicia," she said, her voice going soft and sweet as she spoke the child's name. "She's the reason I came here. She's all I have, and I want her out of danger. This morning I kept worrying that she was in trouble. And I had to know that everything was okay. She's in a little town where my family used to vacation. San Rafael del Mar. Susana is taking care of her, and you made me worry about that," she explained, making him wonder why she was piling on so many details.

She kept her gaze on the hands in her lap. Clearing her throat, she added. "She's five years old."

Five. He processed the information and came to a conclusion that sent a shock wave through his system. "So you went from me to that fiancé of yours," he growled, surprised that he was actually jealous after all these years. "How nice for you."

She raised her head, her lip quivering. "No. I didn't go to Bernardo. After...after being with you, I knew I could never marry him." She stopped, then lurched on. "Anyway, there was no way he was going to marry me when he found out I was pregnant."

The words hung in the charged air between them.

"So who, exactly, did you sleep with?" he said.

Her hand went to her jaw, and she rubbed the sore place where his beard had marked her. The gesture wasn't lost on him.

"Nobody," she said in a voice that he knew she was struggling to hold steady. "I mean, you were the only man I was with."

He pushed back in his chair, gave a harsh bark of a laugh. "Well, we didn't...how can I put this delicately. You didn't lose your virginity with me. I remember being pretty careful about that."

She nodded.

"And now you expect me to believe that somehow I got you pregnant?"

"No. I don't expect you to believe it," she whispered. "That's why it was so hard to tell you." She sucked in a quick breath, then took a deeper one and let it out in a rush. "But it's the truth."

"Sure. Right." He stood, paced to the window, turned and stared at her where she sat hunched in the chair. "You never could be straight with me, could you?" he muttered.

She looked down at her hands. "After you left, I kept feeling sick, and I finally went to the doctor to find out what was wrong. When he told me I was pregnant, I couldn't believe him. I asked how that could be possible since we didn't..." Her voice trailed off, and she cleared her throat before starting again. "He told me that the man doesn't have to be inside the woman. Not if both of them are naked and...and giving each other pleasure... Some of the man's seed can get inside the woman."

He pressed his lips together. He knew what she was saying was possible. But he'd figured the odds were on their side.

"Everything I've told you is the truth. I'm not accustomed to lying," she said with dignity.

He made an exasperated sound. "Except when you got me

arrested? Or when you told Bernardo and your parents a story about where you'd been when Chipotalli erupted?''

Her bottom lip quivered. ''Yes,'' she whispered.

He saw her fingers digging into the chair arms. Her eyes were huge with tears. As he watched, they spilled onto her lower lashes and began to trail slowly down her cheeks, but she didn't move, didn't make a sound.

Seeing her like that almost undid him. Almost. Then he reminded himself what she'd done to him six years ago and what she was trying to do now.

Apparently she was in a hell of a fix, and the only way out of it was lying through her teeth. Now what was she expecting, exactly? That he'd take responsibility for a kid he knew wasn't his?

She swiped her hand across her eyes then stood, swaying on her feet, and he thought she might topple over. Instead, she stiffened her spine and reached under her knit top, pulling out a money pouch. Fumbling inside, she extracted a photograph. After looking at it for a moment, she silently held it toward him.

He almost refused to look. Then he sucked in a breath and flicked his gaze downward. It landed on a color picture that showed a little girl who might have been four or five. She was sitting on a low bench in front of a whitewashed house. The first thing he saw was her dark red hair, shining in the sun and tied with a green ribbon.

A shiver raced across his skin, and it took several seconds before he could focus on the picture again. When he did, he saw her broad smile as she gazed into the camera. And her light-colored eyes. Blue or green. Not dark like her mother's. Light, like his.

Waves of shock and denial rocketed through him. Unable to fill his lungs with air, he could only stare at the little girl in disbelief. It wasn't true. This was some kind of trick. No way had he and Mariana created a child with their make-do lovemaking.

He clung to that conviction by his fingernails, even though

the logical part of his brain ordered him to face facts. There was no other way to explain this little girl, unless Mariana had found a lover who was a dead ringer for him. He dismissed that hypothesis out of hand. There weren't many men in San Marcos who looked like him.

He raised his eyes to her, then looked away. "I—" He didn't know how to finish the sentence, didn't even know what he intended to say.

She walked toward him, took the photograph from his limp hand and slid it carefully back into the pouch.

"I've made my confession," she said in a barely audible voice. "Now I'm going to lie down. Until we have to meet Jed."

He couldn't answer, only watched her sink to the mattress. Rolling to the spot she'd occupied the night before, she pulled up her knees and lay with her back to him, her body trembling.

No longer able to stand, he lowered himself into the chair, staring into space, his thoughts and emotions in turmoil.

A little girl. His daughter. His and Mariana's. The startling reality reverberated through his mind, through every cell of his body.

It was simply too much to absorb. Not after all this time. Not after everything he'd assumed.

He tried to tell himself it didn't matter. Nothing had changed. He knew he was lying to himself. Everything had changed.

His eyes flicked to Mariana as she lay on the bed, her body curled protectively away from him. When he simply couldn't bear to watch her any longer, he picked up the morning newspaper on the table and thumbed through it, looking for any news of the supposed terrorist attack at the airport. There was nothing. The story had dropped off the face of the earth.

But his mind wasn't capable of doing more than skimming headlines. Every time he tried to concentrate on something else, he came back to the bombshell she'd dropped in his lap.

She had a daughter. A daughter who was five years old. *His* child.

MY GOD, it was the final irony. He'd done the honorable thing and not taken her innocence. Now she was asking him to believe it hadn't worked out the way he'd expected.

His eyes kept flicking to the clock, watching the minutes tick by. When he couldn't sit still for another moment, he got up and shaved. Then he started throwing clothing into the bags he'd brought from the store.

Mariana sat up and looked at him with red-rimmed eyes. "What are you doing?"

"Getting ready to leave. We can have lunch in a café while we wait for Jed."

"I'll help you."

"I can do it."

Ignoring the clipped response, she got up and retrieved her dress from the bathroom, along with the toilet articles he'd bought.

They cleaned up the room in silence. When he was satisfied the place looked as anonymous as when they'd first entered, he picked up the bag he'd dropped beside the door.

She snatched up the other bag, following him silently down the stairs and into the parking lot.

After stowing their few possessions in the trunk, he consulted a map he'd gotten from the desk clerk, then started the ignition again.

He pulled out of the parking lot, all his attention focused on his driving. He didn't speak again until they'd taken an entrance ramp onto the highway and were heading south. "Does Jed know what you look like?" he asked.

"Not unless he's seen a picture of me."

"I guess he'll be looking for me, then."

"THANK YOU FOR COMING," the older man said graciously as he stepped aside to usher his guest into the opulently furnished study of his house in Santa Isabella.

"Thank you for doing me the honor," his guest replied, crossing the Spanish-tile foyer with its potted plants and pre-Columbian Indian sculptures liberated from an ancient city in the mountains.

The host led the way to a spacious study, the closed shutters lending an air of cool isolation to the meeting. The two men had never been friends. But they were part of the San Marcos elite—the two hundred families that held the wealth and power of the country. Constantino Reyes had also been one of that select circle—until he had become expendable.

The older man clenched his hand into a fist, then struggled to relax the tension. He wasn't going to suffer Reyes's fate. And his visitor was part of the plan for ensuring his safety, because they had come to understand that if they worked together, they could each get what they wanted.

"Please. Sit down."

The visitor settled himself in a leather armchair on one side of the carved stone fireplace. The host crossed to the sideboard. As he opened a cigar humidor, he covertly studied his guest. The other man was tall, well built, just starting to gray at the temples. He was at the height of his manhood. The height of his power. Yet he still had his vulnerabilities because sometimes he was ruled by his passions rather than his head.

From the humidor on the side table, the older man extracted a fine Cuban cigar, rolled it between his fingers and brought it to his nose, inhaling the enticing aroma.

"Can I offer you one of these?" he asked, extending the humidor. "I have them flown in from Havana."

"Yes. Thank you." The visitor accepted a cigar and for several moments they were busy with the ritual of lighting up and puffing.

The host pointed to the drink trolley under the window. "Brandy? Cognac?"

"I never indulge so early in the morning, but you go ahead."

The words might be taken as a subtle insult. Ignoring it, he gave a small shrug and poured himself a brandy because he needed the liquor in his belly at the moment.

Still, he moved with deliberate nonchalance as he settled himself in the leather easy chair on the other side of the fireplace and crossed his legs. As if intent on savoring the tokens of his wealth and power, he focused on the cigar and the amber liquid in his glass for several moments before asking, "Are you going to give me an update?"

The other man flashed square white teeth. "I have agents in several towns where she could have hidden the child before she left for the States."

"And?"

"We'll find out where she is."

He nodded, took another sip of brandy. He'd investigated this man and found him to be efficient and ruthless, as well as someone who hung on to a grudge by the last shreds of his fingernails.

He was a bad fellow to have for an enemy. So for better or worse, they were stuck with each other.

MARIANA SAT STIFFLY in the front seat of the car, her eyes covertly moving toward Scott as he drove. The traffic was fast and heavy, and more than once a car cut sharply in front of them.

Each time, Scott muttered a curse under his breath, and she had to stop herself from twisting a lock of her hair into a knot.

His hands were clamped to the wheel, and his jaw was set with equal rigidity. Every so often his eyes flicked to the rearview mirror, and she knew he was making sure they weren't being followed. But that wasn't the only thing on his mind. Judging from the expression on his face, she imagined he was counting the minutes until he could turn her over to Jed Prentiss.

Then it would be all over. Despite what she'd told him, she'd never see Scott O'Donnell again. Her throat burned and she felt a giant fist squeezing the inside of her chest, making it impossible for her to draw a breath without feeling the pain.

It was all she could do to keep from gasping for air. The only thing that kept her taking in shallow, controlled breaths was her own pride. Because she would not let him see her anguish. If he didn't want to acknowledge his child, that was his business. But she couldn't let him know how much that hurt.

Chapter Seven

He couldn't stand to see her sitting there small and defenseless like a wounded bird caught in a trap, so he kept his gaze focused on the traffic ahead—and the traffic behind, making sure that nobody was tailing them. Still, he was aware of every shuddering breath she took, every little movement as she took her lips between her teeth or reached to wrap a strand of dark hair around her finger.

The pressure of his hands on the wheel helped anchor him to the present. He found he didn't like it all that much better than the past.

In the San Marcos prison where they'd taken him, all choice had been stripped away from him—along with his self-respect. Six years later, he could make his own decisions, but he had the terrible feeling that any choice he made would be the wrong one.

He slowed as they reached the fringe of the Art Deco district. Even on a weekday morning, there were plenty of cars driving up and down the streets, and it took several minutes of searching before he found a space.

Mariana had been silent since they'd gotten into the car. Now he saw her sit up straighter and smooth the hem of her skintight knit top. He had the sudden impulse to apologize for having gotten her an outfit he knew would make her uncomfortable.

On the other hand, she fit right in with the crowd, he noted as he eyed the casually dressed men and women, some with kids in tow, emerging from cars and strolling toward the commercial area, bent on a pleasant morning of shopping.

It was easy to see why Jed had chosen the location. Lincoln Road was an open-air pedestrian mall with almost as many in-line skaters and bikers as pedestrians, along with a free tram for the lazy. Men and women with shopping bags darted in and out of jewelry stores, art galleries and the inevitable T-shirt shops, many of which advertised their wares in Spanish instead of English. The air was rich with the smell of *café con leche* and the sound of Latin rhythms emanating from many of the doorways.

"This is like being at home," Mariana said as she looked around, wide-eyed.

"Yeah."

He felt her relaxing in the familiar environment, until he saw a policeman coming toward them through the crowd. When she moved closer to him, he slipped his arm protectively around her shoulder, feeling his own heart pounding harder as the man advanced.

However, the officer didn't give them a second glance, and Scott let out a breath, feeling as if he'd passed some kind of test. It took several moments for him to realize that he still had his arm around Mariana, and she was standing with the side of her body pressed to his so that he could feel every curve of her wonderfully feminine shape. Swiveling his head, he saw that her eyes were closed, her lips slightly parted, and he had to give himself a mental shake to make himself drop his arm.

Her eyes blinked open, and she looked around in surprise, like a child coming out of a dream. They were standing in front of a white stucco café with a balustrade along the roofline. The sign in the window advertised Cuban specialties, and there were a number of diners at outdoor tables.

"This is as good a place as any," he said.

"All right," she answered, her voice seeming to come from far away.

He led her to a table shaded by a green-and-white striped umbrella, then took a seat where he could watch the street. Mariana sat with her back to the building, as if she needed the solid wall to prop herself up.

Not prepared for small talk, he gave his order and angled away from the table, scanning the crowd for Jed.

The combination platter the waiter set in front of him might have been good if his nerves had allowed him to taste the food. Judging from the way Mariana was bent over her plate, pushing a piece of plantain around in a circle, it appeared she was having the same problem.

She was sitting three feet from him, close enough that he could reach across the table and touch her again if he wanted to. Yet he felt the gap between them widening with every moment that passed.

"Mariana," he heard himself say.

Her head jerked up, and those beautiful eyes of hers focused so intently on him that he had to drag in a breath.

He felt like a man teetering at the edge of a deep chasm, where one false move would send him plunging to his death on the sharp rocks far below. He could still back away and scramble to safety. But he chose to step forward and peer into the abyss.

"Let me see the picture again."

She stared at him in astonishment, her eyes wide yet cautious. Her hands were shaking as she fumbled at her waist for the zipper of the money belt. It seemed to take forever to open it, and he had to keep from leaping out of his chair and charging around the table to help her. Instead, he sat there, feeling the blood pounding in his temples.

Perhaps she'd taken so much time so she could compose herself, he decided, because when she raised her head again, her face was carefully neutral. But she was unable to control the trembling of her hand as she handed him the snapshot.

Again he saw the little girl with the red hair and the light eyes. This time, he felt his heart slam against the inside of his chest, felt a rush of unfamiliar emotion he'd blocked when he'd looked at her image before.

She was his daughter. There was no denying that simple fact. A child he and Mariana had made together.

"What did you tell her about her father?" he asked, hearing the gruffness of his voice as he cupped the photograph in the palm of his hand.

The color in her cheeks deepened, and she shifted in her seat. "Why do you want to know?"

He couldn't answer the question, not even in the privacy of his own thoughts. "Just tell me," he said in a clipped tone.

"The things I said were to make her feel good about being your daughter. To give her a sense of connection, of…of being wanted."

He nodded, knowing what it was like to be a kid who wasn't wanted.

"I told her she looked a lot like you. I said you were sorry you had to go away before she was born."

Her hand fluttered, and tears glistened in the corners of her eyes. "You have to understand, it was hard for her being different. When she came home crying because some stupid kids teased her about not having a father, I explained that you wished you could be with her."

When her voice cracked, he reached across the table to press his fingers over hers.

She drew in a shuddering breath before going on. "I told her you loved her. I know that was…presumptuous. But I thought you would have." She stopped, gulped. "And I was trying to make sure she understood that she was as good as anyone else."

He wanted to ask if he could keep the picture. But he knew she needed it more than he did. So he handed it back across the table. "It's okay," he said thickly. "You told her the right things."

Mariana stared down at the little girl as if trying to see something new in her face.

He watched her, thinking that his own childhood had been hell. And now he was responsible for making another child miserable. It was almost too much to bear.

"I told her stories about you," she added, her voice soft. "The things I knew. And…" She paused, then seemed to make a decision. "I kept a journal. I wrote in it every week. Things about her when she was a baby—when she walked, her first words. All the things you'd want to know if you ever—"

She broke off, took several gulping breaths. "I'm telling you because you asked. That's all."

"I know that," he answered softly.

For an unguarded moment, her eyes shone. "I know you'd like her. She's…a daughter you could be proud of."

He couldn't dredge up an answer, not when he'd been hit with this surprise less than two hours ago. His heart was thumping too hard and too fast and he wanted to be alone, where he could sort things out in private. But there was nowhere he could hide.

"Scott, I know this is all a shock."

"Yes."

"You don't have to feel any obligation to us."

He gave her a hard stare. The world as he knew it had changed suddenly and irrevocably, and he was trying his best to cope. "Don't tell me what I can and can't feel. I have to figure that out for myself."

"I'm sorry. I was just trying to make this easy for you."

"Don't," he said again, more sharply than he'd intended.

Before the conversation could continue, a tall figure entered the outdoor café.

"Jed's here," he said with a mixture of relief and disappointment.

Mariana nodded and slipped the picture quickly into her money belt as the former agent came over to their table.

"Sorry I'm late."

"No problem," Scott answered, tipping his head up to gaze at his friend. Dressed in cutoffs, a light knit shirt and sunglasses, he was doing a pretty good job of looking relaxed—unless you knew him well enough to see the tension around his mouth.

"What happened?"

"There was a reception committee waiting for me at the airport. I gave them the slip. Then I drove to another branch of the rental place and changed cars."

THE WORDS MADE Mariana gasp, adding to her sense of unreality as she tried to switch gears. She and Scott had been in the middle of a deeply personal discussion about their daughter. Now she'd better remember why she'd come here in the first place.

"Nowhere near as dramatic as your greeting," the newcomer was saying as he pulled out a seat and offered her his hand, which she shook. It was large and firm, but he didn't try to emphasize his superior strength by squeezing too hard.

"I'm Jed Prentiss," he said.

"Mariana Reyes."

"Glad to meet you."

He was sizing her up. She did the same, liking what she saw. He was a big man with an open face, blond hair, blue eyes and an easy confidence that made her feel like she and Scott had an ally. The only thing she wished was that he'd waited a few more minutes before appearing.

The waiter approached and asked if he wanted to order a meal. He declined, but asked for a piece of key lime pie and *café con leche*.

"Might as well get some perks out of this," he remarked, stretching out his legs comfortably and crossing them at the ankles as he looked around the café. The lunch rush was over, and most of the tables around them were empty now, giving them a fair amount of privacy, even in this outdoor setting.

"What, exactly, happened at the airport?" Scott asked.

"A couple of wise guys were looking for me. If I'd known I was so popular, I wouldn't have taken a commercial flight."

"How did they know you were coming?"

He shrugged. "The important thing is that I gave them the slip."

Scott answered with a tight nod.

Jed swung his gaze between the two of them. "You haven't made any more calls since we talked?"

Mariana felt her face heat. "I was going to," she answered honestly. "Scott stopped me."

"Good. Because somebody is going to a lot of trouble to find you."

She felt the blood drain from her face but did her best to return his steady gaze.

"Well, first things first. If we get separated, we'll meet at my car." He gave Scott a description of the vehicle and directions to the location where he'd parked.

"Why do you think we might get separated?" Mariana asked.

Jed shrugged. "I don't. But it's better to be prepared."

Before she could press for more information, he took control of the conversation. "So, you're mixed up with Hector Porfirio," he said, addressing her in a voice that didn't carry beyond the table.

"He was a friend of my father's," she said, automatically using the same low tone.

"Your father was…?"

"Constantino Reyes."

Jed made a low, whistling sound. "One of Sanchez's backers."

"No!" she objected hotly. "He and Sanchez weren't friends. My father was against him."

"Then why did he provide some of the money for the general's private army?"

She heard the question, but she refused to believe it had any validity. Instead, she demanded, "How do you know so much? How do I even know you're telling the truth?"

"For starters, he took a big risk coming here," Scott snapped.

Jed shook his head. "No, she's got a right to ask." He looked around to make sure nobody was within earshot. "I'm a friend of Scott's from Randolph Security. My wife, Marci, works in the same building where he does. But before I settled in Baltimore, I was with a couple of covert government agencies. You don't need to know the names, but at one point I was assigned to the School of the Americas when Sanchez was doing some military training there. He and I got to be friends, as much as an American agent and a San Marcos general could be friends." Jed's expression turned hard. "Then he tried to execute Marci, and relations between us got a little strained."

Mariana listened with fascination, sure that the things he wasn't telling her were at least as interesting as the clipped explanation.

"Over the years, I've kept myself informed on the political situation in San Marcos—and on Sanchez. In fact, a couple of years ago I went back to get some military records for another friend."

"Is that why Hector Porfirio sent me to you?" she asked.

Before he could answer, the waiter arrived with his order.

Jed took a swallow of the hot coffee with milk, then forked up some pie.

"The real thing," he said appreciatively. "You can't get it like this in Maryland."

"Isn't it supposed to be green?" she asked, eyeing the wedge of yellow pie topped with whipped cream.

He laughed. "Don't say that too loudly. They'll know you're a tourist." Deliberately, he took another bite, chewed

and swallowed before lifting his head toward her again.
"Here's the problem," he said. "I only know Porfirio by
reputation. I haven't a clue why he sent you to me." He
paused. "I think he picked me because, if you checked my
credentials, you'd find out I had an extensive background
working in San Marcos. But I have the feeling you weren't
actually supposed to make contact with me."

Slack-jawed, she stared at him. "But his letter made me
think you and he were friends."

"We never met!" Jed said emphatically.

"I'll give you another piece of the puzzle," Scott broke
in. "Six years ago I ended up in a San Marcos prison. A guy
named Ed Thompson got me out. He's the one who sent me
down here to hook up with Mariana."

"I don't recall your mentioning getting in trouble down
there," Jed murmured.

"It wasn't exactly my finest moment."

"Maybe you'd better fill me in."

"The details aren't important," Scott retorted.

"Maybe they are."

Mariana raised her eyes to Scott's and held his gaze for
several heartbeats before turning to Jed. "It's a long story,
as you said about your wife and Sanchez. The important
point is that I was convinced I could save his life by planting
some military maps in his apartment. I thought they were just
looking for an excuse to deport him. I didn't know they
would throw him into prison and torture him."

Jed tipped his head to the side, taking in the frank explanation. "Thanks for being straight with me."

"I promised myself I would be." She gulped. "Back then,
I was too young and too frightened to make the right choices.
I thought six years of hiding from Sanchez's hit men had
made me smarter. Now you're telling me that I was sent to
you by a man who might not have had my best interests at
heart."

Jed's eyes narrowed as he turned to Scott. "Maybe she

was sent here to get hooked up with *you*. Only she would have refused if she knew the truth. So they used me as a decoy.''

Stunned, she tried to understand the devious thinking that had produced such a plan.

"It's going to take a little time to unravel all this," Scott muttered.

"It'll have to wait," Jed said, his voice turning sharp as he stared in the direction of the street. "Keep your eyes on me," he added. "There are two men coming down the street, both wearing light jackets and sunglasses. They're the two who were waiting for me at the airport."

Scott cursed softly. "How did they get here?"

"Damned if I know," Jed answered.

Mariana felt the breath freeze in her lungs.

"Keep your back to the street. Mariana, get up and go inside like you're going to the ladies' room," Jed said. "Go through the restaurant to the back door. Scott and I will follow you. Go."

She pushed herself up, mildly surprised that her knees would hold her weight. Trying not to lurch like a windup toy, she made for the restaurant interior. It was cool and dark inside, and it took several moments for her eyes to adjust. Then she started toward the back.

"You can't come in here," a man said in Spanish as she barged into the kitchen.

When she didn't reply, he tried again in English. But she was already halfway across the tile floor.

The alley smelled like garbage, and she stood staring at the refuse around the Dumpster, thinking that the front of the building was a lot more inviting.

Long seconds passed, and she glanced behind her anxiously, waiting for Scott and Jed to appear.

Finally, Jed pushed through the door, moving at a dead run. Scott was right behind him.

"Come on," he growled.

She didn't need any urging. Following the men, she sprinted down the alley and ducked around a corner, hearing the sound of heavy footsteps getting closer.

They came to a row of buildings that were obviously being renovated. At one, the back door stood open with wallboard and lumber piled in an untidy heap nearby. Tacked to the door was a sign that said, Danger—Keep Out.

Jed dodged inside. Scott stepped aside so she could follow, then pulled the door shut. When he ducked around a table saw and some drop cloths, she followed. Through the window she could see a courtyard where stacks of lumber blocked their escape route.

Jed retraced his steps toward the back of the room, then started up a roughed-in flight of stairs. Before she or Scott could follow him, a noise at the back of the building made them all freeze.

Looking wildly around for another exit, Scott spotted a place where workmen had been building a false wall, forming an enclosed area about two feet wide and four feet from the floor.

God, anyplace but there, he thought, feeling cold sweat break out on his skin as he peered into the dark, confined space. But it was the only option.

"Get inside, Mariana," he hissed.

On hands and knees, she obeyed, while he turned and dragged the table saw a few feet across the floor so it hid the opening, then scattered the sawdust so the tracks wouldn't show.

Finally, teeth gritted, he ducked into the tunnel. As the cold, dark passage swallowed him up, he felt his heart threatening to pound its way through the wall of his chest. The ringing of blood in his ears almost blotted out the sound of men cursing and heavy objects being thrown around outside.

Ahead of him, Mariana flung herself through the wall into

what had to be the next building. On the other side, the space was similar, except there was no exit.

Scott felt the walls pressing in on him, felt the breath being squeezed from his lungs. Somehow he made himself scramble after her and sat gasping for oxygen, his back pressed against the wall.

There was just enough light to see a piece of drywall that was apparently intended to close the gap between the two spaces. Mariana leaned across him and pushed it into place, just as feet pounded into the room where they'd been standing.

He sat unmoving as tactile images of spider feet and sharp-toothed rodents—the tiny monsters of his childhood—crawled into his mind. He could feel them on his skin, on his arms, working their way up his pant legs.

God, no, his mind screamed. But he kept the scream locked inside. And that was a kind of victory, at least. It had taken every ounce of willpower he possessed to follow Mariana into the suffocating darkness, and then to follow her down the tunnel. Knowing she was there had helped, but it hadn't stopped the terror from building.

In his mind he realized he wasn't a helpless little boy locked in a dark closet, being punished for crimes he hadn't known he'd committed. But he'd spent so many hours in the dark, waiting for his stepfather to come and pull him out and beat him again, that the panic attack was a conditioned reflex.

Long ago, he thought he'd slammed the door on that terrible time in his life. But it only took a small, enclosed space to bring the terror screaming back.

He felt Mariana press against him. All he could do was sit in the darkness, desperately holding on to the shreds of his sanity.

The men who'd carted him off to prison had known about his weakness. He remembered the look of satisfaction on their faces when they'd shoved him into a closet-size box and bolted the lid shut—and left him there to simmer in his own juices until they were ready for other tortures.

Outside, footsteps crossed the floor toward them, and he felt Mariana go rigid beside him. Somehow he managed to lift his hand a fraction and bring it down over her trembling flesh. She turned her palm up, knit her fingers with his, squeezed tightly. With superhuman effort, he made his muscles work enough to hold her hand, even as he wondered which of them needed the contact more.

As if her thoughts were in tune with his, she carefully swung around in the darkness so that the front of her body was pressed to his. Then her free arm crept around his neck and tunneled through his hair as her head dropped to his shoulder. His hand came up to cradle her, and she moved closer, soft and pliant in his embrace, as if they were lovers who had crept into this cramped, dark place for the pleasure of being alone.

She moved her mouth to his ear and murmured his name. It was the barest whisper of sound, yet he heard and absorbed.

In the next moment, the spell was shattered. His body tensed again as he caught the sound of something heavy scraping across the floor—and recognized it as the table saw being shoved away from the opening in the wall.

Chapter Eight

Muscles rigid, he waited in the darkness for one of the thugs to come crawling down the tunnel, wondering what the hell he was going to do. Or if he was capable of doing anything besides sitting there and letting them shoot him.

Then, from the floor above, he heard scuffling noises and a shout. Beside him, Mariana sucked in a sharp breath. She gasped when the scuffle was followed by a gunshot, then another.

"Jed!" she whispered, even as heavy footsteps clattered overhead.

Forcing his muscles into action, Scott cupped Mariana's shoulder. "Move over so I can get out," he whispered.

After a second's hesitation, she slid away from the wall-board. Teeth clenched, Scott eased the covering aside and peered down the tunnel. The light at the other end beckoned to him like a lantern in a storm.

"Stay here," he ordered as he started crawling back the way he'd come, the blood that pounded in his ears blocking out every other sound. Reaching the end of the passageway, he started to scramble out, just as he spotted two pairs of feet descending the stairs. With a silent curse, he shrank back into the shadows, knowing that his chances of remaining unde-tected were slim.

Every muscle tensed as he prepared to spring at his attackers, but he held himself in check when he saw that they came awkwardly down the stairs, one leaning heavily on his companion, and groaning with every faltering step he took. His left hand was pressed against his shirt, and blood oozed from between his fingers. He grimaced as he reached the first floor and swayed sideways. His companion fought to keep him erect, murmuring encouragement in Spanish.

"You're gonna make it," he said. "But we gotta get you out of here in case somebody figures out where those shots came from."

The wounded one didn't answer, only gritted his teeth and let his friend steer him toward the back of the building.

Scott made himself wait until they'd been out of sight for half a minute before starting forward.

Behind him, Mariana's voice rose in a firm whisper. "Don't."

"It's okay. They're gone." Pulling himself from the tunnel, he stood and swiped fingers across his clammy forehead.

After scrambling from the opening, Mariana gave him an assessing look. "What happened to you when we went in there?"

"Nothing!" He rubbed his damp palms against the sides of his shorts, then started for the steps.

"I couldn't see anything," she said, hurrying to keep up with him.

"One of them had a bullet wound in the chest. I'm surprised he was still on his feet," he muttered, seeing the trail of blood spattered on the risers. Taking the steps two at a time, he reached the upper story and almost slammed into a huge roll of insulation lying sideways across the floor. Dodging around it, he saw more building materials—some stacked neatly against the walls, some scattered as if a hurricane had torn through the room.

Jed was sprawled against a pile of lumber, his body limp and his head lolling to one side. Like the man on the stairs, his shirt was also bloodstained.

Responding to the movement in the doorway, he raised his head—and the gun in his hand.

"Don't! It's me," Scott called.

The eyes struggled to focus, and the gun wavered, then lowered as Jed sagged back against the wood. Scott sprinted across the room and knelt beside him. Mariana moved quickly to his other side.

"*Dios,*" she wheezed, looking down at the blood on his shirt and the gray color of his skin.

"I hit one of the bastards," Jed muttered, his words slurred. "What happened to him?"

"He's got a chest wound, but I guess they didn't want to stick around for the police."

"You can't either," Jed said hoarsely, starting to push himself up. As he fell back, he cursed.

Mariana soothed a hand across his forehead, her eyes going to Scott. "We've got to get him to the hospital," she said.

Jed lay with his eyes closed for several seconds, then opened them again and focused on Scott, obviously making a tremendous effort to stay with him. "I don't have much time to talk," he whispered. "Something you don't know about me. I've got a virus in my blood...that shuts down my body when...I'm under stress. I can feel it...now."

Scott stared at him. He'd heard that something strange had happened to Jed several years ago—something that had forced him out of active duty as a secret agent. He knew his friend hated to talk about it, except to joke once in a while about a voodoo curse.

"No time. Listen. It's only...my shoulder...you... Mariana. Go. Call 911. Call Marci. She'll know...what... I...need."

"We can't leave you," Mariana said.

"Got to. This is...big. An interna—" He stopped and sucked in a breath. "International conspiracy. Someone high up...in U.S. government... Powerful. You...find out...expose..."

It was obvious that the speech had taken a Herculean effort. He lay back, his eyes closing again as he struggled to get out one more phrase. "Your...obligation is more...important...than me."

"No," Mariana insisted.

"Yes," Jed hissed.

"But we don't have any information!" Mariana pleaded. When Jed didn't answer, she gently pressed her hand to his neck. "His pulse is weak," she whispered to Scott. "He could bleed..."

The injured man's eyes blinked open, and Scott saw he was struggling to hang on to consciousness. "The virus," he whispered, his words so slurred they were hard to understand. "Puts me...out...stops bleeding..." He gathered in a shaky breath and looked at Scott, his eyes fierce. "You go...take gun...take car..." He trailed off, his eyes closing again as he settled back against the lumber, his breath shallow.

"He's delirious," Mariana said.

Scott shook his head. "No. I remember hearing something about this. He's got what he calls a voodoo virus. From some island in the Caribbean. But..." He swore in exasperation. "How in the hell am I supposed to know what to do?"

"Go," Jed whispered urgently with what must have been the last of his strength.

Scott turned his troubled gaze to Mariana. "We'd better do what he says."

"We can't just leave him!"

"Do you think I want to?" he said harshly, his eyes boring into hers.

She shook her head numbly.

Forcing himself to be hard and pragmatic, he felt in Jed's pocket, found his car keys and also his portable phone. After a moment's hesitation, he also took out Jed's wallet and stared at the driver's license.

"He's carrying a false ID," he said in a gritty voice. "His name is Dan Parker."

"Oh," was all she said. Then she made a noise as she saw Scott removing the cash and thumbing through the wad of bills.

"I'll pay him back later," he said sharply. "And this makes it look like a simple robbery." Bending low over Jed, he asked, "Did you hear that? If you can hear me, buddy, tell the cops you were dragged in here and robbed."

There was no response, but Scott hoped that the message had lodged in Jed's mind. Picking up the gun from the floor, he shoved it into the waistband of his pants, pulling his shirt over it. Then, standing, he stuffed the folded bills into his pocket.

"Come on. The sooner we get out of here, the sooner we can call an ambulance," he argued, trying to persuade himself as well as Mariana.

It was almost impossible to turn his back and walk away. The only thing that made him do it was the urgency he'd heard in Jed's voice—and the fierce look in his eyes.

When Mariana stood frozen in place, he took her arm and helped her to her feet.

"Is he going to be all right?" she said, turning and looking over her shoulder as they reached the steps.

"Yes." He gave her the only answer that he could, praying that it was true.

At the top of the stairs, he reached for the gun he'd just put away.

"Wait till I tell you it's all clear," he ordered, then started cautiously down. Pulse pounding, he made a quick inspection of the first floor, then called for her to follow. Moments later, they were back in the alley, walking at a normal pace that belied the pounding of his heart.

On the street, they blended back into the crowd, then located Jed's car not far from the restaurant where the three of them had sat in the sunshine less than half an hour ago. As soon as they were inside, Scott called 911, reported that a tourist had been shot and gave the location.

Refusing to supply his name, he slammed the receiver into the cradle, pulled into the stream of traffic and drove for several miles.

"Now all I have to do is break the news to Marci," he muttered.

When he'd convinced himself he could handle it, he got the number from information, and called Adventures in Travel in Baltimore.

As he waited for Jed's wife to come on the line, he felt Mariana's hand cupping his shoulder.

"I know this is hard," she whispered.

"Yes." Then Marci was speaking, and all his attention focused on the woman at the other end of the line.

"Scott, what's wrong?"

He swallowed, and forced the words he didn't want to speak past his lips. "I'm sorry, but Jed was shot."

"Oh God! How bad is it?"

"His shoulder…but…"

"The virus," she said. "I'll be there as soon as I can. What hospital?"

Scott felt his stomach knot. "I don't know. He made us leave him before the ambulance came."

"You left him?" she said, her voice icy.

"I had to."

There was a long pause, then she said, "Okay."

"Marci—"

"We can't stay on the line. He told me…" She stopped. "I'd better not repeat what he said, except that I know the name he's using."

"I'm sorry he got hurt. I'm sorry we had to leave him."

"I know you are. Thank you for calling. Now hang up," she said, her voice very firm.

"I—"

The connection went dead, and he stared at the phone,

marveling at her courage, and her ability to think straight when he'd just told her the man she loved had a bullet in his body.

Mariana's hand slid to his arm. "Don't blame yourself for Jed. It's my fault."

"I lured him down here!" He turned and glared at her, daring her to contradict him.

"Because he was *my* contact." She swallowed. "Scott, we both feel terrible. But we didn't have any choice."

"Yeah, you're good at thinking like that!" he muttered.

The color washed out of her face, and he wished he could call the accusation back. Shrinking away from him, she huddled against the passenger door, her hands clasped tightly in front of her and her head bent.

"I'm sorry," he said in a gritty voice. "That wasn't fair. Jed *told* us to go."

"What you said is true," she whispered.

He reached to put his hand on her arm, feeling her cringe at his touch. "I'm taking out my guilty feelings on you," he admitted, trying to be as honest as he could.

The silence in the car hung between them. Then he slowed as he spotted a trash can on a side street.

"Pitch the phone," he ordered. "In case they can track its location."

"Is that possible?"

He made a snorting sound. "You know, a couple of years ago there was a movie called *Enemy of the State* where the bad guys were from the National Security Agency, and they wanted to kill this poor jerk because he'd stumbled onto information that could damage them. They used satellites to track him, and when they didn't use satellites, they used the phone system. Every time he made a call, they found him. I thought it was a paranoid fantasy dreamed up by some Hollywood writer. Now, the way things are going, I think we'd better assume the worst."

She picked up the phone from the seat, holding it gingerly

by the antenna as if it were a dead mouse. Flinging open the car door, she sent the instrument clanking into the trash can.

The moment the door closed again, Scott pulled away from the curb and started moving again, trying to stay within the speed limit as his mind raced—making plans, considering contingencies.

Beside him Mariana huddled in her seat. As he watched her, he promised himself that he was going to make things come out right, this time.

On the outskirts of the city, he found a gas station and started contacting hospitals. It took three calls to find out that a man named Dan Parker had been admitted to the emergency room at Municipal Hospital. Unfortunately, the woman who answered would only say that he was in surgery.

As soon as he completed the call, he started the engine and merged into the flow of traffic again.

"Jed's in surgery," he told Mariana as he put some distance between them and the phone. Fifteen minutes later, he pulled off the highway again, into a shopping plaza.

"What are we doing?" Mariana asked as he found a parking space in the sprawling lot.

"A repeat of last night's shopping expedition. We're a retailer's dream. We buy clothing and throw it away the next day." He sighed. "This time you get to pick what you want to wear. I'll meet you near the checkout lines."

She eyed the store doubtfully, then gave a little nod, and he realized she'd probably never been shopping anywhere like this superstore before.

"Do you want to wait in the car?" he asked.

"No. I want to help you. But I may not know what to buy."

"The standard stuff. Underwear. A couple of casual outfits."

After leaving her in the women's department, he made a rapid run through several other sections of the cavernous store, his attention only half on the shopping.

His mind was reeling with the impact of Jed's desperate words. An international conspiracy. All those years ago he'd told himself that he had just been in the wrong place at the wrong time. That there was no way he could answer the questions of his interrogators. But what if the questions really had made sense? What if it all had something to do with the film he'd shot?

He shuddered. The film was gone. Thompson had taken it, and told him it wasn't the reason he'd been scooped up by the police. At the time, he'd wanted to believe it because he'd wanted to put the whole thing behind him.

He stopped still in the middle of an aisle. Was that what he had to do? Go back to Thompson and find out what was so important about the damn film?

He had no answer to the question. And no clue about how to find the bastard. So he set the problem aside and concentrated on simply keeping himself and Mariana alive.

By the time he finished with his purchases, she was waiting near the main aisle, anxiously scanning the shoppers. When she saw him pushing his cart toward her, she relaxed several degrees. But the worried look didn't leave her eyes.

"Got what you need?" he asked.

She gestured toward a meager stack of clothing. "I didn't want to spend too much. And..." She held up a soft green dress. "Is this okay?"

He imagined the thin fabric clinging to her slender figure and swallowed. "Fine."

His own haul was a lot more extensive, and he felt guilty. Not about spending the money but about what he was going to make her do in a little while.

"This place is so big," she whispered as they waited to pay.

"Yeah, you can buy everything from motor oil to tea bags and TV's," he answered offhandedly as he began transferring items from the cart to the counter.

Quickly she began to help him, not paying too much attention to his purchases. But when she saw the package of mahogany-colored hair dye with a picture of a woman on the front, she shot him a questioning look. "Why do we need this? My hair is already dark."

"It's not for you," he said, then lowered his voice. "But let's not talk about it now."

She gave a tight nod and didn't speak again while they were in the store. Back at the car, he shoved everything into the cheap suitcase he'd bought, then stowed it in the back seat, except for the Miami Dolphins cap, which he shoved onto his head with the bill in the back.

When he glanced at Mariana, she was sitting tensely in the passenger seat with her hands clasped in a death grip in her lap.

"I need to ask you a favor," she said softly when he'd closed the door.

He glanced back toward the store, wondering if there was some feminine item she'd been embarrassed to buy in front of him. "Did you need something else?"

She kept her eyes trained on her hands. "No…nothing for myself. It's about Alicia."

He went very still, then raised his head as a flash of movement caught his eye. A man and a woman were coming down the row, their arms full of packages. They stopped at a nearby car, and the guy set his purchases on the roof while he fumbled in his pocket for the keys.

"Mariana, a parking lot isn't a good place to talk," he answered, wondering where, exactly, he'd like to have a discussion about the child he'd learned of this morning.

"I know."

"We need to be more private." He twisted the key in the ignition, and the car roared to life. After looking behind him, he backed out of the parking space and headed for the exit.

Mariana sat with her head bowed and her hands locked together.

He might have told her to go ahead and sock him with

some more revelations he didn't want to hear. Instead, he kept his eyes on the road as he drove toward the city again, not even looking for a place to stay until they were deep into a low-rent area. Then he chose a small, green stucco motel with a faded tile roof.

Leaving Mariana in the car, he strode to the office and asked if there were rooms in the back because his wife wanted to get away from the highway noise. The clerk gave him the key to room 14, which faced a stretch of trash-strewn ground in back.

The room sported scarred night tables on either side of the double bed and several stains on the rug. But when he took a quick look inside the bathroom, it seemed relatively clean.

Turning back to Mariana, he found her facing the window, apparently staring at the closed blinds. Heaving the suitcase onto the bed, he reached toward her, then let his hand fall back.

"I'm sorry this place isn't very nice."

"It's fine."

As she played with a strand of her hair, he clenched his hands at his sides, wondering which was worse—watching her tension or feeling his own stomach muscles tie themselves in knots.

"You were going to say something about Alicia?" he finally made himself ask because the need to know what was in her mind was greater than his need to protect himself.

She gave a helpless little sigh, half turned, then changed her mind. Still with her face angled away from him, she whispered, "Susana is old. And…" Her voice trailed off. He saw her shoulders heave, and she started again. "Today, when Jed got shot, I realized that it could have been me."

"We're going to get out of this!" he insisted.

She answered with a mirthless laugh. "He said it's an international conspiracy. How do *we* fight an international conspiracy?"

"I'm not without resources," he said, even as he wondered

exactly what they were. At the moment, his chief plan was to evade capture.

"I know," she answered, the hope in her voice making his insides clench even tighter. He watched her hands sliding up and down her arms. When she started to speak again, her voice was so low that he automatically took a step closer so he could hear her. "Scott, I went into hiding before Alicia was born. I didn't have much…how do you say it? Prenatal care. She came early, while I was traveling to a village in the mountains."

He tried to imagine what that must have been like. Stepping forward, he wrapped his arms around her waist.

She leaned into him, sighing before she began to speak again. "They got a woman who could help. But the conditions were primitive." She stopped and breathed. "I was in labor for a long time. When the doctor finally came he had to do a—a caesarean. He said there were problems and, I— I can't have any more children."

The pain in her voice cut through him, and he turned her in his arms, stroking his hands across her slender shoulders, feeling the tremors that went through her body.

"I'm sorry," he heard himself say. "That must be…" He let the sentence trail off, unwilling to make things worse by trying to put her feelings into words.

"I've accepted it. It's my…punishment."

"No!" he answered automatically. Over the years, he'd had his own pain to deal with. He'd had no idea what she might have gone through.

Her head moved against his shoulder, but he could hear the tears edging her voice. "Alicia is all I have. She's very important to me."

"I know," he answered, the words coming from deep within him. "You're a good mother. I know that, too."

"I've tried." Her breath hitched and her fingers dug into his arm, clenching and unclenching. "Scott, I know it's a lot to ask. You don't even know her. But promise me that

How To Play:

No Risk !

1. With a coin, carefully scratch off the 3 gold areas on your Lucky Carnival Wheel. By doing so you have qualified to receive everything revealed — 2 FREE books and a surprise gift — ABSOLUTELY FREE!

2. Send back this card and you'll receive brand-new Harlequin Intrigue® novels. These books have a cover price of $4.25 each in the U.S. and $4.99 each in Canada, but they are yours TOTALLY FREE!

3. There's no catch! You're under no obligation to buy anything. We charge nothing — ZERO — for your first shipment. And you don't have to make any minimum number of purchases—not even one!

4. The fact is thousands of readers enjoy receiving books by mail from the Harlequin Reader Service®. They enjoy the convenience of home delivery...they like getting the best new novels at discount prices, BEFORE they're available in stores...and they love their *Heart to Heart* subscriber newsletter featuring author news, horoscopes, recipes, book reviews and much more!

No Cost!

5. We hope that after receiving your free books you'll want to remain a subscriber. But the choice is yours — to continue or cancel, anytime at all! So why not take us up on our invitation, with no risk of any kind. You'll be glad you did.

LUCKY

Find Out Instantly The Gifts You Get
Absolutely FREE!
Carnival Wheel

Scratch-off Game ➤

Scratch off ALL 3 Gold areas

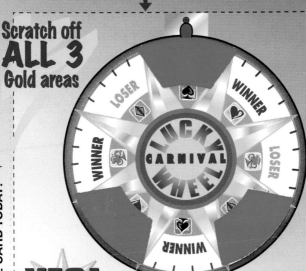

YES!

I have scratched off the 3 Gold Areas above. Please send me the 2 FREE books and gift for which I qualify! I understand I am under no obligation to purchase any books, as explained on the back and on the opposite page.

381 HDL CY43   **181 HDL CY4T**

NAME   (PLEASE PRINT CLEARLY)

ADDRESS

APT.#   CITY

STATE/PROV.   ZIP/POSTAL CODE

Offer limited to one per household and not valid to current
Harlequin Intrigue® subscribers. All orders subject to approval.

(H-I-04/00)

The Harlequin Reader Service® — Here's how it works:

Accepting your 2 free books and gift places you under no obligation to buy anything. You may keep the books and gift and return the shipping statement marked "cancel." If you do not cancel, about a month later we'll send you 4 additional novels and bill you just $3.57 each in the U.S., or $3.96 each in Canada, plus 25¢ delivery per book and applicable taxes if any.* That's the complete price and — compared to cover prices of $4.25 each in the U.S. and $4.99 each in Canada — it's quite bargain! You may cancel at any time, but if you choose to continue, every month we'll send you 4 more books, which you may either purchase at the discount price or return to us and cancel your subscription.

*Terms and prices subject to change without notice. Sales tax applicable in N.Y. Canadian residents will be charged applicable provincial taxes and GST.

If offer card is missing write to: Harlequin Reader Service, 3010 Walden Ave., P.O. Box 1867, Buffalo, NY 14240-1867

BUSINESS REPLY MAIL
FIRST-CLASS MAIL   PERMIT NO. 717   BUFFALO, NY

POSTAGE WILL BE PAID BY ADDRESSEE

HARLEQUIN READER SERVICE
3010 WALDEN AVE
PO BOX 1867
BUFFALO NY 14240-9952

NO POSTAGE
NECESSARY
IF MAILED
IN THE
UNITED STATES

if…something happens to me…you'll find her and take care of her.''

"Nothing's going to happen to you!" he vowed, his arms tightening around her as the earth seemed to dip and sway dangerously beneath his feet.

She lifted her head, searching his eyes, her own dark and pleading for his help and understanding. "Please. I know I don't have the right to ask anything more from you.... You didn't even know you had a daughter—until today." She swallowed. "But please, I can't stand thinking about her alone and afraid."

"I—" He stopped, struggling not to drop through the giant crevasse that had opened below his feet.

"Promise!"

"Okay."

"Say it!"

"I promise that if anything happens to you, I'll take care of her," he said, the raw words burning his throat.

"Thank you." She held on to him for a moment longer, her embrace fierce. "I know this is hard for you," she whispered.

"And for you. You're her mother."

He couldn't say the rest, and the unspoken part of the sentence hung between them, making the air in the little room thrum with the tension that enveloped them both. Unable to cope with the emotions surging through him, he grabbed the suitcase off the bed and bolted into the bathroom.

Chapter Nine

Mariana sat in the chair, her knees pulled up against her chest, as she listened to sounds coming from the other side of the door. A while ago she'd heard packages being opened, then a buzzing noise.

Much later, Scott had turned on the shower. As it cut off, she felt her tension ratchet up another level. He'd gone in there because he didn't want to talk to her. She was sure things wouldn't be any better when he came out. If she could have escaped from the room, she would have done it. But she'd learned her lesson the last time she'd left a motel room without asking.

Finally, the knob turned, and she stiffened. When he stepped out of the bathroom, she couldn't hold back a gasp. He'd used a clipper to shave away most of his hair. What was left was dark brown, exaggerating every angle and plane of his face.

"I wouldn't have recognized you," she gasped.

"Good." He remained in the doorway, rocking back and forth on his heels staring at her, his face twisting. "You have to make yourself look different, too," he finally said. "Before you can leave this room again."

"Dye my hair?" she asked, wondering if he'd bought another package of hair coloring that she hadn't seen.

"Cut it," he answered.

She sucked in a sharp breath, and her hand went protectively to the dark hair that hung in waves around her shoulders. She had worn it like that for as long as she could remember. In all the years she'd been hiding she had never considered the idea of cutting it off.

"No." The syllable was part plea, part protest. He knew how she felt about her hair, didn't he? He had run his fingers through the strands. Told her how beautiful it looked. Spread it around her head against the white pillowcase in that long-ago hotel room. Her eyes drifted closed as that memory swept over her.

The harsh sound of his voice interrupted her reveries. "I'm afraid the answer is yes. If you want to stay alive—for your daughter—you have to look as different as you can. The sooner you get it over with, the better."

Too choked to speak, she stood on shaky feet and walked stiff-legged toward the bathroom. Then she straightened her shoulders. He wasn't asking so much. Her hair would grow again.

When she faced the mirror where a large pair of shears rested on the edge of the sink, however, she felt her hands go numb.

"I can't," she choked out. "If you want my hair cut, you'll have to do it."

He made a low sound of protest. "I'll make a mess of it."

"So will I!" She raised her eyes, meeting his in the mirror. For long moments, neither of them moved, then he turned away and grabbed a towel from the rack. She saw his lips set into a thin line as he draped it around her shoulders.

Closing her eyes, she grasped the edge of the sink, the coldness of the porcelain seeping into her hands.

"I'm sorry," he muttered. "I knew you wouldn't like it. I wouldn't ask, if it weren't necessary."

"In your opinion," she whispered.

"Do you want men with guns coming after you again?"

She didn't answer, only gripped the sink tighter as she felt his fingers touching her hair. Then the scissors seemed to make a hungry sound as the blades bit through the thick strands, and she had to clamp her teeth on her bottom lip to keep from crying out.

Her whole body vibrated with tension as she felt him chopping at her hair, his fingers stroking the strands just before each cut.

Once she heard him curse under his breath, but she didn't open her eyes to see if he'd butchered her. Eventually she would have to look, but not yet.

Her head felt lighter. Or maybe that was simply her imagination. He cradled her face against his chest and she leaned into him. When she felt his fingers stroke the top of her head, a shiver went through her.

"Turn around," he said in a gritty voice.

She obeyed, felt another cut, then another, felt as if he were cutting away at her soul. Tears welled behind her closed lids, but she struggled to hold them back.

He stepped away from her, and she swayed, opening her eyes because it was the only way she could keep her balance.

His face was unreadable as he stared at her. "I'm sorry."

"Are you?" she managed to say, fighting hard against the tears that threatened to spill down her cheeks.

"Yes."

"Why?"

"Because I loved the way your hair looked. Because I always thought of it when I thought about you."

It wasn't the answer she expected.

"You thought about me?" she asked, her voice high and thin as she felt a trail of moisture slide down her cheek.

"Oh yes." He swallowed. "Do you hate me for cutting it?"

The anxious look on his face made something inside her break apart. "No. I could never hate you."

"Thank God."

She stared at him, hardly able to believe the emotions she was seeing in his eyes.

"You don't look any less beautiful," he said, his tone thick and husky.

Her hand went to her hair, and she trembled as she felt where the strands ended so abruptly.

Setting the scissors down, he pushed the towel off her shoulders and into the sink, then reached for her.

She went into his arms, a shuddering sigh escaping her lips as he clasped her to him.

When he lowered his mouth to hers, she made a sound that was part pleading, part invitation.

"Mariana, I was so wrong about you. Forgive me!" he breathed, his warm breath touching her as he spoke. Then his mouth was moving over hers with an urgency that sent a shock wave through her, a tremor that shook the floor beneath her feet.

When he opened her lips, she made a small, needy sound, then gave herself over to the feast that he offered.

Heat leaped between them as it had that morning when he'd kissed her outside the ice-cream parlor. But this time they weren't standing on a public street. They were in the privacy of a motel room.

Her hand slid back and forth across the clipped hairs at the top of his scalp, the bristles abrading her nerve endings and sending little currents of sensation through her body. With a low sound, she slid her other hand across the broad expanse of his back, reveling in the way his firm muscles rippled under her touch.

He flooded her senses—taste, touch, scent. The only thought in her mind was that she needed to get closer to him, as close as she could get. Seeking his warmth and strength, she slipped her hands under his shirt, stroking her fingers upward against his quivering skin.

He seemed to have the same need as she, because his

hands were under her shirt, too, stroking, caressing, then working the clasp of her bra.

When his palms slid around to push the bra out of the way and cup the weight of her breasts, she whimpered with the pleasure of his touch.

"Oh, Scott, it's been so long."

"Yes."

Her nipples were already hard knots of sensation as he stroked them, then rolled them between his thumbs and fingers, wringing a gasp of pleasure from her.

Stepping back, he pulled his shirt over his head, while she did the same with hers.

She touched his chest, tracing the lines of the scars that he'd gotten because of her.

"I'm sorry," she whispered. "So sorry. I never meant for you to get hurt."

"It was a long time ago," he said as he swept her into his arms. The feel of his hair-roughened chest against her breasts made her knees buckle. But he held her up, held her tightly against his body as he lowered his mouth to hers again for a wild, demanding kiss. She wanted that urgency—that feeling of recklessness—because it meant she might get what she had dreamed of for so long. Yet she was afraid, too.

Closing her eyes, she swayed against him, then let him lead her out of the bathroom and across the rug toward their inevitable destination.

She had ached for this. Still, in the moment when they ended up beside the bed, she felt her body stiffen.

He lifted his head, his eyes coming back into focus. "Mariana?"

The unfamiliar look of his face framed by the dark, short hair made her shiver. This wasn't the Scott she had known. Not at all. Yet it was the man she loved, she told herself.

Ducking her head, she tried to gather her scattered thoughts so that she could speak coherently.

She knew he felt her hesitation, and his hands dropped

away from her body. When he started to step beyond her reach, she closed her fingers over his forearm.

"Scott."

"I'm afraid I got carried away back there," he said in a tight voice as he gestured toward the bathroom. "But you don't have to pay for my protection—if that's what this is all about."

"No. Don't think that. I want to be with you," she whispered. "So much. So many nights I've dreamed of lying in your arms again, with nothing between your body and mine."

She saw the wary expression change to a question. "But?" he asked in a strained voice.

She couldn't find the words to tell him all her uncertainties. The only thing she could do was whisper, "I have a scar. From when I had Alicia. It's so ugly."

He shook his head, gathered her close, his hand stroking over her back, then reaching to caress the cut end of her hair. "Nothing about you could be ugly," he murmured. "Never."

She laid her head against his shoulder, then turned her face so that she could brush her lips against his hot flesh. She had longed for this moment, and she would take what he was offering now.

He crooked his finger under her chin and brought her mouth up to his so that he could give her tiny soft kisses that slowly became deeper, more intimate.

When he lifted his head, she was gasping for breath—and so was he.

Bending, he swept the covers aside, then began to ease her to the bed.

"Wait." She reached for the snap at the front of her shorts, and fought it with shaking hands. Wrenching it free, she skimmed the garment away, along with her underpants. He was watching her, watching the hands she couldn't quite keep steady as she saw his gaze travel over the curve of her abdomen.

"It's not ugly. I can hardly see it," he said.

When she made a doubtful sound, he reached to trace the indentation of her waist and the curve of her hip, then the line of the scar. "You've grown into a very beautiful woman—with a gorgeous body."

She felt herself blush, felt the heat creep down her neck to the tops of her breasts.

"I want you naked, too," she said.

"So you can see how my stomach muscles are holding up?" he teased.

She shook her head. "Because that's not how we started last time."

He gestured toward the rigid flesh straining behind the fly of his jeans. "Yeah, well, there was a reason for it back then. There still is. I don't want to go too fast."

"But I want…everything I couldn't have before," she said again, hearing the note of desperation in her own voice.

He stroked his hands up and down her sides, sliding over her ribs, her hips, her thighs as he bent to brush his lips against hers—once, twice. "We will," he promised. "Everything we couldn't do before. But not until you're ready."

"I am ready."

"Let me be the judge of that," he murmured as his lips moved to her jawline, her ear, down her neck, sending currents of sensation coursing through her.

He did kick away the rest of his clothing before he brought her down to the uneven mattress. But he caught her hand when she tried to touch him intimately. Instead, he gathered her in his arms and began to touch her and kiss her in all the ways that she remembered so well.

She cradled his head against her breast as his lips opened over one taut nipple, the wet heat and the tugging pressure making her cry out as she arched into the heady pleasure of it.

He murmured hot, sexy words as his fingers slid up her leg and found the moist heat where her body begged for his touch. And as he began to caress her, she opened her mouth against his shoulder, stroking her tongue and lips against his hot flesh.

Then the need to communicate became urgent. "Scott... I'm going to...no more..." she finally gasped, recognizing that he was going to send her over the edge. "Please. I want to do this the right way. Now."

He raised his head, his gaze locked with hers. "There is no right way."

Still, she felt an enormous sense of relief as he moved between her legs. Her eyes were still locked with his as she felt his erection probing her most intimate flesh.

This was what she had longed for, dreamed of, although she'd thought she could never have her heart's desire. But here he was, pressing against her, pressing *into* her.

The stab of pain took her by surprise, and she cried out, her body stiffening.

Above her, Scott froze.

"Mariana?" he asked, raising his head, his face stunned as he gazed down at her.

She clasped her arms around him, held him tightly. Moving her hips, she took him deeper inside her, silently asking for more.

"My God, Mariana, you—you should have told me," he said in a strangled voice.

"I didn't know how to," she managed to say but could dredge up no more words. The power of the moment overwhelmed her as she absorbed the reality of her body joined with his.

His face was above hers, taut with strain and perhaps a little of the emotion she was feeling.

She stroked her knuckles against his cheek. "Show me the rest of it," she whispered.

Slowly he began to move, pulling back and then coming

forward in long, gliding strokes as he watched her face. When he saw that he wasn't hurting her, the pace quickly became more urgent, more demanding.

He had brought her pleasure before, showed her the responses of her body. But this was more. Ecstasy that surged through her in time to the rhythm of his body surging into hers.

Joyfully, she met each thrust and retreat, wringing a strangled exclamation from him as she matched his rhythm.

Then his hand was between them, stroking and pressing the spot he had taught her was the center of her sensations.

A hot tide swelled within her, carrying her up and up to heights she remembered. The same—but different.

"Don't stop," she gasped, hardly knowing that she had spoken aloud. "Don't stop."

His answer was unintelligible, lost in the tight spiral of urgent need as she frantically rocked her hips against his, begging for release.

It came in a burst of rapture that made her cry out and dig her nails into the slick skin of his shoulders. Wave after wave crashed against her, lifted her, carried her to a place she had only imagined. And this time he was there with her—right with her, his own hoarse cry mingling with hers.

She floated back to bed in his arms, clinging to him in the aftermath of the storm.

"Thank you," she gasped. "Thank you for giving me that." The words were inadequate, but she knew that saying more would be dangerous.

His lips skimmed her cheek, and he started to shift his weight off her, but she circled his lower back with her hands, holding him where he was.

"Stay with me," she whispered. "Stay inside me a little longer."

"I'm too heavy for you," he answered. But he didn't leave her, only shifted to his side, his arms cradling her so that he could take her with him.

She closed her eyes and rested her head against his shoulder, allowing herself to revel in the moment.

SOME TIME LATER, her eyes blinked open. Scott was still lying beside her, cradling her in his arms, his green eyes warm as he watched her.

"Was I asleep?" she murmured.

"Yes."

"I didn't mean to."

"I liked holding you."

"I liked everything."

"Yes."

"You should have told me," he repeated his earlier words. "I never dreamed you would be a virgin. How was that possible?"

She tried to laugh and failed. "I guess I never do things the regular way, do I? I told you, Alicia had to be delivered by caesarean section."

His arms tightened around her, and she tucked her face against his shoulder. She was thinking she'd just managed to do something the "regular way." And she longed to tell Scott how much that meant to her.

In reality, she longed to take the conversation to a deeper level—to say all the things that were in her heart. She wanted to know what making love had meant to him. She wanted to know about the future. But she couldn't ask how he felt now. Or make the declaration of love bubbling inside her, bursting to be set free. So she closed her eyes, nestling in his arms while she had him beside her.

They both slept, then. But when Mariana woke, she knew immediately that Scott's mind was on other things.

"What are you thinking about?" she asked.

He hesitated for several moments. "That we should eat."

She was pretty sure that hadn't been the topic uppermost in his mind, but she didn't challenge him.

"I stuffed some sandwiches in the suitcase, along with the

clothing.'' He laughed. ''They really did have one-stop shopping. I'll go get some sodas from the drink machine.''

Climbing out of bed, he picked up the clothing he'd discarded on the floor and grabbed the ice bucket sitting next to the television set.

While he was gone, she pulled the covers over the red stain that marred the sheet and dashed into the bathroom. Quickly she washed herself, then began to dress. She had just pulled on her shorts when he came back with the ice bucket and sodas.

After removing a slightly crushed paper bag from the suitcase, he shifted his weight from one foot to the other.

''Are you okay?''

''Yes.''

''I mean…''

''I know what you mean. I'm fine.''

He studied her as if he was trying to make sure she was telling the truth. Then he walked to the table and started taking out the sandwiches. ''I got roast beef on rye and turkey on whole wheat. Which one do you want?''

''Could we share?''

''Sure,'' he answered. She knew the rejoinder was supposed to be casual, but she felt tension coming off him in waves.

While he got glasses from the bathroom and filled them with ice, she unwrapped both sandwiches and rearranged the portions, then took a small bite of the turkey, trying to convince herself she could enjoy the food.

But her own worries were more compelling than the meal.

Perhaps he caught the uncertain expression on her face, because he asked, ''What are *you* thinking about?''

She chewed and swallowed the bite of sandwich, wishing she could turn aside the question as easily as he had. But she'd sworn to herself that she would never lie to him. ''About…about Alicia. I can't help wondering if she's okay. Scott, do you think she's safe?''

"Yes."

"You're just saying that."

"What do you want me to say?" he asked, his voice clipped.

She stared at him, sure he wouldn't want to hear her answer. She wanted to hear him say he loved her. She wanted him to say he forgave her. She wanted him to say he would be a real father to their child.

The silence stretched. Finally, when the tension became more than she could bear, she stood, collected some things from the suitcase and shut herself in the bathroom.

Chapter Ten

For the first time she dared to look at her hair. Her vision swam as she inspected the ragged cut. Snatching the scissors still sitting on the toilet tank, she evened the cut ends a little. When she'd done the best she could, she ran the shower and stepped under the spray.

By the time she came out, she was feeling more in control. And once she'd towel-dried her hair, she decided it was passable. At any rate, it would grow. Besides, right now it was the least of her problems.

When she stepped into the room, Scott was sitting in the chair, with a newspaper open on his lap. But apparently a good deal of his attention had been focused on the bathroom door, because he glanced up as soon as she stepped back into the room.

They stared across the ten feet of space that separated them.

"You look good," he finally said in a voice that was almost normal.

"Well, not too bad," she corrected. "Not as bad as I thought. You did a good job."

"You evened it up." He stood, crossed to the dresser and leaned against the edge.

She nodded.

The conversation died again. After several seconds, he

cleared his throat. "Actually, there's something else I've been thinking I should say to you."

Every muscle in her body seized as she waited for him to tell her things she didn't want to hear.

SCOTT KNEW he had to tell her now. He might never have another chance.

"I've spent the past six years blaming my prison stay on you. Now I'm ready to admit the only person I have to blame is myself." He said it in a rush, in one breath, and he was amazed that he had managed to make the confession at all.

Turning away from the shocked expression on Mariana's face, he paced to the window, stared at the dusty slat blinds, then lifted several so he could peer out.

"How can that be true?" she asked.

"Because it all goes back to Thompson, the man who sent me to the Miami airport to meet you," he heard himself admitting. "He was in on it from the beginning, and he's in on it now." He ran a hand through his hair, momentarily startled by the way the short bristles felt against his fingers.

"I guess I thought I was going to win an Emmy for my outstanding work capturing the nuances of San Marcos culture. Anyway, it was really important to me. But I kept getting turned down for financing." He stopped, sighed. "Then, finally, when I'd just about given up, Thompson came out of the woodwork with an offer to bankroll me with federal funds."

"From a government agency? Which one?" She asked the question that he should have pursued more thoroughly six years ago.

"He said he was with the State Department. He gave me a number to call and check his employment. I did that. But I didn't investigate too deeply, because I wanted the money." He turned back to face her. "Can you understand that?"

"Yes. It was very important to you."

He nodded. "He gave me enough cash to buy equipment,

go to San Marcos and hire a small staff. The only stipulation was that he wanted to see any film I shot. At night, after you had left, he came in to look at it.''

"That's not so bad."

"Yeah, well, maybe it was."

The dull ache that had started in the front of his head was pounding through his entire brain now, making him ball his hands into fists. Opening them again, he flexed his fingers. "I've told myself there was nothing sensitive on any of my film, nothing worth being jailed and tortured for. But I don't know for sure."

"You mean you don't know if you shot anything sensitive?"

"No. I mean, I don't know what was on some of the film. When I decided to go up to Chipotalli to do some scouting around, it was because you told me you had the day free— and you could come with me. But the next day I was supposed to go to Nagola Province to visit General Sanchez's compound." He told her the secret that he'd kept hidden all these years. "I knew I was rushing it, but I told myself I had time enough to do both. When I realized we weren't coming back for at least twenty-four hours, I sent Pepe in my place."

"You changed things around to be with me," she whispered, going to him and resting her head against his shoulder.

"I would have rearranged the Gregorian calendar to be alone with you," he said.

She allowed herself to feel the impact of the confession for several seconds, then asked, "And you trusted Pepe to take care of the filming for you?"

"Maybe I shouldn't have. At the time, I told myself he was competent and efficient," he argued, hearing the hollow sound of his own voice. "You saw him differently?"

"I never liked him. He was…" She shrugged as she tried to find the right words. "Strange. Intense. I never knew why he was interested in filmmaking."

"He told me how much he wanted to learn the business.

He was a good worker. But I knew you and he never got along.''

"He resented my social position," she said, and he sensed that she was struggling to keep her tone mild.

"Well, he didn't give me any trouble. And he knew what he was doing." He paused, his vision turning inward. "I never got a chance to find out what he filmed in Nagola Province. And I made the decision not to discuss it with Thompson, either."

"Why not?"

"I figured I had enough problems, and I didn't want to do or say anything that would prevent me from getting out of San Marcos," he answered with brutal honesty. "Besides, Thompson told me there was nothing sensitive on any of the film he'd seen."

He had tossed out the statement as a sort of confirmation that it was true, but something about the way Mariana shifted her weight from one foot to the other put him on alert.

"What?" he said.

She lifted her face to him. "I—I haven't thought about any of this in years. But I heard the government men talking about film. They ransacked the office and took away everything they could find."

"So they got the footage Pepe shot," he said, hearing the relief in his own voice. "Then that's not what this is about—"

Before he could finish, she hurried on. "Scott, that's not how it happened. Pepe didn't come back until after they'd left. When he found out you'd been arrested, he got scared and took off. After he disappeared, I searched the Jeep. And I found some film that he'd packed in the wrong boxes."

The impact of her revelation reverberated inside his head. They'd asked him over and over about the film when he was in prison. He'd had no way to answer their questions. "What happened to it?" he asked in a hoarse voice.

"I hid it."

''Why would you do something like that?'' he demanded, suddenly conscious of how much he had told her.

''Because *they* thought it was important. And I didn't want to get you into any more trouble than you already were.'' She reached to twist at a strand of her hair, found it had been chopped off and made a small sound in her throat.

He crossed to her and seized her hand, folding her fingers and pressing them against his lips. ''So the film's been missing all these years. Where did you put it?''

''I gave it to Juan Tiemplo, an old servant of my father's.''

''Does he still have it?''

''I don't know. I think he would have kept it if he could. He and I were friends. But I haven't seen him in years.''

His fingers tightened around her hand as he struggled with the sudden tension twisting his insides. He'd told himself that it would be a cold day in hell before he set foot in San Marcos again. Now, suddenly, it looked like his only option.

''We have to find out what's on that film. Maybe it's from Sanchez's compound. Maybe it's something different— something Pepe shot instead of the assignment, or in addition to it.'' His mind swam with new possibilities.

''Maybe it's not important,'' she countered.

''Is that what you think?''

She shook her head. ''It doesn't matter what I think. We can't look at it.''

He searched her eyes. ''Why not?''

''How would we get to San Marcos? If they're watching the airports here, they're doing the same thing at home.''

''I get the feeling Jed was prepared to arrange transportation,'' he answered, hoping it was true. Now that he knew the footage existed, he had to see it for himself, no matter what the risk. Because if Jed was right and they were caught in the middle of some international conspiracy, the film might well be the key to saving their lives.

He took a deep breath and let it out in a rush, trying to calm himself so he could think through the implications.

"It's not just the film," he mused. "Something's changed. Something that made Thompson and his boss change their minds about how to handle the 'situation.' Something that made them come up with the plan to get us both branded as terrorists and blown away at the Miami airport."

He felt her fingers digging into his arm. "What are we going to do?" she asked.

He thought about it for a while, then checked his watch to make sure there was still time to get what he needed.

"I'm going down to the hospital and talk to Jed."

"Scott, it's too dangerous. We don't know—"

He cut her off before she could finish. "It's an acceptable risk."

"Then let me do it."

He gave her an incredulous look. "You don't even feel comfortable in a department store. What makes you think you can impersonate a nurse?"

When she gave him a defeated shrug, he started to add another telling point, then decided that it was a mistake to share any more of his thinking. But she'd caught his expression and wasn't going to let him off the hook.

"You were going to say something else," she said.

He swallowed. "You have to stay safe—so you can go back and pick up Alicia."

"I—"

His jaw firmed. "I'm not going to argue with you. And if I'm going to pull this off, I have to leave."

"When will you be back?" she asked, her voice hitching.

"As soon as I can." Crossing to the desk, he scribbled a name and number on a piece of stationery. "This will get you in touch with Randolph Security. If anything happens to me, call them."

"You said nothing would happen to you!"

"Yeah. But if I'm wrong, you'll need help."

She took a shallow breath, then a deeper one. When she

wrapped her arms around his back and held him tight, he felt her heart pounding—and his.

His arms came up to embrace her, and he heard himself saying, "You could give me a kiss for luck."

"Scott," she whispered, lifting her head, seeking his mouth. He meant it to be a light kiss. It turned deep and intimate and ended when he wrenched his mouth away, though he wasn't able to turn her loose yet. As he clasped her body to his, he sensed that she would stay in his arms as long as he wanted to hold her there.

"Are you trying to keep me here?" he asked, his cheek pressed to hers so she couldn't see his face as he struggled to control the emotions surging through him.

"Yes," she admitted, her tone throaty.

"I'll be back soon. Lock the door behind me."

He stepped away from her, turning quickly to avoid eye contact. Before he could change his mind, he opened the door and bolted outside. Then he waited in the humid darkness until he heard the sound of the lock clicking and the safety chain sliding into place.

IT WAS DARK, and Alicia was supposed to be asleep. She'd put on her nightgown and gotten into bed. And Tiá Susana had read her a story.

Now she lay in the narrow bed with the doll, Maria, that Mama had given her. She could hear Tiá Susana and Tiá Dolores talking.

Then Tiá Susana went out, and Tiá Dolores was listening to the radio.

Alicia listened to the soft music from the front of the house and talked to her doll, telling Maria that everything was going to be all right. She had almost drifted off to sleep when a knock at the door made her eyes snap open. At first Tiá Dolores didn't say anything. But when the knock came again, louder and more urgent, her aunt called out in a high, nervous voice, "Who is it?"

A man said something through the door, and Tiá Dolores opened it. Then Alicia could hear the two of them talking in the front room. Although she couldn't make out anything they were saying, the low buzz of their voices made her heart start to pound like a drum inside her chest.

When Tiá Dolores came down the hall, Alicia pulled up the covers and closed her eyes.

Tiá Dolores brushed the hair back from Alicia's face. "Wake up, *niña*," she said, trying not to sound worried.

Alicia opened her eyes and blinked. "What?"

"You have to get dressed."

"But Tiá Susana said I needed my sleep," she said, her arm tightening around her doll.

"I know. But you have to go out."

"I want to stay here!"

"Please, little one. Don't give me an argument."

SCOTT TRIED to keep his mind off Mariana as he drove into the city, but it was impossible not to picture her sitting tensely on the bed in the motel room waiting for him.

Was it safer to have left her or to have let her come along? He prayed it was the former.

In the space of a few days, everything he'd thought about her had changed. He'd believed she'd gotten him thrown into prison. Finally he'd admitted it was his own fault. More than that, he could see that all her problems stemmed from her association with him.

He pounded his palms against the wheel. All these years he'd pictured her married and living with Bernardo Cortez. Now...

Now he knew the truth. He'd ruined her chances for marriage by leaving her pregnant—even if he'd talked himself into believing that what they'd done in that hotel room was safe. He hadn't had intercourse with her. But he'd come damn close. Too close, as it turned out.

She'd borne his child—a little girl named Alicia. And the

two of them had been on the run since he'd escaped from San Marcos and gone back to his nice safe life in Baltimore. The image of mother and child huddled in the darkness together made his head pound, and he forced his mind away from the disturbing picture.

There was no way he could have known about the child. And he couldn't afford to let the guilt swamp him now, because he had to stay focused to stay alive.

At a phone booth ten miles from the motel, he called the hospital and found that the patient named Dan Parker had been moved to room 303 and was in stable condition.

Then he used another phone to call stores that sold uniforms. To his relief, one was still open, so he drove to the shop and bought a doctor coat. Next he took a roundabout route to the hospital, making sure that no headlights stayed in back of him. When he reached the sprawling complex, he circled the perimeter, checking the parking lots, the exits, the traffic flow, before finding a parking spot near an entrance where he could watch the comings and goings of employees.

Half an hour later he squared his shoulders and headed for the emergency-room entrance, feeling the wind tear at his new white coat as if protesting his deception.

Doing his best to look as if he owned the place, he strode confidently toward the double doors. His steps faltered momentarily when he caught sight of a guy with unkempt dark hair leaning against the wall, watching the exit. It wasn't anyone he recognized, yet something about his face and posture reminded him of the two men from Lincoln Road.

Trying to keep his features relaxed, he walked briskly through the door, his ears peeled for signs of pursuit.

The man stayed where he was, and Scott breathed a sigh of relief as he strode across the waiting area where a security guard was talking to the woman at the admissions window.

Scott kept his pace steady and confident, secretly relieved when he saw a sign to the elevator. Luckily, at this late hour, there were few people in the halls.

Once the elevator doors closed behind him, he felt as if he'd won a major victory. Yet he couldn't banish the unpleasant prickling sensation that had started at the back of his neck.

It was because he didn't want to confront Jed, he told himself as he walked down the hall. Locating room 303, he passed it and exited onto the stairwell where he could watch the doorway. A few moments later, a nurse came down the hall and disappeared into the room.

When she came out and returned the way she'd come, he made his move, stepping into 303 before his emotions could get the better of him.

It was a private room, and his eyes lit on the high-tech bed where Jed lay with his eyes closed, a white bandage around his head, and tubes and wires going in and out of his body.

Scott had told himself he was prepared for what he was going to see. But the way Jed looked, lying there so still and pale, made him fight for breath. At the same time, the white bandage confused him. From what he remembered, Jed had been hit in the body. What had happened to his head?

Scott didn't even realize anyone else was in the room until a low, feminine voice said, "The nurse just checked him. What are you doing here?"

Caught completely off guard, he swung his eyes to the woman sitting beside the bed. Marissa Prentiss. Marci. Before she'd married Jed, her travel-agency job had served as a cover for secret assignments from the State Department.

He'd always seen her as calm, cool and collected. Now dark smudges marred the skin under her eyes, and her rumpled shirt and skirt looked as if she'd thrown them on a couple of days ago. As she stared up at him, her expression went from questioning to alarmed, and her hand slid into the pocketbook that rested on her lap.

When he realized she didn't have a clue who he was, he found his voice. "It's Scott," he said.

Her eyes studied him. "Scott?"

"If you don't recognize me, I guess I get an A-plus from the Sherlock Holmes School of Disguises," he said, hoping to dissipate the tension that had crowded into the room with him.

She whispered his name again, took a closer look at his face and hair. The hand that had crept into her purse slid out again and rested on top.

Scott shifted from one foot to the other. "Why does he have a bandage on his head?" he asked anxiously.

"It's a prop. In case..." She swallowed. "In case somebody comes looking for him. Hunter, Steve and Matthew from Randolph Security came down here with me. I sent Hunter out for dinner. The other two guys are at the airfield."

Scott nodded tightly. "How did you get the hospital to allow a false bandage?" he asked.

"Well, they think Jed is a special agent in the Miami area under deep cover. And Randolph Security agreed to do a free evaluation of their vulnerability to unauthorized access." She shot him a quizzical look. "Judging from the fact that you got in here with no problem, I'd say they need it."

"Yeah. Why don't they have a guard on Jed?"

"Too conspicuous." Marci glanced from Scott to her husband. "He's not as bad as he looks," she said reassuringly. "I brought his medical records with me. So they know about the virus he has and why it's keeping him unconscious." She gave a small laugh. "Actually, they're excited about the chance to, uh, study him."

"How long before he comes out of it?"

"It depends on the extent of the trauma to his body. The surgeon removed the bullet. And there's no damage to internal organs or anything like that," she answered with a note of relief.

"Good." Standing beside the bed, Scott laid his fingers briefly over one of Jed's still hands. "I'm sorry I got you into this mess."

He thought he caught a tiny flicker of eyelid movement, but it might have been his imagination.

He looked at Marci, and he repeated the apology, knowing it was completely inadequate.

"He knew this could be dangerous," she answered.

"He talked to you about it?"

"We always talk," she said emphatically. "He's kept up with the situation in San Marcos, and he thought there were compelling reasons to come down here."

Scott nodded. When he sensed another facial movement from the unconscious man, he turned quickly back to the bed.

"I think he can hear us."

"Yes," Marci answered. "At least some of the time." She moved to her husband's side and touched his cheek. "Everything's fine," she murmured. "Scott came to see you. He's got a boot-camp haircut and he's dyed that gorgeous red hair industrial brown. So don't freak out if you open your eyes."

"Good description," Scott said.

Jed's lips moved, but nothing came out.

"He's trying to say something," Marci whispered as they both leaned closer.

The man on the bed seemed to be struggling up through layers of fog, but he couldn't break through the barrier of his imposed sleep.

"Jed?" Scott asked hoarsely. "Is there something you need?"

His head moved on the pillow.

"Something you want me to know?"

In answer, Jed's facial muscles contorted.

"Is he in pain? Is that it?" Scott asked.

Marci stared at him with concern. "Maybe I should get the nurse."

"Go on. I'll be right here with him."

She left the room, and Scott leaned over his friend. "Take

it easy," he said. "Everything's going to be okay. Do you need some pain medication?"

"N-no."

Before Scott could ask another question, Marci rushed back. "I saw two men coming down the hall, ducking into the patients' rooms," she breathed, snatching her purse from where she'd laid it on the window ledge. "They don't look like hospital staff."

Scott swore under his breath. It was insanity to assume that the gang of thugs searching for him had figured out he was here. Yet somehow he didn't think the men Marci had seen were simply checking the rooms to make sure that all the food trays had been picked up after dinner.

His gaze shot to the man lying on the bed who was now moving restlessly, then to Jed's wife as she extracted a small handgun from her purse and concealed it in the folds of her skirt.

She moved to the bedside, explaining in low tones what was happening.

Above the sound of her voice, Scott could hear the searchers coming, and he felt a pulse begin to pound in his temple.

God, now what? A shootout in Jed's hospital room? Cursing himself for not staying in the motel, he stared at the closet, the bathroom, discarding each as an adequate hiding place.

There was only one more possibility. Leaping to the window, he turned the crank, opening the casement as wide as he could. Hoping nobody was standing on the ground below, he kicked the screen free, hearing it land with a soft thud on grass or dirt.

Hands on the metal frame, he ducked through the opening, scraping his shoulder and then his knee in his haste to escape from the room. Outside he discovered there was only a tiny ledge, so narrow that he had to turn his feet to the side as he shuffled along the wall.

The rough stucco pulled at the fabric of his doctor coat, trying to hold him back, but he tore away and kept moving.

It was windy outside the building. In fact, he could feel another Florida storm blowing up. The white coat whipped around his hips, and he clenched his teeth, pressing his back against the rough wall.

Focusing on a light in the distance, he dug his hands into the side of the building and held on as tightly as he could, wishing he had suction cups on his fingers.

Behind him, he heard the window closing. Moments later, there were more sounds in the room. He heard Marci say, "My husband's very sick. What are you doing here?"

The question elicited a gruff answer, but Scott couldn't catch the words. Every muscle in his body clenched as he awaited the unmistakable sound of gunfire.

Chapter Eleven

The shots didn't come.

Still, Scott's ears strained for some sounds from within as he hovered in the darkness, his pulse pounding, his nails clawing at the side of the building. One of his feet began to tingle, then went numb as the wind picked up, whistling around the corner of the building and whipping at his trouser legs and coat sleeves.

A splattering of rain hit his face, and he braced for another deluge. Before it could drench him, the window opened again, and his whole body tensed.

"Scott? Are you out there?" Marci called.

"Yes," he answered, letting out a ragged sigh as he shifted his weight. His muscles were stiff, and his foot felt like a block of wood as he concentrated on inching back toward the window.

"Are you okay?" Marci asked when he stood in the room once more.

He nodded. "Are you?"

"Yes."

"What did they say they wanted?"

She gave a short laugh. "They said they were doing a room check, whatever that's supposed to mean. I didn't try to keep the conversation going."

He swore under his breath. Had the guy at the door spotted

him? Or were the thugs simply checking every hospital room in the Miami area?

"Do you think they were looking for me specifically?" Scott asked.

Marci shrugged. "That's my best guess. At least they didn't realize who Jed was."

Before he could ask another question, footsteps sounded in the hall again, and they both went stock-still.

A large male shape filled the doorway, and Scott cursed himself for returning to the room so soon. After several seconds, it registered that the newcomer wasn't one of the guys who had been searching the ward. It was Hunter Kelley from Randolph Security.

"This is Scott," Marci said quickly.

The hand that had slid inside Hunter's coat stilled as he studied Scott. "You look like a mess," he said in the blunt way he had.

Scott laughed. "Bad hair day."

The security man took in the expressions on their faces. "I think I picked the wrong half hour for my dinner break. What happened?"

Marci gave a rapid explanation.

Hunter addressed Scott. "I think we'd better get you out of here. For your safety—and Jed's."

"Yes." He started toward the door, but stopped when the man on the bed made a moaning sound.

"Sc…" he said, his voice edged with desperation. Yet that was all he could get out, despite what looked like a massive effort to make himself understood.

Jed's lips twitched, the muscles exaggerating his expression into a grimace.

Alarmed, Marci moved forward and took his hand. "Please, Jed. You're scaring me. I'm afraid you're going to make yourself worse."

His mouth relaxed and he lay with his eyes closed, breathing shallowly, letting her know that he'd gotten the message. When he seemed calmer, Marci asked, "Did you want to tell Scott that Steve Claiborne is waiting at Stanford airfield with a plane to take him and Señorita Reyes to San Marcos? Is that it?"

Jed gave a tiny nod, yet it was obvious to Scott that there was more. Or maybe he was reading too much into this unorthodox exchange.

"Did you want to tell him something about Sanchez?"

Again Jed reacted. He sucked in a breath, then let it out, along with the syllable "Film."

"The film!" Scott practically shouted. "You want to tell me about the film."

Jed grimaced.

"I'm sorry," Marci said. "This can't be good for him."

Hunter stepped closer. "I'm afraid you have to leave now. We don't know if the men are coming back."

Scott nodded, knowing Hunter was right. Yet what Jed was trying to tell him might make the difference between life and death.

As he stepped toward the door, he saw Marci's face twist. "Wait," she said.

He looked up to find that her eyes were troubled. Then she seemed to make a decision. "Scott, you know I was a special agent before I married Jed. I'm still cleared for pretty sensitive information." She sighed. "The trouble is, this should be a discussion between you and Jed."

The man lying in the hospital bed made a strangled sound, and his eyelids flickered.

Marci went to his side, took his hand. "It's okay," she murmured. "I'll tell Scott the rest of what we discussed in Baltimore."

She turned back to him, her expression set. "You may not know that Jed worked with General Sanchez at the School of the Americas. Then he was sent back to San Marcos with him to instruct his troops."

Scott waited tensely for her to get to the point.

"Jed found out that Sanchez was training his men to wage war on their own people. He didn't want any part of that, so he managed to get recalled to the U.S. before he did anything that he knew he'd be sorry for later." She stopped, swallowed. "But he heard that there was someone in the U.S. military willing to take his place. Someone who liked training troops for rough stuff."

Scott stared at her. "Who?"

"I wish I knew. It was kept confidential. But Jed's guess is that it was somebody who's desperate to keep his involvement hidden now. Somebody pretty high up with a lot to lose."

"So I'm fighting the U.S. military?" Scott asked. "That's just great."

"No. Just somebody with a questionable past he wants to hide. Probably an officer."

"Is there any more you can tell me?"

She shook her head. "That's all I know. Except that Jed thought you could find out more in San Marcos than you can here."

She reached in her purse, and Scott thought she might be going to offer him her weapon. Instead, she pulled out a piece of paper.

"This is a map of the airport," she said. "Steve's in hangar three."

"Thank you. For everything," he said, meaning it. Then he squeezed Jed's hand. "Take care of yourself," he whispered before striding to the door.

"I will be back in a few minutes," Hunter told her as he moved toward the door.

Scott followed him down the back stairs. Two minutes later, he was standing on a sidewalk at the rear of the building. The air was damp and the ground was wet, and he realized that he'd barely missed getting caught in the storm, although he'd been so focused on Jed that he hadn't even heard the rain.

As he made his way back toward the car, Hunter stayed close beside him, his eyes alert for signs of the men who'd come sweeping through the ward.

Halting beside the car, Scott turned to the other man. "Take care of Jed and Marci."

"I intend to."

They clasped hands. "And good luck to you," Hunter added.

"Thanks." Scott knew he was going to need it.

He shucked the lab coat and tossed it into a trash can, then got in the car and backed out of the space.

It didn't occur to him until he was about a mile from the hospital that if the goons had figured out he was visiting Jed, there might be some way they could find Mariana, too. Which meant that they had to clear out of the motel room—fast.

His throat squeezed, and he jammed the accelerator to the floor, before forcing himself to ease below the speed limit again. Getting stopped by a patrol car was an invitation to disaster.

He drove at a steady pace, his mind churning as he thought about Sanchez, the film—and the man who had been driving the car when he and Thompson had been in the back seat.

The man's voice was no help. It had been electronically distorted. And the features had been hidden, too. But he'd sat ramrod straight behind the wheel. And his tone had held the confidence of a commanding officer.

Scott spat out a curse.

The whole setup fit with what Marci had told him. Yet he still didn't have enough to go on to nail the guy. And who would believe him anyway—without proof?

His thoughts flashed back to Mariana, alone and unprotected in a motel room. By the time he pulled into a space at the opposite end of the row from their room, he was almost sick with worry.

It was only thirty yards to the motel room. He closed the

distance at a trot, his eyes focused on the slits of light he could see through the blinds. His knock was low and quick.

"Scott?" an anxious voice came from the other side of the barrier as one of the slats parted.

"Yes. Let me in."

She slid aside the chain and twisted the knob.

As soon as the door opened, he pushed inside the little room and was swallowed by her wide-eyed expression.

"What happened?" she gasped as she searched his face. "Is Jed okay?"

He closed the door, fumbled for the lock, answered her question with one choked syllable. "Yes."

"But something went wrong. Tell me."

"Nothing important," he heard himself say. At that moment, he wasn't capable of saying anything more coherent. Surging forward, he swept her into his arms, letting out a strangled exclamation as he pressed the willowy length of her body to his.

He had come home, he thought with a kind of dizzy knowledge.

Even as he gathered her close and ran his hands eagerly up and down her back, she clung to him with fierce possessiveness. When she lifted her face, he was lost in the depth of her dark eyes. They were brimming with anxiety and at the same time tinged with a smoldering passion.

"Scott," she breathed. "*Gracias a Dios,* Scott."

"I'm here. Everything's all right."

"Yes." He felt her body mold itself to his. And as he watched in fascination, the anxiety in her eyes receded, and the smoldering passion surged.

Responding to the silent invitation, he brought his mouth down on hers—hard and urgent.

He could feel the relief in her kiss, and the need. Shamelessly, he took advantage of her generosity, devouring all the sweetness that she offered so unstintingly, his hands sliding over her back, then cupping her bottom as he pressed her to him and began to rock her body against the hard length of his arousal.

She tried to say something, but he knew that words were poor substitutes for action. He angled his mouth first one way and then the other, tasting and taking, even as he strove to give back in equal measure.

Her fingers brushed eagerly back and forth across the bristles of his hair, sending currents of sensation zinging through him.

He needed her. Not simply because his body clamored for hers. He needed to bind this woman to him for all time.

Tilting the upper part of his body away from hers, he slipped his hand under her shirt and cupped his palm around one of her breasts, entranced by the contrast of the wonderfully soft globe crowned by the swollen stiffness of her nipple. He caressed her with his fingers and thumb, fceling her tremble at his touch.

He heard her make a whimpering sound, felt her arch forward into the caress, and gloried in the knowledge that he had kindled the same fire in her that threatened to consume his body.

Her hands moved to his ribs, restlessly stroking along the hard ridges. His nerves were so sensitized to her touch that he felt the impression of each individual finger like a branding iron on his skin.

Bending, he found one distended nipple with his mouth, but felt frustrated by the layers of fabric that kept her skin from his.

Mindless desire consumed him. Without considering the consequences of his actions, he began to move her across the floor to the bed, and banged his shin against the metal frame concealed bencath the edge of the spread.

Pain zinged along the nerve endings of his leg, returning some measure of sanity to his brain.

He blinked and looked down into Mariana's passion-drugged face. "We can't," he said, his voice barely more than a throaty rasp.

He watched her vision come back into focus, saw her struggle for breath.

Her hands gripped his forearms tightly as her eyes sought an explanation in his. "Why not?"

"We have to get out of here. Quickly," he answered, his own breath coming in burning gasps as he looked around the room, trying to assess how fast they could clear out.

"What happened at the hospital?" she asked breathlessly. "Tell me!"

"We don't have time to talk about it now. I'll give you a report in the car." He squeezed her shoulders reassuringly. "Jed's fine. I'm fine."

Stepping away, he crossed the carpet and entered the bathroom, noting immediately that she'd cleaned up the mess from the hair cutting and dyeing. Good.

After gathering up the toilet articles they'd bought, he turned to the trash can. It was brimming with red and black hair, along with the packaging from the hair dye. If anybody saw the contents of the can, they'd know exactly what measures he'd taken to change his appearance, and Mariana's.

Her gaze followed him as he lunged out of the room and grabbed a plastic bag from the department store, dumping the contents into the suitcase she'd opened on the bed.

"Finish packing," he called over his shoulder as he stepped back into the bathroom and emptied the trash can into the bag.

He had just finished washing out the can and emptying it in the toilet when the sounds of their preparations were interrupted by the shrill ringing of the phone on the bedside table.

The hairs on his head were so short they already stood on end. But that didn't stop the prickling sensation that raced across his scalp. Leaping out of the bathroom, he found Mariana taking a tentative step toward the phone.

Before she could make it across the room, he grabbed her arm and pulled her to an abrupt halt. "Don't even think about answering it," he rasped.

She nodded and pressed back against him.

"Finish packing," he said.

She snatched the bag she'd set on the end of the bed as the phone continued to ring, the noise filling the small room, making it feel as if the bell were actually sucking away all the molecules of air.

Trying to ignore the choking sensation, Scott stuck his head back into the bathroom, looking for an exit besides the front door. The only option was a narrow window about two feet above the toilet tank. Slamming down the toilet seat, he climbed on top and flipped the catch. When he tried to push up the sash, it stuck.

His frustrated curse brought Mariana to his back, the suitcase in her hand.

"What is it?"

"The damn thing won't open, and breaking it will be a dead giveaway that we went out that way."

With a grunt, he shoved again, then had to brace himself to keep from tumbling forward when the sash gave.

After pushing the window as wide as it would go, he jumped down and gestured for Mariana to take his place. "You go first."

She didn't ask for an explanation, only shoved the suitcase outside before maneuvering her body through the opening and into the darkness beyond. For a moment she looked as though she wasn't sure how to lower herself on the other side. Then her head and shoulders disappeared.

Thank God he'd had the smarts to pick a room on the ground floor, Scott congratulated himself as he climbed onto the tank. For the second time that evening, he began squeezing himself out a window and into the humid darkness. Too bad he wasn't auditioning for a job as a cat burglar. Bracing awkwardly with one hand on the frame, he pushed the window as far down as he could before lowering himself to the gravel. Mariana was waiting for him.

"You think they're here?" she whispered.

"Or on the way."

He cupped her shoulder, then looked around to get his bearings, seeing that they were in a narrow breezeway between two sets of rooms. Gesturing for Mariana to follow him, he started toward the car. As he approached the end of the building, he slowed his pace and listened for signs that anyone else was about. Then he cautiously peeked around the corner.

As far as he could tell, the coast was clear. Relieved, he took a step toward the pool of illumination from a floodlight near the roofline. Before he could step into the light, Mariana's hand grabbed his arm, holding him back as a car careened into the driveway. Streaking past them, it sped toward the back of the motel where their room was located. It was a Mercedes-Benz, with a souped-up engine, from the sound of it.

The car looked out of place in the parking lot of a cheap motel. So did the two hard-faced men in the front seat and the third one in the back.

It was them. If not the same guys, then their cousins. This time with reinforcements.

He sucked in a harsh breath, then reached into his pocket and felt for the car keys, his fingers clamping around the cold metal.

Mariana was watching him, and he wished he could say something reassuring. All he could tell her was the truth. "I made sure I wasn't followed. So I don't know how they found us."

She edged closer to him while he silently thanked God that he'd come to his senses and hustled the two of them out of the motel room, instead of throwing her on the mattress and ravishing her.

For a terrible moment, he imagined the two of them in

bed, lost to everything but each other, and the door flying open as the goon squad rushed in.

Then he clenched his teeth and forced his mind into more constructive lines.

"Stay here," he ordered, moving her so that her back was pressed against the wall and as much of her as possible was in the shadows.

She tightened her grip on his arm. "Scott, you're not going back there!"

"No, but I have to get the car. And we have to time this carefully."

Easing his face around the corner, he saw two of the men get out of their vehicle and head for the motel-room entrance. One rapped on the glass panel in the middle of the door. When there was no answer, he bent toward the lock, either with a key or some sort of pick.

"Okay, this is what we're going to do," Scott told her. "I'll get the car and drive back this way. When I pull up opposite the corner, you bring the suitcase and jump in."

"Why can't I go with you?"

"So there's only one person coming down the sidewalk."

He rummaged in the bag, pulled out the baseball cap he'd bought and jammed it on his head. Then he shoved his hands into his pockets and ambled toward the car with a flat-footed gait.

It was only a few dozen feet, but it felt like a last walk to the executioner. When he saw the guy in the back seat of the Mercedes glance up, he had to force himself to keep moving at the same nonchalant pace.

The man kept his gaze trained on Scott for several seconds, then looked toward the motel-room door.

Scott made it to the car and opened the lock. As he eased out of the space, he prayed that the guys inside the room would wait just a half minute longer. Slowing at the corner, he saw Mariana watching him. When he hit the brake, she sprinted for the passenger side of the car. She'd almost made it when the motel-room door opened, and the men came out.

One of them pointed toward the fugitives, and they ran toward their car.

"Get in!" Scott shouted, even as she flung open the door and threw herself into the front seat, the suitcase landing in the back with a thunk.

As she pulled the door closed, he sped up the driveway, wondering what his chances were of outrunning a Mercedes-Benz with a supercharged engine.

When he reached the front of the building, he had to make a split-second decision. Run for it or hide. Either plan had its risks. But maybe the best chance would be to do the unexpected.

HOW MUCH HEAD START did they have, Mariana wondered as she fumbled for her seat belt with the car careening up the driveway and around the corner. Before she could snap the buckle, she was thrown against Scott. He seemed not to notice as he hunched forward, his knuckles white on the steering wheel.

He'd rounded the building, and she expected him to zoom onto the highway. Instead he slowed.

She knew she should keep silent, yet she couldn't stop herself from gasping, "What are you doing?"

"Taking a big chance."

To her astonishment, he whizzed past the exit and up the row of cars that were parked at the front of the motel. When he came to an empty spot, he pulled in and cut the engine.

"Get down," he ordered as he hunched low behind the wheel. Slipping off the seat, she knelt on the floor, cradling her head on her hands. Scott's fingers brushed her hair, stroking and winnowing through the strands as long seconds ticked by.

The squeal of tires made her whole body go rigid. Beside her she could hear Scott's breath rasping in and out of his lungs. Although he kept his hand on her hair, his fingers stopped moving.

Many times when she and Alicia had been on the run, she'd prayed to God to deliver them from evil. She prayed now, silently, the familiar words easing her tension a little.

Then she realized Scott was speaking. "I can see them," he whispered. "They're at the exit. They're waiting for a break in the traffic so they can pull onto the road."

When he let out a long, whistling breath, she relaxed a fraction.

"They're on the highway," he said, starting the engine and backing out of the parking space.

Pushing herself up, she climbed back onto the seat and collapsed against the headrest, still half expecting the men to come flying around the edge of the building in their big car.

"How did they find us?" she asked.

"I wish to hell I knew," he ground out.

"If they did it this time, they can do it again."

"We won't be here. We'll be in San Marcos."

"How?"

"A private plane."

She wanted to ask more questions, but the way he clipped out his answers told her he wasn't interested in explanations at the moment. So she sat back in her seat and watched the line of traffic moving past them on the highway. When he found an opening, he eased into the flow.

He stayed on the main road for only a few miles before turning off again and weaving through an area of warehouses and large businesses. Several cross streets later, he was heading in the same direction as the Mercedes, but using another route.

There were things she wanted to say. Personal things. Instead, she took the coward's way out.

"Is it all right to ask you some questions about the hospital?" she asked.

"Yes," he answered, although his tone wasn't exactly full of encouragement.

She cleared her throat. "How was Jed?"

Beside her, he seemed to let go of some of his tension. "Well, I told you about the virus he has. Right now he's in some kind of state bordering on unconsciousness." He sighed. "I'm pretty sure he can hear what's going on. And he wants to communicate. But he can't make himself understood. He kept trying to tell me something. From the way he was acting, it was pretty important."

"What *did* he say?"

"He wanted to tell me about the film. But he couldn't get more than that one word out."

She nodded, then asked, "What else did you learn?"

He was silent for several moments, then plunged into a clipped recitation. He told her about talking with Jed's wife, about the thugs showing up, and about scrambling out onto the windowsill. She didn't ask what floor he'd been on because she didn't want to know.

"How did they know you were there?" she asked.

"It could be the guy stationed at the entrance recognized me." He made an exasperated noise. "All I know is that nobody followed me back to the motel."

She laid her hand over his. "I know. I know you were careful."

His head swung toward her. "I have to ask… You didn't make any phone calls, did you?"

"Of course not," she said. "And I didn't go out of the room either."

"It's okay. I wasn't accusing you of anything."

She turned to face him, needing at least some reassurance. "Do you trust me?" she asked.

"Yes."

His answer meant a lot. "Thank you," she said in a thick voice.

He turned his hand up and pressed his fingers to hers. "I got you into this, and I'm going to get you out of it."

"You didn't get me into anything!"

Ignoring her exclamation, he went on. "I thought I had everything all sorted into neat black-and-white piles. But I didn't really understand the mess I'd stepped into." He lifted one hand from the wheel, turning it palm up. "Now I understand that coming to work for me screwed you up with Bernardo Cortez."

She lifted her chin. "I haven't thought about *him* in years. I never would have been happy with him," she said vehemently. "I sensed it back then. I'm sure of it now."

"Why?" he asked, tension creeping into his voice.

"To start with I didn't love him. And he didn't love me. It was an arranged marriage. He wanted me because we'd be uniting two powerful San Marcos families. And he thought that my father could advance his career. He would have gotten me pregnant as quickly as possible and then taken a mistress, or run around with a lot of other women."

His eyes left the road and flicked toward her. "That's a pretty cynical assessment. You're sure about all that?" he asked, tossing off the question as casually as possible. But the pose didn't fool her.

"I'm sure about my feelings," she insisted, her voice soft but firm. Then before she lost her nerve, she added, "There's only one man I've ever loved."

The statement hung in the darkness between them, and she ached to hear Scott say something as bold.

When he didn't speak, she lowered her head. Last night, he had made love to her. Then when he'd come back from the hospital, he'd held her in his arms. Still none of that meant that he was planning any kind of permanent arrangement with her, and she had no right to push him, or make demands, for herself or for her daughter. All she could do was show him that she wasn't the same addle-brained young woman who had gotten him carted off to jail all those years ago.

She saw him pat his pocket and start to reach inside for a piece of paper. Then a green sign came into view at the side of the highway, and he slowed to read it. It said they were three miles from the turnoff to Stanford Field.

"Is your friend expecting us?" she asked.

"Jed told him we were coming," Scott said slowly, yet she caught the uncertainty in his voice.

"But?" she asked.

He ran a hand over the short bristles on the top of his head. "I thought the haircut was a good idea at the time, but I can't say it's bought us anything except trouble. Marci and Hunter didn't recognize me. Neither will Steve, which means if he's expecting trouble, he might shoot first and ask questions later."

Mariana sucked in a sharp breath. "What are we going to do?"

"Proceed with caution."

She didn't like his reply—or the question that wormed its way into her mind. "Is there any way the men who keep finding us can figure out that we're here?" she asked.

"I hope not," he said, but the tone of his voice made her realize he'd been considering the possibility.

She didn't ask what he was going to do about it. Instead, she tried to relax as he slowed to make another turn. In the moonlight she could see small planes parked in a row along the side of the road. But at this time of night, there was no activity around them.

Scott pulled onto a blacktop road that ran alongside several large, metal buildings.

"Do you know where he's supposed to be?"

"Hangar three. I've got directions, but I'll have to turn on the light to read them."

They both peered into the darkness, then she saw a sign with arrows pointing to various hangars. "Over there."

He made the indicated turn, then pulled to the gravel shoulder well short of the hangar. Cutting the engine, he reached for his door handle, then stopped. "I don't like going in there cold. So you wait here until I give you the all-clear."

"Can't you call to him?"

"Not if somebody else might be listening."

She knew this wasn't the time or place for an argument, so she made a sound that he might have taken for agreement. Then, waiting until he was about thirty feet away, she climbed out of the car and quietly closed the door. The night was dark and sultry. Almost immediately, she felt her clothing sticking to her body.

Nervously, she reached to wind a strand of hair around her finger, then stopped abruptly when she grasped at empty air. Hand pressed against her side, she followed Scott toward the hangar. By the time he reached the entrance, she was almost on top of him.

He turned and gave her a narrow-eyed look but said nothing as he drew her away from the doorway and into the shadows. From their vantage point, she could see the interior of the hangar was cavernous and illuminated by only a few banks of fluorescent lights hanging high up near the ceiling.

Most of the floor space was occupied by small and medium-size planes. About thirty feet from the door was a battered metal desk, and behind it sat a dark-haired man. His chair was tipped back, and his feet were on the desk. As they watched, he yawned.

Scott pulled away from the window. "That's Steve Claiborne," he informed her. "Too bad he and I don't know each other better."

"Why would they send somebody who doesn't know you?" she asked.

"Because they needed a pilot to fly Marci down to be with Jed, and Steve must have been available."

She nodded, then studied the casual posture of the man

named Steve. "Well, he doesn't look like he's expecting trouble."

"My guess is that he's got a gun within easy reach. Maybe if I walk in with my hands up, he'll give me a chance to tell him who I am before he blows me away."

"Or I could go in," Mariana suggested.

"No," he answered instantly.

"He won't shoot a woman," she argued, hoping that the assumption was true.

"Maybe," Scott muttered.

Before he could come up with a better suggestion, she took several quick steps forward—out of his reach and into the dim light of the hangar.

The moment her toe touched the concrete, the man's chair legs hit the floor and his hand came into view. It held a gun—pointed at her chest. What had made her think that he was half-asleep? Maybe he'd even spied them lurking around the doorway and had been waiting for them to make their move.

His eyes narrowed as he looked her up and down, taking in everything from her short-cropped hair to the sandals strapped on her feet. In that instant, her mind went blank.

It took several agonizing seconds before she could even remember his name. "Mr. Claiborne?" she finally asked, feeling her pulse drumming in her ears.

"Who wants to know?" he answered. "Come over here so I can get a better look at you."

When she stayed planted to the floor, he growled, "Hurry up!"

She followed directions, stopping when he said, "That's far enough."

Resisting the urge to tug at her clammy clothing, she said, "Mr. Claiborne, I'm Mariana Reyes." Somehow, saying her name made her remember the rest of what she should tell him. Still, she could hear the quaver in her own voice as she continued. "I know you have to be careful about who you let in here. But I'm the woman Jed Prentiss came down to Miami to meet.''

''Prove it,'' he ordered, the weapon still trained on her.

She wasn't exactly prepared to comply, since she didn't have any identification, or anything else that could prove who she was. But she did have information. ''I can tell you what happened when Scott and I met Jed. We were ambushed, and Jed was shot.''

''The other side knows that,'' he snapped. ''Give me something a little more unique.''

She thought for a moment, wishing she had planned this better. ''I know about that sickness Jed has. The virus in his blood—''

Before she could finish, she heard a harsh voice from behind her snap a sharp order. ''Hands in the air.''

A suffocating wave of fear swept over her, threatening to choke off her breath. *Dios,* no. The bad men had tracked them here. And now it was all over.

From the corner of her eyes, she saw Scott moving slowly forward. Another man was right behind him. A tall man with a grim face and a square jaw. As the two of them came abreast of her, she saw that the newcomer had a pistol pressed into the middle of Scott's back.

Chapter Twelve

Mariana stood rigidly in place as Scott and the hard-looking man drew abreast of her.

"Here's another one," he observed dryly, making it clear that he was with Claiborne. "He sent his woman in and stayed outside in the darkness."

The suggestion that Scott might be a coward was so outrageous that Mariana forgot there was a gun pointed at her heart. "He did not!" she objected vehemently. "It was my idea. I came in here before he could stop me!"

All eyes were focused on her, and she raised her chin defiantly, even though her insides were quivering.

Scott kept his hands even with his shoulders as he locked eyes with the man behind the desk. "I'm Scott O'Donnell. Jed sent me."

"Funny, you don't look much like O'Donnell," Steve Claiborne retorted.

Scott barked out a laugh. "Yeah, well, when your face is plastered all over a wanted poster, you try to change your appearance. I've shaved off most of my red hair and dyed it the color of burnt toast." He leveled his gaze at Steve and continued. "You and I met at a party at the Randolph Estate. We had a discussion about movies. You think Sean Connery is getting too old to play action heroes. Your wife is Abby Franklin. You have a daughter who was kidnapped a few years ago. You like Indian food. At least, you were scarfing up the tandoori chicken wings from the buffet table. And if that's not enough of an introduction, there's a note from Marci in my pocket. You can have your buddy take it out and read it.''

Steve held up his hand. Coming around from behind the desk, he walked toward Scott, stopping about three feet away, and studied him intently.

"How many chicken wings?'' he asked.

When Scott screwed up his face, Steve uttered an apology as he clicked the safety catch on the pistol and stuffed the weapon into the waistband of his slacks. "Your own mother wouldn't recognize you,'' he muttered.

Mariana let out her breath in a shuddering sigh as the other man also put away his weapon and came around to face Scott. Holding out his hand, he said, "Matthew—Matt Forester. I'm the new guy at Randolph Security.''

Scott hesitated, then took his hand and shook it.

"No hard feelings?'' Forester asked.

"I guess I have to be thankful you didn't shoot me in the back.''

"I try to avoid that,'' the other man answered laconically. Then he inclined his head toward Mariana. "Especially when there's a beautiful woman present.''

She flushed to the roots of her cropped hair, and Scott moved to her side and slipped his arm around her. "This is Mariana Reyes,'' he said.

"I'm afraid I've gotten Scott into a lot of trouble,'' she added in a low voice.

"Mutual trouble,'' Scott corrected.

"Marci filled us in on the way down from Baltimore,'' Steve answered. "It looks like somebody is pulling out all the stops to shut you up.''

Scott's mouth tightened. "Unfortunately, Jed was the one who got hurt.''

"He knew the risks,'' Matthew answered.

"Maybe he thought he did," Scott countered. "Two goons were looking for me at the hospital. Three more showed up at our motel less than an hour ago. If our luck is holding, they'll be driving down the access road to the airport in a couple of minutes."

Steve looked thoughtful. "What car are you driving?"

"The one Jed rented in Miami."

"Any chance they could have gotten to it with a directional finder before they went after you at Lincoln Road?"

Scott made a whistling sound. "That's a very plausible explanation for why they're dogging our heels. At least it's better than my paranoid fantasy that they have a satellite dedicated to tracking us."

"The lesser of two evils," Steve agreed.

Scott's eyes narrowed. "It doesn't explain why they cut us some slack last night."

"There are two possible scenarios," Matthew mused. "Either they weren't sure which car to go after and had to tag several or they were being greedy. They were hoping you'd lead them back to Jed, and they could tie all of you up in a nice neat package."

"I guess they weren't counting on his fake name and head bandage," Scott said. Then his eyes narrowed. "I've got another set of possibilities for you. Either they slipped up letting us get away from the motel a little while ago, or they're trying to find out if anybody else is helping us."

Steve nodded. "I've already done a preflight check and filed a flight plan that will cross their wires. That should buy you some time when you arrive in San Marcos."

"Appreciate it," Scott replied, but he didn't look entirely happy.

"More problems?" Steve asked.

Scott turned his palms up. "Unfortunately, I'm going to need some expensive video equipment."

Steve didn't miss a beat. "We have a couple of choices.

Stopping in a U.S. city or making for somewhere like Belize.''

''We're more likely to find what I want in the U.S.,'' Scott answered, then cleared his throat. ''We're talking about laying out fifty thousand dollars.''

''I think we can pick up what you need in Tampa,'' Steve said.

''Randolph Security has been considering a portable editing setup. In fact, I was going to consult with you on it.''

''If you say so,'' Scott said. ''But if anything happens to it in San Marcos, I'll reimburse you when we get back to Baltimore.''

Matthew Forester had stepped out of the hangar during the discussion. He came trotting back, holding the suitcase Mariana and Scott had brought from the motel room. ''I've moved your car over by the other building.'' He gestured toward the suitcase. ''You're traveling light.''

Scott nodded, then Steve led the way out of the hangar and toward a small jet.

Mariana stuck close to Scott as they climbed aboard, her mind in a kind of daze at the speed things were happening now. The plane was another shock. Even when she'd been the daughter of a rich San Marcos businessman, she'd never seen a private aircraft like this—a Gulfstream Five, Steve called it.

He caught her looking around wide-eyed at the luxurious cabin and grinned. ''This baby has a lot of special modifications. There's even a bedroom in the back. After we take off, you and Scott might want to get some sleep.''

She fought a blush, then glanced at Scott. Heat flared like green fire in the depths of his eyes, kindling an equally potent fire in her midsection. He took a step toward her, then checked himself. She wanted to reach for him. But this was hardly the time. So she settled into one of the padded seats in back of the pilot's chair.

As the men conferred in low voices, she leaned back and

tried to unwind. The attempt was cut short by a pair of headlights knifing through the darkness.

"A car's coming," she breathed.

"It could be a pilot or a mechanic reporting to work early," Steve muttered. Despite the reassurance, she saw him speeding up preparations for departure.

She strained her eyes into the darkness, watching the progress of the headlights. They stopped moving, and she assumed the car had drawn up next to the rental.

Dios, Matthew must be right about some sort of tracking device on the car. Which meant Sanchez's men could have come bursting in on her and Scott last night when they were making love! As she contemplated that scene, she felt her throat close.

The plane did a quick turn, and began to taxi down the runway. In the distance, she thought she heard small explosions—like shots being fired. But the plane was already in the air, climbing into the night sky.

They were safe. For the moment.

THREE HOURS LATER they were on their way to San Marcos, after a stop in Tampa where Matthew had somehow procured the equipment Scott needed. He was a resourceful man, a good man to have on their side, Mariana thought as she tried to relax her hold on the armrests of her seat.

She felt like an overwound spring about to snap as she sat and listened to Scott fill the men in on their wild adventure.

Did they really need to know so many details? she wondered as she pressed her fingers into the rubbery plastic. She wanted to break into the conversation and ask Scott why he was making excuses not to be alone with her, because by now she was sure that's what he was doing.

Which confirmed the assumptions she'd been making all along. If they got the evidence they needed, Scott would leave her and go back to the U.S. Then she would never see him again. She felt her throat tighten, then her chest, making it impossible to fill her lungs with air.

Glancing up, she saw him deep in conversation with Matthew, apparently oblivious of her presence a few feet away. She watched him until her eyes began to burn. Ducking her head, she struggled to keep her raw emotions from showing—a skill she'd had plenty of practice perfecting as her father's daughter.

When she felt more in control, she jerked to her feet and bolted into the tiny bedroom at the rear of the plane. She'd had a look at it before. Most of the floor space was taken up by a double bed. She had to edge around it to get to the little bathroom beyond. After using the facilities and washing her hands and face, she kicked off her sandals and climbed into bed in her clothes.

Lying there in the darkness, she pressed her clenched fist against her mouth to hold back the sobs that threatened to wrack her body. Despite her best efforts, tears leaked from her eyes and trickled down her cheeks. At least she kept herself from making any noise.

For six years she had structured her life to keep her child safe. She hadn't asked much for herself. She hadn't expected much—until fate had thrown her and Scott together again.

He had said he trusted her. He had said he understood why she'd planted those papers in his apartment all those years ago. And he had made exquisite love to her. For her, the joy of finally taking that ultimate step was beyond description. She wished she knew what it had meant to him.

She knew it was selfish to want him with her now. She knew she shouldn't be thinking about herself. Yet knowing that he was only a few yards away sent heat curling through her body.

Scott, please, she silently called to him. *Just give me a few more hours alone with the man I love. Don't deny me that.*

She didn't know how much later it was when she heard the knob turn and looked up to find Scott standing in the doorway. Forcing herself to breathe evenly, she watched him through slitted eyes. He stood staring at her for long moments, and she wondered if he had simply opened the door to see if she was sleeping. Her breath frozen in her chest, she waited. When he silently closed the door and turned the lock, she let the air trickle out of her lungs. In the dark, she saw him move around the bed toward the bathroom. When he emerged again, he wedged a towel in the crack of the door to keep it open, sending a thin shaft of pale light across the end of the bed. Then he pulled off his shoes.

The mattress shifted as he lay down beside her. He didn't touch her. In fact, he left as much space as possible between the two of them—the way he had the first night in Miami.

She could see him lying with his hands folded across his chest as he stared at the bulkhead. If he had come here to get a few hours' rest, she should leave him alone, she told herself sternly. Yet the warmth of his body and the scent of his skin teased her senses, leaving her dizzy with longing. Her mind had stopped functioning rationally. All she knew was that if he wouldn't come to her, she would come to him, and give him the only thing she had to offer—her love.

"Scott?"

"You should get some sleep," he answered in a gritty voice.

"I know."

In the dim light, she turned and brushed her lips against his cheek, feeling his muscles clench. But he said nothing more. And neither did she.

Perhaps there was nothing left for the two of them to say. But she had stopped thinking that words would solve any of her problems.

She had never played the seductress. When she'd first known Scott, she'd been too young and inexperienced. In the years they'd been apart, there hadn't been any man she'd wanted.

As he lay there beside her, she could feel his tension and

hear the quick intake of his breath. Still, she wasn't sure what would happen if she tried to convince him that there was something more constructive to do in this bed besides sleep.

The thought that he might turn away from her now sent a jolt of pain through her heart. But she couldn't stop herself from silently asking for what she wanted. Eyes closed, she slid her lips along his cheek. Shifting her body so that she lay half on top of him, she found his mouth and teased the seam of his lips with her tongue. When it remained closed, she grew a little bolder—and a little more desperate. Drawing back a fraction, she took his bottom lip between her teeth, giving him small, nibbling bites and then sucking his flesh into her mouth.

His body stayed rigid; his hands stayed at his sides. Still, she felt his heart rate accelerate and heard a growl well up from deep in his throat. Encouraged, she sought access to the warmth of his mouth again. And when she felt the fine tremors shiver through his body, she couldn't hold back a little sigh of satisfaction.

Long ago, in a hotel room near Chipotalli, he had set out to discover what kindled the flame of her desire. Now she did the same, using the knowledge he'd given her.

She discovered how much he liked the stroking of her tongue against the sensitive skin at the inside of his lips, and that the nibbling of her teeth along the edge of his tongue sent another shiver through him.

If she was affecting him, she was driving herself wild. A sweet, fierce longing pulsed through her body. Her breasts felt hot and tight, and she pressed them against his chest, hoping to ease the ache a little. It didn't help. It only made her long for more.

Eyes closed, her mouth still playing with his, she slid her hand down his body, finding him hard behind the fly of his pants.

When she touched him there, she heard his indrawn breath, felt his hips strain upward to press himself more firmly against her hand—and she knew that she had the power to send him over the edge.

But not like this. Not when she had discovered the ecstasy of his body moving inside hers, driving her to heights of pleasure she hadn't known existed.

Before she could contemplate her own audacity, she pulled her knit shirt over her head. She knew he was watching her intently as she dropped the shirt onto the floor because she felt his gaze on her like licks of hot lightning. With her lip clamped between her teeth, she unhooked her bra and sent it after the shirt.

She was wondering exactly what she was going to do next when he pulled her down again so that she was lying half sprawled across him.

Somehow in the seconds during which she'd been occupied, he'd pulled off his own shirt so that she was lying with her breasts nestled against his chest.

"Oh!" The exclamation sighed from her, even as he cupped his hands around the back of her head and brought her mouth to his. Then he was kissing her with all the pent-up feelings she'd sensed when she'd been trying to provoke him. Only now he had taken over, and all she could do was cling to him and let him sweep her along on a tide of passion.

His kiss was thorough and thrilling. Before she could catch her breath, he bent to rub his face against her breasts, then capture a swollen nipple in his mouth. She cried out as he began to suck on her. Clasping his head in her hands, she stroked the bristly ends of his hairs against her fingers, adding to the ripples of sensation coursing through her.

He feasted on her like a starving man, lavishing his attentions first on one breast and then the other, even as his hands found the snap at the top of her shorts and released it.

He had the shorts and her panties off almost as quickly as he had removed his shirt.

Naked, she gazed up at him in a kind of daze as he knelt

over her, his fingers trembling as they stroked the line of her hip.

She reached up to touch his face, trace his lips as she felt them curve into a smile. Then he was bending to kiss his way down her body, his tongue stroking her tingling skin and dipping into her navel before finding the pulsing core of her and focusing his tender attentions there.

She strained against him, calling out his name as a deluge of sensations poured over her, until she knew that she was in danger of drowning in the strong current he had built.

"Scott, no," she gasped. "Please. Not like this. Not when I can have you inside me."

He lifted his head, his fierce gaze meeting hers. Then he was pulling away, tearing off his remaining clothing before coming back to cover her body with his.

He entered her in one swift thrust that brought a deep sigh of satisfaction to her lips. Her arms circled his broad shoulders as she rocked her hips upward.

He began to move, setting a controlled pace that drove her mindless with need.

"Scott, oh, Scott," she gasped. "Please, now."

Deaf to her pleas, he made her wait, building the pleasure by slow degrees until she was calling out, begging for completion.

Still he kept her on the edge, making her ride the storm until she surged against him in desperation—and shattered into a lightning bolt of sensation that was sweet and sharp and all-consuming. Then she felt him follow her into the heart of the tempest, heard his hoarse shout of pleasure—and her joy was complete.

He lay on top of her, breathing hard, and she clasped her arms around him, wishing that she would never have to let him go. When he shifted to his side and cradled her in his arms, she stroked her lips against his shoulder.

"Thank you for that. I have a hard time asking for things I want," she answered softly.

"I know. So do I." He settled her more comfortably against his side, his fingers playing up and down her arm. "Will the light keep you awake?" he asked.

"No," she replied. But the question and his tone of voice sent her thoughts flashing back to the day before, when they'd ducked into the tunnel to escape the gunmen.

He must have sensed her disquiet because he finally said, "If you want me to turn it off, I will."

"I'm fine."

"No you're not. What's wrong?"

Though she felt her chest tighten, she lifted her face toward him. "I was thinking that you left the light on because you hate dark, closed places."

He sat up, glaring down at her. "How do you know that?"

Wishing she'd had the sense to keep her mouth shut, she blurted, "From the way you acted when we were hiding in the tunnel."

The challenge in his eyes made her add, "And from my father."

"Your father?"

She pushed herself up so that her shoulders were nearly level with his, dragging the sheet with her to cover her breasts. When...when I first started working for you, he gave me a report on your background."

Scott made a low sound. "You never mentioned it to me."

She placed her hand over his, her eyes apologetic. "I knew you weren't proud of your family. I didn't want to upset you by bringing it up. Besides, it didn't matter to me."

He was silent for several moments before asking, "So what else do you know about me?"

She watched the shaft of light waver as the plane hit an air pocket. "I know your parents divorced when you were eight. I know your stepfather punished you in ways that nobody should punish a child."

"Like what?" he challenged.

"Like locking you in the closet. Like starving you. Like beating you."

His mouth hardened. "I survived."

"Because you got help. You got into that film program for young people and started winning awards."

"You knew all that, too?"

"Yes. It made me so proud of you. I kept thinking about how much you'd overcome."

He shook his head. "I thought I'd put the past behind me, but I was fooling myself. The guys who threw me into that prison cell must have read the same dossier your father had. They knew how to bring it all back, play on the weakness I thought I didn't have."

"It's not your fault," she breathed. "Everyone has things they fear."

"Well, in a few hours, we'll get to see how well I deal with them," he muttered, turning to punch up the pillow, then lying down with his back to her.

"Scott. I shouldn't have said anything," she whispered, realizing suddenly that when they'd started the conversation, she hadn't even considered what going back to San Marcos must mean to him. They were flying to the country where he'd been thrown into prison and tortured. *Dios,* he must feel as if he was walking back into a cougar's den. With her leading the way again.

When he didn't reply, she put her hand on his shoulder and felt his muscles spasm. "Go to sleep," he said. "While you have the chance."

BY THE TIME she woke up, he had cleared out of the bedroom. When she took a quick peek out the door to the private cabin, she saw him holding a mug of coffee and talking in low tones to Matthew.

Slipping back inside, she washed as best she could in the small sink and changed into the green dress she'd bought, since that would look less conspicuous than shorts or slacks in her own country. Then she hurriedly began to tidy up the cabin, bent on making it look as if they'd only been sleeping peacefully in here all night. She knew the prudish impulse was silly. It didn't matter what the men from Randolph Security thought about her relationship with Scott. Yet in the back of her mind she couldn't help thinking that when Scott returned from San Marcos alone, she didn't want his friends to know there had been anything between them in the first place.

She was still trying to understand her own logic when Matthew tapped on the door.

"We're going to be landing in half an hour. You should come out here soon and strap in."

"Thanks. I'll be there in a minute," she told him, hastily finishing smoothing out the covers.

Matthew was waiting for her with a sweet roll and a mug of coffee, and she saw he'd fixed it the Latin way, with lots of hot milk.

"Thank you," she said again, her gaze straying to Scott as she lowered herself into the seat next to him.

His head was buried in a map, but he spared her a tight nod as she nibbled on the roll and sipped the lip of coffee.

"We're landing to the north of Santa Isabella," Matthew told her. "At a private airstrip. And we've arranged some inconspicuous transportation into the city. I'd volunteer to go along…"

"But the two of us will be better off alone," Scott finished, his voice tight.

When he raised his head, she saw the lines of strain etching his face.

All at once, there were things she desperately needed to say. She wanted him to know that she had absolute faith in him. She wanted to tell him how much she loved him. But when she glanced at the two men in front of them who sat in the pilot and copilot seats, she knew they were close enough to hear any private conversation.

"Scott," she murmured.

He turned his head toward her, and she covered his hand with hers, even as she tried to tell him with her eyes that everything was going to work out all right.

SCOTT TURNED BACK to the window and studied the volcanic peaks in the distance and the dark green jungle vegetation speeding below the wings of the plane.

One of the mountains must be Chipotalli, he thought with an odd kind of detachment. But he had no idea which one, since it wasn't presently spewing black ash into the air. That would certainly have been an appropriate welcome. A warning from the ancient gods.

Then the jungle was rising up to meet them as the plane descended. In the distance he spotted a slash of black cutting through the foliage. The plane banked, then made for the end of the tarmac.

It was a good landing, he told himself. Still, as the wheels touched down on the abandoned runway near Santa Isabella, he felt a jolt of sensation like a hammer blow reverberating through his body. He flicked a quick glance at Mariana to see if she'd detected the change in his expression. She was staring straight ahead, and he hoped she was thinking about her daughter. Because he didn't want to get into a conversation about the joys of landing in the country where they'd march him in front of a firing squad if they caught him.

He hadn't told Mariana he'd left with the understanding that a death sentence was waiting for him if he ever set foot here again. And he didn't intend to share that piece of information with her now.

He just wanted to get a look at the damn tapes, figure out what was so incriminating and put the plan into action that was rattling around in the back of his mind. Until all that happened, he and Mariana were walking targets. But he wasn't going to explain any of that to her, either. Because the only thing worse than getting through the hours he had to spend in San Marcos was talking about it. With Mariana or anybody else.

He'd made several other vows last night—one of which he'd broken as soon as she'd done that sexy trick of taking his lower lip between her teeth. He'd told himself he couldn't make love to her again until the bastards stalking them were in custody. Now he was hanging on to his other commandment, not to make any promises about the future, until he was sure that they had one. So he sat rigidly in his seat, feeling as if the temperature of his blood had dropped ten degrees since the wheels had touched down on the cracked runway.

They came to a stop next to a rusting iron building, the interior dark and shadowy. Parked in the shade of one disintegrating wall was a green van that said it belonged to a bottled-water company. Was that their transportation? As Steve taxied toward the building, Scott found himself watching out the window, unconsciously waiting for armed men to come swarming out of the building.

Instead, the plane rolled through the open doorway and came to a stop. Then Steve cut the engine, and they were surrounded only by shadows and silence.

Scott shifted in his seat and studied Mariana's face. It was as tense as his probably looked.

He gave her hand a quick squeeze, then unbuckled his seat belt, stood and stretched as if they were tourists landing at a Costa Rican resort. "Where are we?" he asked Matt, who was busy opening the hatch.

Warm, damp air flooded into the plane, immediately making Scott feel as if his shirt had been stuck to his body for hours.

"About thirty miles north of Santa Isabella. This place belongs to a consortium of businessmen. It's used on an occasional basis."

Scott was smart enough not to ask which kind of business

as he climbed down the short flight of steps to the concrete pad and held out his hand to assist Mariana.

Matt gestured toward the delivery van. "Your transportation," he explained. "That way you have plenty of room for the video equipment—and anything else you decide to bring back."

"Thanks," Scott answered.

"We'll wait as long as we can," Steve added as he joined the group.

"I understand," he answered, knowing that if they got wind of trouble, they'd have to pull out.

Glancing at Mariana, he was pretty sure that she had taken in the meaning of the conversation. But she didn't comment.

"Can you find your way to the guy with the tapes from here?"

"If I can look at a map," she said.

Steve brought one out and showed her their location. In a few minutes, she'd found a route into the city that would take them to the house of Juan Tiemplo.

"Too bad we can't warn him we're coming. It's going to be a shock to see you after six years," Scott said as he donned the sunglasses and broad-brimmed hat that helped to hide his face from view.

Mariana nodded tightly as he thumbed through the San Marcos currency Matt had given him. Jed's gun was tucked out of sight under the loose-fitting shirt he wore. The weapon made him feel marginally safer, but only marginally.

Mariana shot him a concerned glance. "How are you?"

"Fine," he said tightly, afraid he'd just let her know he was a lot less cool than he pretended. Turning away, he strode toward the van, and she followed.

Without giving himself time to brood, he started the engine and pulled onto the dirt road leading to the highway.

Beside him, Mariana smoothed her fingers across the map, then bent to study the route. His own hands locked around the steering wheel as he turned onto the pockmarked highway that led into Santa Isabella.

Grateful that she didn't bombard him with questions, he drove in silence through the green of the jungle which gave way gradually to small farms, then clusters of low houses, then the squalor of a city where more than half the population lived in poverty.

As the traffic increased, he was forced to slow down—and remember that the vehicle that got to the intersection first was the one with the right-of-way.

Driving in San Marcos made Miami look like a driving-school test course, he mused as he slammed on his brakes to avoid hitting a rickety truck piled high with crates of chickens. It pulled to a stop in front of a roadside restaurant where a skinned pork carcass hung from a hook near the door. The smell of smoke-cooked meat made his stomach roil, as he suddenly remembered why he hadn't eaten barbecue since his visit to San Marcos.

"We should turn here," Mariana announced, the first words she'd uttered in more than half an hour.

As she pointed to a small traffic island adorned with a carved stone cross, he saw a policeman standing in the intersection directing traffic, his green uniform pants tucked neatly into polished black boots and his sidearm prominently displayed in a large black holster. Despite the heat and humidity, Scott felt goose bumps rise on his arms. Beside him Mariana had gone rigid.

"He's not looking for us. He's just directing traffic," he muttered, then was utterly astonished—and profoundly relieved—when the man paid them no more attention than the Jeep to their right and the old Japanese sedan to their left.

He told himself nobody was on the lookout for the delivery truck. He told himself that the men who had captured and tortured him couldn't still be in power six years later. But he only half believed the reassurances. And he was glad when Mariana directed him off the main traffic route and into a sleepy neighborhood of low stucco houses with red-tiled roofs.

They turned onto a narrow street that wound upward into the hilly part of the city. There were no house numbers, and she stopped several times to ask questions of women walking along the edge of the road.

Finally, they came to a freshly painted white bungalow with neatly tended flower beds of hibiscus and poinsettias in front.

"There." Mariana pointed. "I think that's it."

He circled the block, looking for someone watching the house. "Are you sure that's it?"

"Yes. It looks the same. He loves his flowers."

Scott made one more slow pass, then pulled under the shade of a mimosa tree.

"Let me go in first," Mariana said.

"You can knock on the door. But I'm going to be right there," he told her, unwilling to let her take any more unnecessary chances. Every time he thought about her risky stunt of charging into the hangar ahead of him, he had to keep from grabbing her shoulders and asking her what she could possibly have been thinking.

He stayed right behind her as they proceeded up a neatly weeded stepping-stone path, then stopped at a recessed doorway where she rapped her knuckles against the dark-stained wooden door. Once. Twice. Three times, she knocked, then gave Scott a worried look before calling in a strained voice, "Juan?"

There was no answer, and he was suddenly seized by a very bad feeling. Gently moving Mariana out of the way, he tried the knob. It turned, and he drew the gun before easing inside. The moment he stepped across the threshold into the small hallway, he saw the body crumpled on the tile floor.

He tried to shield Mariana's view. But she must have smelled the coppery scent of death. Pushing around him, she stared at the crumpled figure on the floor of the hallway—a white-haired man clad in a neatly pressed blue shirt and gray slacks.

"Juan!" she gasped, kneeling beside the old man who lay on his side, his knees bent and his head centered in a pool of blood.

"He's dead," Scott hissed, trying to pull her away. "We've got to get out of here!"

"No." She was already reaching out to touch the still chest.

Scott looked from her to the body. The man had been dead for several hours. He knew that much. But he didn't know if the killers were still in the house.

When he tried to pull her away, she fought against him and pointed to a folded white rectangle that stood out against Juan's blue shirt.

"I see our timing was perfect," Scott muttered. "What the hell is that? A suicide note?" he asked, his eyes flicking to the bullet hole in the center of the man's forehead. There was no corresponding weapon in the dead brown hand.

Unfolding the paper, Mariana began to read, then sucked in a strangled breath.

"What?"

"They have Alicia," she told him in a barely audible whisper.

Chapter Thirteen

"Who? Let me see! Maybe they're bluffing." Snatching the note from Mariana's hand, Scott scanned the black letters scrawled across the white paper. It was written in Spanish, but he had no trouble translating. "'We have your daughter. If you want to see her alive again, bring the tapes to San Rafael del Mar. Your deadline is 2:00 p.m. tomorrow.'"

"Where's San Rafael del Mar?" Scott demanded.

"It's the town where I left Alicia with Tiá Susana! Don't you see? That proves it!" she shouted, her voice rising in hysteria. "They found out where I'd taken her, and they came and got her."

He took her by the shoulders, moved her away from the body and into the next room, all his attention focused on her. "It doesn't prove anything," he muttered, sure he was lying.

Her eyes raised to his. They were large and dark and full of tears, and he felt himself melting into their depths. Helpless to do anything else, he reached for her and folded her into his arms, feeling the sobs take her as he rocked her, stroked her.

"It's all right. It's going to be all right," he said, because it was the only thing he could say.

Mariana clung to him, her grip strong as roots burrowing into rock. "I shouldn't have left her," she sobbed out. "I never should have left her."

"You couldn't take her with you!"

"I don't even know who has her." She lifted her shimmering eyes to his. "Who is it? Who?"

Scott could only shake his head.

She jerked away from him. "We have to go there. We have to get her."

"With the tapes," he said through clenched teeth. "We'd better find the damn tapes."

She stood there for several more seconds, and he wondered if he'd gotten through to her. Then her eyes cleared, as if she'd remembered why they had come here in the first place. "How did they know to go after Juan?" she asked, her voice cracking. "After all this time?"

"I don't know. But we'd better collect what we came for and get out of here."

He raised the gun chest-high in front of him, the cold metal making him glad that they had some means of defense. Still, he didn't like this setup. What if the killers were out there—waiting to swoop in as soon as he and Mariana had accomplished their mission?

She nodded, then looked around, her breath hissing out in a little gasp. He followed her gaze, seeing with a shock what he hadn't noticed before. The living room had been taken apart—with malice. Books and smashed pottery lay beside overturned bookcases, the sofa and chair cushions had been ripped apart. The bedroom was the same. Scott wondered if there was any possibility of finding the tapes.

"He did a favor for me," she whispered as she surveyed the mess, then looked back toward the hall. "And they killed him."

"I'm sorry."

She gave Scott a bleak look. "I thought when we left the U.S…." Her voice trailed off. She cleared her throat and started again. "They followed us here."

"No. There wasn't time for them to follow us. This was done by somebody in San Marcos. So tell me where to find the tapes, then I'll stash you somewhere safe and look for them.''

She raised her chin. ''There *is* nowhere safe, and that being the case, I feel safest with you.''

The simple statement made his throat constrict. She had put her trust in him, but he knew there was no guarantee he could keep either one of them alive.

She must have thought he was going to argue with her, because she went on quickly, ''Besides, I can't leave you here. Juan and I discussed more than one hiding place.''

''Then let's hurry,'' he said, trying to damp down the conviction that they were tempting fate by staying in this house of death. ''Which place is most likely?''

''Out here.''

When she led him to the back door, he stopped and surveyed the garden before letting her show him toward a storage shed partially hidden by trumpet vines. The interior, too, had been ransacked. But she ignored the mess, bending to clear debris from the middle of the floor. ''Under the paving stones, I hope,'' she said, kneeling to lift a flat slate set in gravel.

''I'll do that,'' he said, handing her the gun. ''Do you know how to use this?''

''My father made me practice on the firing range, in case somebody broke into the house.''

''Good. Then stay out of sight behind the door and cover me while I work.''

She did as he asked, fading into the shadows while he found a shovel and began to dig. It seemed forever until he unearthed what looked like a giant butterfly cocoon of plastic shrink wrapped around a metal box. It reminded him of the suitcases he'd seen going in and out of the Santa Isabella airport, where travelers used the technique as a protection against theft. In this case he hoped it was equally effective against moisture.

Climbing into the hole, he tugged the box, finally wrestling it to the floor of the shed with a thunk.

Seconds later, a noise outside made him realize his instincts had been right in the first place.

"Stay where you are, and raise your hands," a voice said in Spanish from the doorway.

Scott could only stare in shock at the man standing there with a pistol in his hand. It was Pepe Fortunato, his former employee.

Dumbfounded, Scott regarded the man who had made himself indispensable six years ago. He was a little grayer, a little heavier, but basically he looked like the same efficient assistant, ready to do any job Scott gave him. He even had the same broad smile on his face. Only now the curve of the lips didn't match the coldness in his dark eyes.

Scott blinked, hoping that this was some sort of hallucination. "Pepe? What are you doing here?"

"Waiting for you to show up." He gestured toward the box. "I've been looking for that! I figured you might as well do the work of finding it for me."

Before Scott could answer, Mariana shouted a warning. "Scott, down!"

The exclamation was followed by the almost simultaneous sound of two shots being fired. One slammed into the metal chest in front of him, but he was already dodging to the side and reaching for the shovel, which he launched at Pepe like a missile. It hit him squarely in the chest, and he made a grunting sound as he pitched backward, hitting the wall and sliding to the floor.

Grabbing the shovel, Scott brought it down on Pepe's gun hand. The man screamed and went limp as the weapon clattered to the flagstone floor.

"Are you all right?" Scott shouted to Mariana. Her face was wraith pale, but she appeared to be unharmed.

"Yes," she quavered. "Are you?"

She handed him the gun, her eyes wide as she stared at the man on the floor. "Did I hit him?"

"I don't know."

Scott wanted to wrap her in his arms and tell her how brave she'd been. But there was no time for a tender moment between them. "You did just fine," he said, then narrowed his eyes as he stared down at Pepe, who was struggling to sit up. There was a red gash at his hairline, but the wound was superficial.

"You grazed him," Scott told Mariana. "He'll be all right." Making his voice hard, he continued for the benefit of the man on the floor. "If you'd killed him, we couldn't ask him any questions."

His next words were addressed directly to Pepe. "There are worse things than death. I don't have any problems putting bullets in various parts of your anatomy where it will hurt the most. You killed a helpless old man. And your friends have been following us all over Miami."

"Not me," Pepe gasped. "I didn't kill him. And I don't know who's been following you in Miami."

"Convince me," Scott growled. Without taking his eyes off the man, he spoke to Mariana. "I saw some rope in the mess on the floor. Get it and tie him up."

She searched the debris and found the rope.

Under orders from Scott, Pepe sat up and put his hands behind his back while Mariana tied him to a metal cleat attached to one wall. When the prisoner was secure, Scott knelt beside him, his voice deadly calm.

"If you didn't kill Juan, who did?"

"Men like her father!"

"No!" Mariana gasped.

Pepe ignored her. "It's all on the tapes," he said. "Evidence against the men who control this country and use any means possible to stay in power. How do you think someone like your father acquired his wealth?" he snarled, his eyes boring into Mariana.

"He had plantations. Mines. He worked hard administering his financial interests."

Pepe snorted. "You think he worked hard. You don't know the meaning of the term. He took the wealth from the land and lived like a king, while the people worked for wages that wouldn't support their families. The price of a pair of your high-heeled shoes would have fed and clothed a peasant family for a month."

Scott saw her cringe, and glared at Pepe. "You're acting so self-righteous now. You're the guy who ran away when the police came. That's how you lost control of the blasted tapes. So just stick to the subject at hand. If you didn't kill Juan, who did?"

"I don't know their names," he said with what sounded like genuine disappointment. "I've had his house watched for years, because I knew Mariana had contacted Juan after they dragged you off to prison. Yesterday I got a call that men in black cars had arrived in the middle of the night. When I got here, it was all over." He sounded tired and his skin looked bloodless.

Scott clenched and unclenched his fists. He wanted to wreak violence on this man. But not with Mariana watching. "Let's see," he muttered. "You expect me to believe you've been watching this place for six years, but you haven't made a move until now."

"I don't expect you to understand. But I have my principles," Pepe answered. "Juan Tiemplo was a man of the people. I questioned him many times, and he always denied that he knew anything about the tapes. I accepted his word, but I paid one of his neighbors to keep me informed—just in case."

Scott made an angry gesture with his hand. "Enough of your convoluted reasoning. What's on the film?" he demanded. "What did you shoot that day when you went to Sanchez's compound that has everybody so scared?"

"I don't know," came the barely audible reply.

Scott stared at him with disgust. "What do you mean you don't know? Do you think I'm stupid enough to believe that?"

"I did some filming during the day. The stuff they wanted me to see. Schoolkids playing. Women using the modern laundry facilities. Crafts projects. But I heard people talking about a meeting of some bigwigs at night after I was supposed to leave." He stopped and sucked in a breath before continuing. "I parked down the road and came back to the grove where they'd set up chairs. But I was in the bushes. I had to turn up the mike and hold the camera above my head and hope I was getting the scene."

Scott swore under his breath. "People are trying to kill us to get that film. You're saying you held a twenty-thousand-dollar camera over your head like an umbrella. And you don't even know what's on the tapes. That's perfect."

Turning away, Scott looked around for some convenient way to move the box with the film. When he saw a wheelbarrow leaning against the wall, he rolled it forward.

"Wait. What are you doing?" Pepe wheezed.

Scott didn't bother to answer.

The man on the floor tried to stand and fell back against the wall. "Don't leave me. We could join forces. You have the film. I have the connections to do something important with it."

Scott gave a harsh laugh. "Not likely."

He glanced at Mariana who looked almost as sick as their captive. "We'd better get out of here before somebody else we don't want to meet shows up."

"What about him?"

"I can tell the Randolph men to scoop him up after we leave."

"Please...no," Pepe called. "Turn the tapes over to the People's Party. They will know what to do with them."

Ignoring him, Scott wheeled the box out of the shed.

Five minutes later, after he'd checked for suspicious vehicles on the street, they were in the van and speeding away from the house.

"We have to go to San Rafael del Mar," Mariana said as they rounded the corner.

"Yes," Scott agreed. "But first we have to look at the tapes."

He saw her face contort and laid his hand over hers. "I know how worried you are," he said.

"How could you?" she challenged, her voice full of anger and despair.

He shifted his gaze from the road. "Because I know what kind of mother you are. I know this is eating you up from the inside out. But we can't just go charging into their clutches. We have to look at the tapes first and see what we're up against. It's the only way to make sure that all of us are going to be safe."

"All of us," she echoed.

"You. Me. Alicia."

"You haven't even met her," she whispered.

"I want to," he answered, knowing it wasn't just a perfunctory response to keep the woman beside him from going into hysterics.

She turned her eyes on him, searching his face for the truth of his words, and he felt his throat tighten.

"I know you said you had a journal. But…could you tell me some more about her now," he asked in a thick voice. "Tell me the things I missed when she was little. Like her first word."

He saw a tiny smile flicker on her lips, saw her gaze turn inward. "Her first word was *ga*. For *gato*. She likes cats."

"Did you have one for a pet?"

"We never could. We moved too much."

His hands tightened on the wheel. He didn't want to think about how unsettled their life had been. He didn't want to think that Alicia's father should have been there, taking care of her and Mariana.

Obviously sensing his tension, she went on quickly, "She used to go around naming everything in sight. Animals. People. Flowers. But when she was little, she'd only say half the word, so I was the only one who could understand her at first. Now she's learning to read. And I helped her write a storybook."

"Isn't she young for that?"

"A little. But she's smart."

"Like her mother."

Mariana gave a little nod as she launched into a description of the picture book she and Alicia had worked on together. He let her talk, partly because he knew it eased her tension and partly because he was greedy for details.

MARIANA WATCHED Scott as he worked with impressive efficiency, connecting leads between two Beta tape machines, two monitors and a portable-computer editing system.

He'd started cursing when he first opened the boxes and confronted the unfamiliar equipment. But it hadn't taken him long to figure out how to make it all work together.

They were in a small hotel on the outskirts of the city, where they'd rented an empty suite of rooms on the first floor. She'd handled the negotiations with the owner, spinning a story about being in a competition to make a documentary film on San Marcos wildlife.

In exchange for an exorbitant payment, Señor Madero had been eager to cooperate. He'd even helped carry some of the equipment.

Since then, there had been nothing for her to do besides watch Scott work—and worry. Alicia. Fear for her child's safety never faded, but it flared at quiet times like these. Really, she'd wanted to jump up and pace the room, but she made herself remain still, to keep from distracting him.

"I'm ready," he finally said, putting a tape in the player.

With a mixture of relief and apprehension, she pulled up a chair beside him and they began watching the film.

There were eight tapes in the box, carefully packed in layers of protective plastic. The first three were of locations Scott had shot early in his San Marcos stay, and he fast-forwarded impatiently through the footage.

Mariana yelled, ''Stop,'' when a gate came into view announcing General Sanchez's residence. But then there was nothing beside scenes of well-turned-out soldiers marching in formation on a parade ground.

''That can't be what they're worried about!'' Mariana whispered.

''Unless they're so paranoid they're not thinking straight.''

Unable to deal with the tension, she stood up. ''I'm going to see what we can have for…is it lunch or dinner?''

''Whatever.''

When she came back she was carrying a tray of sandwiches and coffee. Scott barely glanced at the food.

''You have to eat,'' she murmured.

''If you do,'' he answered as he fast-forwarded through a scene of women working in a large, modern kitchen. ''This is even better!'' he muttered sarcastically. ''Subversive cooks.''

She forced herself to take a bite of beef and avocado, glad that the greasy vegetable made the food easier to swallow.

Scott watched her for a moment, then picked up his own sandwich. They both chewed and swallowed without enthusiasm and sipped the *café con leche* as they focused on the screen.

At the same moment, they both realized that the scene had changed abruptly. First the camera jerked, then it steadied.

''Go back!'' Mariana cried out, even as Scott rewound for several seconds.

In the new setting, there was much less light, and leaves blurred the edges of the screen. The picture was barely steady, but she could see that the footage was of men in crisp officers' uniforms filing into rows of folding chairs that had been set up outside facing a low platform with a striped green awning.

When the audience had taken their seats, General Sanchez, splendid in his green dress uniform, strutted onto the stage to thunderous applause.

Mariana felt a shiver travel over her skin. This was film shot long ago, she told herself. Yet the man had the power to make her tremble.

The camera jerked, and she held her breath, afraid that the screen would go blank. But the picture steadied as Sanchez smiled and held up his hand for quiet. When the crowd was silent again, he gave a brief speech praising the efficiency of his men in wiping out subversive elements in the countryside.

His words brought a choked exclamation to Mariana's throat. "Pepe was right," she gasped out.

Scott reached for her hand and felt her fingers close around his. "Unfortunately," he muttered as the scene jerked again.

When the speech ended, young enlisted men carrying submachine guns, and wearing camouflage uniforms tucked into high black boots came out onto the low stage.

For a terrible moment, she wondered if the soldiers were going to spray the audience with bullets. Then she saw they were only serving as an honor guard for the group of men filing in to take their seats on the platform. Some wore the uniforms of high-ranking army officers. Some were dressed in conservative business suits.

The camera wavered violently then righted itself, and she saw a face she recognized. "Hector Porfirio," she said, pointing to one of the businessmen. Beside her, she saw Scott's features go rigid.

"*That's* the man who sent you to Jed?" he said.

"Yes. Do you recognize him?"

"He was there in the prison when they interrogated me," Scott spat out.

She closed her eyes, unable to face him. *Dios,* what a fool she'd been to trust Porfirio.

Then she heard Scott curse and blinked open her eyes. He was pointing toward the screen, and they both watched Pablo Omera join the elite group of Sanchez backers. "Another familiar face. This is turning into old-home week."

The newcomer was the government official who had devoted his time to pestering Scott about rules and regulations.

"He was at the office all the time, looking over my shoulder. He had to approve every location where I shot any footage. I thought he wasn't going to give permission for me to go to Sanchez's compound. Then he changed his mind."

"I assumed he was just a minor bureaucrat throwing his weight around," Mariana breathed as the two older men on the screen clasped each other's arms.

"Yeah, well, it looks like Omera and Porfirio are buddies," Scott said.

Apparently Pepe was having trouble holding the heavy camera steady. But though the picture wavered, the film kept rolling.

More men came in, and Mariana was able to call off some of the names. Some had since been convicted of crimes against their own people. Others were still in the army or in high government positions.

Then a tall, ramrod-straight man in a United States Army uniform joined the group, and Scott drew in a sharp breath.

"You know him?"

"It's Anthony Bennington," he breathed. Reaching out a hand, he stopped the tape, freezing the image on the screen.

The name meant nothing to Mariana. "Who is he?"

"Well, apparently, he was a colonel back then. Now he's a respected U.S. general. The rumor is that he's launching a presidential campaign." He studied the man, his eyes narrowing. "Marci told me Jed thought a U.S. military officer had helped train Sanchez's assassination squads. It appears to have been Bennington."

He stared at the image still on the screen. "A lot of things suddenly make sense. I'd say Bennington is the guy with the most to lose here. This six-year-old tape is probably the only evidence that he was connected with this gang of thugs.''

He pounded his fist against the tabletop. ''I'm willing to bet he was the man in the car with Thompson. The man who wanted to get the two of us together. No wonder he's been able to track our every move. He's got the resources of the U.S. intelligence community at his disposal.''

Scott started the tape again, and more images flashed by as he filled her in on Bennington's background.

The picture wavered dangerously again, then righted itself in time to catch another man standing in the background. As Mariana focused on him, she felt her stomach twist and heard a choked sob escape from her lips.

Chapter Fourteen

Mariana felt her pulse pounding in her ears, even as Scott turned to her.

"What is it? What did you see?" he asked urgently as he pulled her close and wrapped her in his arms.

Her teeth were chattering too hard for her to speak. All she could do was lay her head on Scott's shoulder and try to catch her breath.

Scott moved his lips against her cheek, stroking his hands through her hair. "What is it?" he repeated.

Gulping in air, she managed to say, "My...my father."

His body stiffened. "The film's pretty jerky. Are you're sure?"

She wrenched away from him, stopped the tape and slapped her hand against the screen, pointing to the man in the shadows. "Of course I'm sure! Don't you think I recognize my own father?" She pressed her hand to her mouth, feeling as if the surface of the screen had seared it. "He said he was going away on a business trip that day—the day Pepe did the filming. That's why I could go with you to Chipotalli."

"He took your mother to Sanchez's compound?" Scott asked skeptically.

"No, he sent her to visit my aunt."

Scott gave a curt nod.

She stared at him, her eyes bright with tears. "I thought he was an honorable man. Now I know he was one of them. Pepe was right. He was helping them murder our people."

"Then why did they kill him?" Scott countered.

"How do I know what men like that would do?" she whispered. Really, she had no other answer. She only knew that everything she'd been taught was a lie. Her father's friend had set her and Scott up to be killed as terrorists. When that hadn't worked, they'd stolen her daughter.

Not they. Hector Porfirio—her old family friend who had offered his help if she ever needed it. His generosity had only been a trick to get the cursed film.

"He's going to kill Alicia," she sobbed.

"No!" Scott's arms tightened around her and rocked her comfortingly.

"If anything happens to her…"

"Shh. Nothing's going to happen. I promise." His lips brushed her hair, and his hands soothed across her back.

She clung to that because the only alternative was madness. Sucking air into her lungs, she expelled it in a thin stream and struggled to pull herself together.

When she thought she could keep from sobbing, she straightened.

"Okay?" Scott murmured.

"Yes," she managed to say and knew that he was willing to accept the lie.

He gestured toward the video equipment. "I'm going to do some work on the tape."

"Can I help you?"

"No. I want you to get some sleep."

"I don't think that's possible."

He squeezed her shoulder. "I know this is tearing you apart, but one of us has to be rested. When I finish here, you can drive us down to San Rafael del Mar, and I can get a few hours' sleep."

She nodded, wondering if he was making up reasons for

her compliance. Really, he must know she hadn't had much experience driving a van. But she didn't voice the doubts; she only turned away and sat down on the sofa in the alcove of the main room, where she pulled off her shoes and unfolded the comforter draped across one arm.

Once she laid her head on the pillow, her mind kept circling from one awful fact to another. Her father. Porfirio. Omera. They had all betrayed her. And now Porfirio had her daughter. The reality of that made her start to tremble.

Sometime early in the morning, she finally slept, then woke to the sound of birds chirping in the trees, and the whisper of voices. Sitting up, she blinked as she saw Scott and Matthew Forester packing up the video equipment.

"What are you doing?" she asked.

"Arranging a little surprise for Anthony Bennington and company," Scott answered. "Something that will convince him and his San Marcos friends that if they harm us or Alicia, the whole world will know why."

Mariana nodded, then returned her questioning gaze to Matthew. "I don't understand. I thought you were supposed to wait for us where you landed the plane. How did you get here?"

"That was the fallback plan, in case we didn't hear from you. But we also agreed that we could risk a quick phone call on a secure line."

"You should have told me," she said, her gaze moving between the men. "What else are you holding back?"

"Jed's awake," Matthew said. "Marci says he's going to make a full recovery."

"Gracias a Dios," she breathed.

Scott squeezed her hand. "That's a load off my mind," he muttered. Picking up a Beta cassette, he handed it to Matthew, along with the portable phone.

"No more calls?" she asked.

"Steve and I are flying this tape back to the States," Matthew answered. "As soon as I pick up your friend Pepe."

Mariana grimaced as she thought about the man still se-cured in Juan's shed. "What are you going to do with him?"

"Take him with us. We'll turn him loose when you've got your daughter back."

"Thank you," she whispered.

"No problem," Matthew answered, obviously uncomfort-able with her gratitude.

Scott gave her fifteen minutes to get ready. She managed in ten while the men finished packing the van and the Volvo in which Matthew had arrived. To Mariana's surprise, he took the van; they took the car, which was loaded with one VCR and a monitor in the trunk.

Scott asked her to drive, and until they got out of town, she was a mass of nerves, constantly expecting a police car to pull in back of them with its lights flashing. When she finally turned onto the road to San Rafael del Mar, she felt a small sense of relief—though nothing could assuage the fear and dread that she wouldn't reach Alicia in time. She had to pray Scott's plan would work.

"Are you going to tell me what Matthew is going to do with the tape you gave him?" she asked Scott as they headed southwest toward the Pacific coast.

"Yes."

As he outlined the plan, she felt herself teetering between fear and optimism. What he proposed was risky. When she started to ask him another question, she saw that he'd drifted off to sleep, his face half hidden by the floppy hat and sun-glasses he'd put on again.

The bouncing of the car over the rough road didn't wake him. But she fought a clogged feeling in her chest when his mouth contorted from what she assumed was a bad dream.

She wanted to reach out and brush her finger against his cheek, but she kept her hands on the wheel, and her jaw set against her own needs.

He'd told her to wake him before they got to their desti-nation. So she pulled into a gas station about twenty kilometers from town where they could fill the tank and use the facilities.

He woke with a jolt as soon as the car stopped, and she saw the gun he'd tucked in his waistband appear in his hand.

"Scott, it's okay," she whispered urgently. "We're just stopping for gas."

He turned his head and focused on her.

"Put the gun away," she whispered as she saw a man inside the station stand up and amble toward them.

Scott blinked, looked down at the weapon, then shoved it out of sight just as the attendant stepped up to her window.

With a silent sigh of relief, she asked the man to fill the tank.

"SORRY," Scott muttered, hoping his voice sounded normal. The longer he stayed in San Marcos, the harder it was to hang on to his sanity.

They were on the road again in a few minutes, and he watched Mariana's set jaw, her white knuckles as her hands clenched the wheel. He wanted to say something that would help her, but he didn't even know if he could help himself.

She jerked to a stop in front of a low stucco house, then leaped from the car and tore up the short walkway. He stayed right behind her, hearing the sound of shuffling feet in response to her frantic knock at the door.

"Susana, where is Alicia?" she demanded, grasping the shoulders of the old woman who opened the door.

"*Madre de Dios*," the woman whispered. "What are you doing here?"

"I came to get Alicia."

The woman's face contorted and her lower lip trembled. "You'd better come in."

They followed Susana into a small living room where another woman sat in an overstuffed chair, her hands clasped in her lap.

"Don't blame Susana. It's my fault," she said as soon as she saw Mariana.

"Dolores. Tell me what happened!"

The old woman wrung her hands. "It was two evenings ago. Susana was at the church. And a man came to the door. He said it was urgent. He had a letter from your father's friend, Señor Porfirio."

Mariana's knees gave way, but Scott was at her side, easing her onto the couch. He came down beside her, kept his arm around her as if the contact could ward away the icy feeling spreading through his veins.

"I'm sorry. I thought I was doing the right thing." Dolores lifted pleading eyes to them.

"Tell us exactly what happened," Scott demanded, making a supreme effort not to shout out his anger and frustration.

"He persuaded me that Alicia was in danger, that he was going to keep her safe." Dolores's lip quivered. "Then Susana came home and told me I was an *idiota*."

Mariana made a low moaning sound, and he held her more tightly.

"I couldn't sleep all night," Dolores continued. "Then a boy delivered a letter this morning." She reached in the pocket of her long woven skirt and extracted a crumpled piece of paper.

Scott snatched it away and started to read. With a shaky hand, Mariana pulled the paper down where she could see it, too.

The message was similar to the one that had been pinned to Juan Tiemplo's body. Ironically this one was signed "Your friend."

Dolores started to weep.

"They won't hurt Alicia," Scott said, speaking urgently both to Mariana and the old women. "They want our cooperation. And they think they can get it by holding her. But we're going to get her back, and stop them in their tracks."

"That's easy for you to say," Mariana cried out. "Your plan is too dangerous. You have to call Steve and stop him. We have to give them the tapes."

"That will just get Alicia killed, and us too," he said, trying to hold his voice steady. "If you stop and think, you know that as well as I do. She's only okay as long as they assume they can buy our cooperation."

Her face twisted in anguish, and he knew she didn't want to hear his attempt at logic; she wanted to hold her little girl in her arms, kiss her and tell her that everything was going to be all right.

"Maybe you're willing to take that chance," she snapped. "But she's my daughter, don't you understand?"

When she tried to wrench away from him, his hand tightened on her arm, and he turned her to face him, desperate to make her understand that he knew exactly how she felt. "She's my daughter, too," he said in a voice that he couldn't quite hold steady.

"You didn't want her. You tried as hard as you could not to get me pregnant. You didn't even know you had a daughter until a few days ago."

The accusation was like a hot whip flailing his skin. Somehow he managed to say, "Mariana, look at me." When he saw that he had her attention, he continued, "I haven't met her! I haven't held her in my arms. But I want to—and I will," he vowed, astonished at the strength of the emotions surging through him.

He'd forgotten that anyone else was in the room. Then a low sound from one of the sisters made him look up.

Dolores swiped a hand across her eyes as if trying to clear her vision.

"Alicia's father," Susana breathed, her eyes flicking between them. "You told me you would never see him again. And…and I thought he had red hair—like your grandmother, the one who came from Germany."

It was Scott who answered the question. "You'll have to

wait till my red hair grows out. As for the other part, she thought she'd never see me again, because we didn't part as friends." He swallowed. "Did she tell you my name?"

"She never said it to me. But Alicia knows. It's a secret they have."

"Well, it's never too late for introductions. I'm Scott O'Donnell."

Susana's cold gaze pierced his flesh, but he refused to look away.

"Well, Scott O'Donnell, you left her with a child in her belly. And when she was in labor and out of her mind with pain, she called for you. She needed you there—to take some of the agony away."

The accusation stabbed at his heart. "I'm sorry I wasn't here," he told her.

"She needed you," the old woman repeated. "Not just for the pain when she couldn't deliver the child and the doctor had to rip her open. All these years. She needed you by her side."

He tried to draw in a breath, but breathing was impossible with hot pincers tearing at his guts. He wasn't going to defend himself, but Mariana did it for him.

"Don't make him feel guilty about leaving me," she gasped out. "He didn't know about Alicia. All he knew was that government agents asked me to plant military maps in his apartment. The police came and found them and hauled him off to prison. You know what they can do. I've seen the scars on his body to prove what happened."

"*Madre de Dios,*" Dolores whispered, her eyes searching Mariana's face. "Why?"

Scott was the one who answered. "She did it because she thought they were going to release me right away and send me out of the country. She knew they were after me, and she thought she was saving my life," he said quickly, wanting these two women who loved Mariana to understand, although he knew that the short explanation was hardly enough. It hadn't been enough for him when he'd first heard it, but during these days he'd spent with Mariana he'd come to understand the motivation of the woman who'd borne his child.

"Let's stop focusing on things we can't change," he said. "What we have to do now is get Alicia back, and convince these men they have nothing to fear from us."

All eyes were on him again.

"What are you going to do?" Susana asked.

He'd given that very question considerable thought as he'd worked last night. "I'm going to throw a private party at the best hotel in town," he answered, elaborating on the information he'd given Mariana in the car.

"How do we know the guests will show up?" she asked.

He choked out a laugh. "They've found us every time we turned around. Why should today be any different?"

"Then why don't they come here and get us?" she pressed. "They must know we've come to Dolores's house."

He had come prepared with answers to questions like that. "For one thing, they know we're not going anywhere without Alicia. For another, the important players may not have arrived yet."

Mariana's lips trembled. "Why don't they just kill us and get it over with?"

"Because they have to make sure we've brought the tapes and that we're not trying to pull some desperate stunt." Of course, that was exactly his intention. But he didn't point that out. Instead, projecting a show of confidence, he stood. "Come on, we have a lot to do."

THE CALL CAME on the portable phone as Pablo Omera sped toward San Rafael del Mar ensconced in the comfortable leather upholstery of his luxury sedan.

"They've set up a meeting at a hotel called the Corona del Mar," Bernardo Cortez informed him. "O'Donnell rented a private banquet room on the first floor. Off the side entrance."

He glanced at the driver, who was facing forward, his attention focused on the road.

"I know the place. It's quite charming—the only luxury hotel in town. But why there?"

"They probably think it's safe." Bernardo laughed. "I've already got the place surrounded by police."

"Have the others arrived?"

"Thompson and Porfirio will be here soon. How close are you?"

He checked his watch. "Less than an hour away."

"Good. That gives us time for a strategy session."

"Where is the little girl?" asked Omera.

"I have her in a safe place."

"Alive?" he pressed.

"Of course. For the moment."

Omera didn't ask for more details, because he didn't like using an innocent child as a pawn in a high-stakes game. And he didn't like thinking about what Bernardo might have done with her, given his hatred of the mother. It was Bernardo who had researched the background of every former servant in the Reyes household, and frightened some of them into talking. Bernardo who had been willing to spend his family's wealth to find where Mariana had hidden her little girl.

Pablo hung up and poured himself a brandy from the portable bar, downing the fiery liquid in one gulp. At last, everything was falling into place. That was the important thing.

Six years ago he'd made a mistake by allowing the tapes from Sanchez's compound to disappear. By the time he'd realized that Mariana Reyes had hidden them, she had already faded into the San Marcos backcountry.

He'd told himself it didn't matter. As long as the tapes were hidden, they couldn't hurt anyone. And really, they might be harmless for all anyone knew.

But the American colonel who had helped instruct the assassination squads had changed the rules. He was a general now with political aspirations, and his enthusiastic support of General Sanchez was an embarrassment. Specifically, he wanted to make sure nobody in his own country ever learned that he'd taught San Marcos elite troops how to kill their countrymen.

He'd made it clear that if he went down, everyone else was going down with him. So the scramble to find the missing tapes had started.

Pablo's hand clenched the empty glass, and he concentrated on making his muscles relax. This elaborate cover-up operation had been jinxed from the beginning, starting with the plan to get O'Donnell and Reyes branded as terrorists so they'd have nowhere to turn. That had gotten screwed up when that fool in Miami almost killed them, then let them get away, before they could be induced to talk. Bernardo was sure that the girl would have cracked if she'd been forced to watch her lover tortured. But the pair had escaped. And when they'd eluded capture, Bernardo had enthusiastically pushed for plan B—kidnapping the daughter.

Pablo shuddered. Bernardo had a private score to settle with Señorita Reyes. She'd impugned his family's honor by bearing the American's bastard child. More than that, the end of Bernardo's engagement to the daughter had left him without a hold over the father, who'd had the nerve to withdraw his support from Sanchez, once there was no longer a chance of an alliance between the families.

Bernardo had made sure that the right people understood the magnitude of Señor Reyes's betrayal and that they'd punished him properly. But that hadn't been enough for Bernardo. He'd wanted revenge on the daughter as well. Unfortunately, she'd disappeared before he could snatch her up.

But now, six years later, it looked as though he was going to get what he wanted. And there wasn't anything Pablo could do about that. He wouldn't interfere with Bernardo, just so long as they accomplished their primary mission—getting the tapes and destroying them.

"Is MARIANA SLEEPING?" Scott whispered.

Susana nodded.

"Good."

No way was he going to let her get anywhere near the gang of thugs assembling at the hotel. So he'd arranged for the old woman to mix a sleeping powder in the tea she'd given her.

"And the hotel manager knows what he's supposed to do?" he asked.

"*Sí.*"

"Then I'm going to load the equipment in the car and put on my party clothes. I want you to wake her in an hour. I want all of you out of this house. Go to a friend—somewhere safe until...until I come back with Alicia," he said with as much conviction as he could muster.

When the old woman's eyes grew frightened, he patted her arm. "Everything is going to work out okay," he said, silently praying it was really true.

He carried out the VCR and the monitor, then came back to the house and washed before changing into his only fresh shirt and slacks. When he started back to the car again, he found Mariana sitting in the front seat, a set expression on her face.

"What are you doing here?" he said, wrenching open the door. "You're supposed to be...resting."

She snorted. "You mean drugged, don't you? Susana never was much good at lying to me. I knew she was up to something when she brought me that cup of tea."

Cursing under his breath, he tugged on her arm. But she only wrapped her hands around the edge of the seat and held fast. "You're not going without me. So take your hand off me before I scream."

He dropped his arm to his side. "It's too dangerous. They could refuse to watch the tape. They could realize I've taken out the good part and given it to Steve. Anything could happen."

"If it's dangerous for me, then it's dangerous for you." She raised her chin, her eyes dark and angry. "I won't let you make decisions for me."

"It's for your own good, dammit!" he practically shouted at her, then tried to get a grip.

She looked at him with narrowed eyes. "If that's what you think, then you're making the same mistake I did six years ago," she said in an even voice. "You're making decisions for me that I have the right to make. Is that why you've been lying to me? Keeping the important part of your plans secret?"

"You've heard the important part!"

"Have I?" she mocked him. "How can I be sure?"

Feeling as if he'd been rammed in the stomach with a railroad tie, he stared down at her, knowing that any answer he gave would be wrong. Stiffly, he walked around the car, yanked open the driver's door and slid behind the wheel.

He wanted to explain that it had been unforgivable to blame her for his troubles when he'd come to San Marcos as a wet-behind-the-ears kid thinking he was going to make the documentary of the century.

Back then, he had fallen in love with her, but he hadn't really understood who she was. Since they'd met again, he'd come to realize that the last person she ever thought of was herself. She had tried to save him six years ago. Now she was trying to save her daughter.

He ached to tell her he had fallen in love with her all over again—with the real Mariana Reyes. He wanted to explain that his prime motive was to keep her out of harm's way because she was very precious to him. But the lump in his throat would have made it difficult to talk. And he wasn't sure if she'd believe him at that moment, anyway. So he simply started the engine and backed out of the driveway— heading for a confrontation in hell.

Chapter Fifteen

As Scott drove toward the hotel, his head began to pound, and he clenched his teeth to keep the pain from exploding behind his eyes. He'd known the only way he could handle being in the same room with men who had arrested and tortured him was by setting the whole thing up—taking control of the situation and by making sure Mariana was safe. As far as he could see, the operation was going wrong before it even got started.

That was just one more thing he couldn't explain to Mariana. And he sure as hell wasn't going to admit that he was scared spitless. So he focused his eyes on the road and gripped the wheel to keep his hands from shaking.

The hotel buildings and grounds were like something out of a tropical fantasy. The beds of flowers and lush greenery shimmering in the sunshine had a surrealistic quality as he pulled into a parking area screened from the street by tall pink and white blooming oleander bushes. Since the lot was almost empty, he found a place only about twenty yards from the entrance.

"Stay here until I check the place out and get things set up," he told Mariana. Without waiting for her agreement, he climbed out, dragging in a lungful of salt-tinged air.

Opening the trunk, he took out the box with the VCR and started toward the hotel. A man in a parked car studied him with pointed interest, then said in Spanish, "The hotel is closed today. For a private party."

"I'm just making a delivery," Scott answered in the same language. "Can you tell me where to find the party room?"

The guy waved toward a side door. "In there. Halfway down the hall on the right."

"Thanks," he answered, glad that for once the disguise was working the way it was supposed to.

Inside, he had no trouble finding the elegant little dining room that Susana had rented for him. There was a guard at the door and several more men inside who didn't look as if they'd been to hotel management school. They all eyed Scott as he set down the VCR on a sideboard opposite a buffet table laid out for a sumptuous feast, but none of them interfered with him as he left to retrieve the monitor.

He was almost back to the car when he felt the blood in his veins turn to ice. A police car had materialized at the end of the parking lot, its lights flashing. Another one glided into position at the entrance, sealing off the area. Almost simultaneously, a tall man strode to the car where Mariana sat and yanked the door open.

"Get out," he growled. "Did you think you could fool me? Did you think I wouldn't recognize you with your hair chopped off like that? I would recognize you in Hades with your head shaved." In a louder voice, he called out, "It's *her*, you fools. The guy with the short brown hair must be O'Donnell. You let him get away."

Scott was reaching for the pistol tucked into his slacks when he felt the unmistakable pressure of a gun in the small of his back. "Hold it right there," another voice advised. "Keep your mitts where I can see them," his captor added as a trained hand lifted the pistol from his waistband.

When Scott shifted position, the cold metal at his back dug deeper into his flesh. "Don't do anything stupid."

"I won't," he answered. He didn't need to turn around to know who was behind him. It was Ed Thompson, the son of a bitch who had gotten him into this in the first place. When he'd planned this little sting, he hadn't counted on Thompson flying in for the festivities. That was a piece of very bad luck.

"I think you and your friends may want to have a look at the videotape before you knock us off," Scott observed in as cool a voice as he could manage, "because there's nothing Pepe shot that was incriminating—unless you're worried about assistant cooks at Sanchez's compound cutting off too much of the potatoes along with the skin."

"We'll see about that," Thompson answered.

His friend yanked Mariana out of the car, and she gasped in pain.

"Leave her alone," Scott choked out. "She hasn't done anything."

"She betrayed me with you. She bore your bastard," the man with his hand clamped on Mariana's arm answered, his voice low and dangerous.

Scott sucked in a strangled breath. This could only be Bernardo Cortez, the man who had planned to marry Mariana—until he'd found out that she was pregnant with another man's child. God, what was *he* doing here?

A smile flickered on Cortez's lips as he ordered Mariana to put her palms on the top of the car, like a policeman in some cop show. When she complied, he moved his hands over her body, pretending he was searching for weapons where none could be hidden.

"Don't," Scott ordered.

Cortez smiled more broadly and continued what he was doing.

Mariana's eyes searched for Scott's. "I'm sorry," she mouthed.

He wanted to say the same thing, but all he could do was watch helplessly as Cortez pawed her.

"What are you doing here?" she asked in a voice that sounded high and strangled.

"I had the opportunity to help out some dear friends," he answered with an offhand lift of his shoulder.

"That's enough," Thompson growled. "We should go inside and get started."

Cortez was hardly more responsive to him than he had been to Scott. "Maybe in *los Estados Unidos,* you run the show," he said in a deadly calm voice, "but not down here. What are you afraid of? A raid from the People's Party?" He gave a sharp laugh. "There won't be any trouble from them—or anybody else."

When he'd made his point, he took Mariana's arm and marched her toward the side entrance.

"Bring the monitor," Thompson told Scott.

Feeling like a trapped animal with the dogs closing in, he followed orders.

The same guard was in the lobby—and a man dressed as a waiter, who scurried out of the way as he saw them coming.

Nodding to the guard, Cortez ushered Mariana into the private dining room. Scott and Thompson followed.

Scott set the monitor next to the VCR, then turned to find Mariana stretch her hand toward her former fiancé.

"Bernardo, please. If you know where Alicia is, tell me," she begged in Spanish.

"Of course I know! I'm the one who collected her from that dithering old woman. If you want to get the brat back, you'll have to cooperate with us."

Mariana gasped. "Do you hate me so much?" she asked in a quiet voice, her face bruised and wounded-looking.

For a moment he looked as wounded as she. Then the pain was masked by anger. "You had the audacity to push me away, then let another man have your body, when you belonged to me," he said, his voice low and dangerous as his gaze landed on Scott. "But now I have the pleasure of making you both pay."

"*You* planned this?" Scott said.

"No. I made some strategic suggestions."

Scott caught the malevolent gleam in his eye.

"Alicia better be all right," he said tightly.

"So, you're finally taking some responsibility for your bastard daughter."

"I took responsibility the day I knew she existed!" he answered, moving to Mariana's side and putting his arm around her, feeling a little shiver go through her. Her skin was like ice, and he pressed his hand over her arm.

Cortez watched them with narrowed eyes. He seemed about to speak, but clamped his mouth shut when two more men entered the room. Both were short and slender, with lined faces and hair going gray. One was Pablo Omera, the official who had dogged Scott's every move six years ago. The other was Hector Porfirio.

As Thompson gave them a deferential nod, Scott felt his heart pound inside his chest, felt the walls of the room close in around him. Suddenly, it was six years ago, and he was back in prison being dragged from his cell to the room at the end of the hall.

Porfirio had been there, conferring earnestly with the guards. Probably he'd been the one giving the orders.

His hands balled into fists, Scott took a step forward, then felt Mariana's fingers digging into the flesh of his arm.

"Don't," she whispered.

With a tight nod, he made himself stay where he was, since getting himself killed wasn't going to solve their problems.

Mariana raised her voice. "Señor Porfirio, I trusted you. Why did you betray me?" she asked.

The eyes that focused on her were sad. "You're such a beautiful woman. I would have saved you if I could, my dear. But there are larger issues here than my personal desires."

It was all Scott could do to keep from smashing a fist into the man's hound-dog face. But he held himself in check. Mariana's life depended on what he did next. So did Alicia's.

The next words came from Omera. "You better have the tapes," he said in a strained voice.

"I do. If you mean the tapes Pepe Fortunato shot at the Sanchez compound."

"Of course. Those tapes. Do you think I care about your charming pictures of village dancers and Indian women weaving tablecloths?"

"Well, village dancers and tablecloths are about as meaningful as this footage. I've looked at it. There's nothing earthshattering, as far as I can see. But you're welcome to look for yourselves."

"We intend to," Porfirio retorted.

"Then I'll hook up the machine," Scott answered. He wanted to stay by Mariana's side. Instead, he gave her hand a squeeze, then stepped away from her and took a quick look at his watch.

Thompson saw him do it. "You have another engagement?" he asked.

"No," he said in a low voice, and Thompson stepped closer. Scott shot him a glance as he started connecting the components.

"So what led you to Juan Tiemplo's?" Scott asked.

"We found out Pepe Fortunato was interested in him." Thompson's eyes narrowed. "He should have turned over the tapes, then we wouldn't have needed your little girl."

Sure, Scott thought. *And you'll be happy to let us go, now that we know so much.* Instead of voicing his thoughts, he kept working, pretending that he was having trouble with the hookup. "I'm curious about something else," he said. "Porfirio was supposed to be a friend of Mariana's father. Why did he turn on him?"

"Señor Reyes was never really one of us. He went back to his old politics, once there was no chance of an alliance with the Cortez family," Thompson said.

"What's taking so long?" Omera demanded from the bar where he was downing a large glassful of amber liquid.

"I'm almost through," Scott answered as Thompson reached for the remote control. "It's working," he announced. "Show time." To Scott, he said, "I'll take over from here."

As Cortez dimmed the lights, Scott looked around for Mariana. She was huddled on the couch. Crossing the room, he sank down next to her. He'd done what he could. Now he'd see how his doctored tape played in San Rafael del Mar.

First the screen showed a road carved through the jungle, then a gatehouse with a military crest.

"Fortunato was there," Omera growled. "There's the proof."

"Of what?" Scott muttered. "Don't make any judgments until you see the whole thing."

No one answered. He could feel the tension in the room when Thompson began to show footage from Sanchez's compound, then the relaxation as the bland scenes unfolded. Men working in the fields. Soldiers drilling on a parade ground, a two-room schoolhouse full of happy children, women washing clothes in a communal laundry, a small hospital, the kitchen.

Then it was nighttime, and the camera pushed through bushes. But just as the scene at the outdoor meeting came into view, the camera jerked upward, and the film cut off abruptly as if the photographer had been discovered and suddenly forced to stop filming.

"There's no more," Scott said, hoping he sounded convincing.

Thompson fast-forwarded over blue screen.

Then he rewound to the moments just after the kitchen and played them once again.

"A guard must have found him and thrown him out," Porfirio said in the darkness, his voice suffused with relief.

"Thrown him out of what?" Scott asked.

"That's none of your business," the older man snapped.

"I don't know what you were looking for on that tape," Scott said. "Were you hoping he got something incriminating on Sanchez?"

"Yes," Omera whispered.

Scott knew it was a lie, but he didn't challenge the man, instead he reached for Mariana's hand and gently squeezed it.

"So now that you don't need our daughter any longer, where is she?" Scott asked in a voice he struggled to hold steady.

He could feel Mariana go very still.

Porfirio swung around and looked at Cortez. "I think it's fair to say we can return her."

"There could be more tape," the other man said. "Or he could have doctored it."

The words sent a chill through Scott's blood. When he'd thought of this scheme, it had seemed so logical. Now fear constricted the muscles of his throat and chest. God, how much longer could he keep this going?

"When would I have doctored your damn tape?" he asked in an even voice, hoping nobody else knew exactly when they'd arrived at Juan's house. "All I've had time to do since we found it is fast-forward through it once and drive it down here. If you want, you can check the cassette for tampering. You can even check it for length."

Before any of them could answer, a new voice rang out from the doorway, "We're going to end this farce right now."

Everyone turned to the door as the lights flicked on. When Scott's vision cleared, he saw Pepe Fortunato blocking the exit, a gun in his hand.

"No," Mariana breathed, her eyes wide with disbelief.

Scott was having the same reaction as he stared at the man. They'd left him tied up in Juan Tiemplo's shed, and the Randolph men were supposed to have scooped him up. Apparently things hadn't gone exactly as planned.

"How did you know we were here?" Mariana asked in a strangled voice.

Fortunato laughed. "I saw the note in the pocket of your

friend Juan, so I knew where you were going. When I got to town, everybody was talking about the big meeting at the hotel.''

Scott uttered a curse.

The newcomer's eyes bored into Scott. "Where's the tape I shot?'' he demanded.

"That *is* the tape.''

"I don't think so. It ends too soon.''

"You're the one who's lying,'' Scott answered, stalling for time. "You want to prove something that's not true because your damn political cause is more important than reality. Maybe you've even deluded yourself into thinking that you really shot more footage, instead of getting tossed out on your ass by General Sanchez's men.''

"Stop lying. Why are you lying? Sanchez and these men are enemies of the people.'' He gestured with the gun in his hand. "And the proof has got to be on my tape—that Señor Omera should never have let me shoot,'' he said, his voice rising in desperation. "He should have kept us away from the compound on that day. And he's been trembling in his shoes ever since.''

"It wasn't my fault,'' Omera roared. "Porfirio gave the clearance. Then he forgot that the meeting date was changed.''

The men were standing, each looking as if he was ready to kill the other. Thompson appeared to be contemplating which to assassinate first.

"It's time you stopped punishing us for the mistakes you made,'' Scott said in an even voice. "I haven't done anything wrong. Neither has Mariana.''

Before he could say anything more, someone came running down the hall in back of Pepe shouting excitedly. "CNN. CNN *en Español!*''

Pepe whirled. As he turned his back, Thompson reached for his own gun and fired.

Pepe staggered, but he turned and pumped bullets into the

room. The only thing Scott could do was grab Mariana's arm and pull her to the floor beside the couch, placing his body protectively over hers.

For endless moments, the room was alive with the crackle of gunfire and whizzing bullets. When one plowed into the sofa near Mariana's shoulder, Scott gathered her closer to him. He could feel her body trembling, feel his own heart pounding against her back.

Every second stretched to an hour of his lifetime—of hers. But finally the shooting stopped.

"Stay down," he warned Mariana, expecting the cops to come charging through the door.

They didn't show, and he cautiously pushed himself up. When Mariana grabbed his shirt, holding him on the floor, he gently untangled her fingers and peered around the edge of the sofa.

Pepe was lying in the doorway. Thompson was sprawled in a pool of blood next to Omera, and Cortez was lying nearby, also surrounded by blood. None of them looked as if they'd survived the shoot-out.

Scott helped Mariana up as Omera and Porfirio pushed themselves shakily to their feet. Apparently neither of them had been hit.

"It's all over," Scott told the two remaining conspirators. "Pepe was right. There was more tape—of your secret meeting with Sanchez. You and General Bennington. I sent it back to CNN headquarters in Atlanta on the plane that brought us down here, along with an explanation I taped last night about what's been happening to us this week. And I've been stalling for time until they could get it on the air and expose you. That's why we needed to be in this hotel—because it was luxurious enough to have a satellite TV hookup. They got the Spanish broadcast. I taped an English explanation too—for U.S. consumption.

"The whole world knows that you and Bennington were working with Sanchez, training troops to go after your own people. Bennington is ruined. And your government won't be able to cover it up.''

Omera roared, ''You can't get away with this.''

''I already have. If you kill us or harm Alicia, everybody will know about it.''

He gestured toward the empty doorway. ''Even your cop friends know when to bail out on you.''

''No!''

Scott was enjoying Omera's reaction so much that he almost failed to see a flicker of movement at the edge of his vision. Cortez had slowly pulled himself up and was aiming the gun at him.

It seemed Mariana saw it too. A scream rose in her throat as she launched herself at the man on the floor, kicking the weapon from his hand just as it fired. The shot went wild.

Scott leaped to her, pulling her away from Cortez, turning her to him so that he could sweep his eyes over her body. ''Mariana. Oh God, Mariana, are you all right?''

''I think so,'' she answered in a shaky voice.

''That was…you could have…'' Reaction sent a tremor through him. Pulling her into his arms, he held her tightly against his body, even as his gaze flicked to the man on the floor who lay still and pale, his eyes closed.

''It's over,'' Scott said again as he raised his eyes to the two older men who stood there looking dazed.

''All you have to do is tell us where to find Alicia and I won't have to kill you.''

Omera shook his head. ''I don't know.''

''You're lying,'' Scott said through clenched teeth, grabbing him by the collar and giving him a savage shake. ''Where is my daughter?'' he bellowed.

''I'm sorry. Please believe me. The only one who knows is Bernardo,'' the other man gasped.

Chapter Sixteen

Mariana moaned low in her throat, then dropped to her knees beside Cortez. When Scott started to come down beside her, she motioned him back. He nodded, staying out of the man's line of sight.

"Bernardo," she said, her voice low and pleading as she took his hand and rubbed her thumb over his pale flesh. The touch of his skin made her stomach roil, yet she forced herself to keep the contact. "Bernardo, you have to tell me—where is my little girl?"

For several seconds, there was no response, and she waited beside him, hardly daring to breathe. Then his eyelids flickered. His eyes were glazed as he struggled to focus on her.

"I beg you. I beg you on my knees. Where is Alicia?" she asked again. "She's just a child. She needs me."

He made a sound that was half laugh, half cough, and blood oozed from his mouth.

"Bernardo, do you hate me so much that you can't give me back my daughter?" she whispered. "Do you want to die with this on your conscience?"

His lips moved, and she bent over him, her ear turned toward his face so that she could catch the word. He spoke in a voice so low that she could barely hear, but she was able to catch his dying words.

When she lifted her head, she saw Scott's tense features.

"He's dead," she whispered, fighting the dazed feeling that threatened to swamp her.

Scott pulled her up and turned her toward him, holding her body protectively against his as tremors shook her.

"Did he tell you where she is?" he asked urgently.

Her lips trembled. "He—he made it a riddle. He said Alicia is in the place where he tried to kiss me. He said I wouldn't remember because it was of no importance to me."

"Do you remember?" he asked, and she saw he was holding his breath as he waited for the answer.

Her mouth hardened. "I remember every nasty thing that happened with him. If he's telling the truth, she's in a cave. Down by the ocean." Her eyes lifted to Scott, and her hands clamped on his shoulders. "She's in the dark. And cold. All by herself. With the water pounding on the rocks. I know she has to be so scared. We have to hurry."

"Yes."

Turning as though one mind controlled them both, they started toward the door. The room was empty now, she saw with surprise. Omera and Porfirio had vanished. Perhaps they were on their way home to stuff money into suitcases, if they were like other former members of the San Marcos power structure. She hoped they'd be stopped if they tried to leave San Marcos. But she couldn't worry about that now. She had more important things to do.

Pepe's body was blocking the doorway, and she faltered.

Scott lifted her and carried her over the dead man.

Once she was past the scene of carnage, she sighed in relief. But in the next second, she felt as if the breath had been knocked out of her.

"Mariana? What?"

"The tide," she gasped, turning her face toward the west—toward the ocean. "When the tide comes in, you can't get into the mouth of the cave. It's underwater."

"Are you sure?" Scott demanded.

"Yes," she choked out, then felt another jolt of terror hit

her. "Maybe it's not just the ocean side," she gasped, picking up speed as she sprinted toward the parking lot. "Maybe the whole cave fills up."

"We don't have any idea when the tide is coming in," he argued as they reached the car and he pulled open the door. "It could be going out, for all we know."

"No. Because Bernardo had to be able to take Alicia inside. So it was low tide hours ago."

"Is there another way in? If the water's too high at the mouth?" he asked urgently, throwing the gears into reverse with a grinding noise that set his teeth on edge.

Her vision turned inward as she remembered the hateful setting. Bernardo had chosen well if he wanted a place that made her insides raw. "I remember when we were inside," she whispered. "There was a hole in the roof. I remember the light coming in and thinking it was like a church, and how could he touch me with such disrespect in a place like a church?"

Scott squeezed her hand. "We'll get Alicia out," he growled, then turned his attention to the winding road.

She sat beside him, her rigid body jerking every time the car rounded a curve. "The fishermen," she whispered.

"What about the fishermen?"

"They have boats. They can get into the cave."

"Yes. Good."

They rode in silence for several minutes. Then Scott was speaking to her, his voice seeming to come from far away. When she heard what he was saying, her head whipped toward him.

"I asked Thompson why Porfirio turned on your father," he said as he swung onto the road that led to the coast.

"Thompson said your father betrayed his friends and reverted to his old politics. I have the feeling he was only going along with them to please the Cortez family. So maybe he had second thoughts about what they were doing. Maybe he even decided to tell what he'd seen at the Sanchez compound.''

"You don't know for sure," she whispered.

"It makes sense," he persisted as he rounded another curve and she saw the water.

"There's the harbor where they dock the boats!"

As he screeched to a halt, sending gravel flying, she drew in a strangled breath.

"What?"

She gestured toward the protective cove where boats should have been anchored. "There's nobody here. They're all gone." Fighting panic, she turned back to Scott. "I didn't realize they'd all be out at the same time."

"We don't need them," he told her, leaping from the car and trotting down to the dock, scattering a trio of gulls as he snatched a coil of rope.

"Which way do I go? How far can we drive?" he asked as he threw the rope in the back seat, slipped behind the wheel again and spun out of the parking area.

She pointed to a dirt track that followed the curve of the shoreline. "I'm not sure how far you can take the car."

Waves crashed against the dark rocks that guarded the coastline.

Her eyes darted to the water, then back to the natural features—the rocks, the low twisted trees, the occasional prickly pear cactus.

"There. I think it's there," she shouted, and he slammed on the brakes, bringing them to an abrupt halt.

Both of them leaped from the car and trotted toward the water. The tide was indeed coming in, with big swells pounding against the coastline and roaring into the yawning mouth of a waterline cave.

Mariana's heart thumped inside her chest as she stared at the relentlessly invading water. "Alicia!" she called. "Alicia!" But the wind snatched the words from her mouth and carried them away. She might have sunk to the rocks, defeated, but Scott grabbed her arm.

"Show me the hole in the roof," he ordered.

Scrambling to the top of a cliff, she searched back and forth across the uneven ground. But if there was a passage leading into the ceiling of the cave, it wasn't obvious from this angle.

"Call to her again!" Scott urged.

Going stock-still, she sobbed out her daughter's name again in a voice that rose toward panic. "Alicia? Are you down there? Alicia?"

From far away, a tiny voice drifted toward them. "Mama? Is that you, Mama?"

"Alicia!" Mariana cried. "Where are you? Tell me where you are!"

"In here," the high, piping voice answered above the crashing of the surf.

Following the sound of her daughter's cry, she scrambled toward a crevice hidden by the shadow of a rock.

As HE CAME UP behind her, Scott could hear the booming of the waves like thunder crashing in the enclosed space. Damp air rose to meet him, making a cold sweat break out all over his body. Without a flashlight, he could see only a few feet into the opening. His hands clenched at his sides as he stared down into his worst nightmare.

Ignoring the terror that threatened to swallow him whole, he wound one end of the rope around an outcropping, wondering what he was going to do if he got halfway down and found it wasn't long enough.

Mariana crouched beside him, cupping her hands and calling down into the darkness. "Alicia, are you all right?" she asked urgently. Flopping onto her stomach, she stretched out her hand into the damp and darkness.

"I'm scared," the thin voice drifted upward, almost

drowned out by the swishing of the water. "The mean man tied me with a rope."

Scott cursed under his breath.

Somehow, Mariana kept her voice calm. "I know it's scary. But we're coming down to get you."

"Not him!" she gasped, her voice filling with terror. "He said he was going to teach you a lesson you'd never forget. But I don't understand what he was talking about. Why did he put me down here?"

Mariana sucked in a strangled breath. "He won't hurt you again," she said, then glanced at Scott as he tested the rope. "Can I tell her you're here?"

"Yes."

Her eyes locked with his for a moment, then she said. "Your father is with me. He came to get you out."

"My father?" she asked breathlessly, sounding as if she thought Mariana was telling her some fairy tale.

"*Sí,*" Scott answered as he tossed the rope down the hole and watched it disappear into the darkness. "I came back to help you and your mama—because I missed you very much."

Another wave crashed, the noise leaping up to meet them where they stood on the rocks. When Alicia spoke again, she sounded more frantic. "The water's coming in here. It's splashing where I'm sitting."

"I'll get you out," Scott told her. "Can you see a hole in the ceiling where the light is coming in?"

"Yes."

"Can you see the rope dangling down?"

"Yes."

"Is it touching the floor?"

"No. You should make it longer," the child answered.

"I can't. This will have to do." He tugged on the line once more, and it seemed securely fastened around the rock.

"Scott," Mariana breathed, her hand on his arm.

"Scott...what you said...about dark places. Can you go down there?"

"Of course!" he said.

He knew from her face that she was thinking about the way he'd been in the tunnel.

"I can do it!" he said, knowing that it was the only option. She nodded.

"If I tie the rope around her waist, can you pull her up?"

"Yes."

"I'll tell you when."

He turned away then, because he couldn't stand the look of uncertainty in her eyes. Wrapping his hands around the rough fibers, he stepped over the edge. Teeth clenched, he lowered himself down the vertical tunnel, into the blackness. The sound of waves crashing reverberated through the rocks as choking blackness closed over him. Nothing in the world would have induced him to venture into that cramped, closed space. Nothing except his daughter.

Above the roar of the waves, he could hear a child whimper.

"Everything will be okay," he called to her, amazed that he could speak around the clogged feeling in his throat. Gripping with his hands and legs, he kept lowering himself into the thick, clammy darkness, fighting the feeling that the rock walls were pressing in on him, crushing the life out of his body.

Closing his eyes helped, but the descent seemed to take forever. Finally, there was no more rope for his legs. Shifting his weight, he opened his eyes and waited for them to adjust to the dim light. Then he looked down and found he was only a few feet from where water was swirling over dark rock.

He jumped the rest of the way, half falling into water that snatched at him and sucked him forward.

"Alicia?" he called urgently.

"I'm here."

He turned his head toward the sound. In the dim light, he found a small figure huddled on a rock shelf several feet above the water. His own fear dissolved as he saw her cringe from a wave lapping at her feet. Emotions pummeled him, emotions as strong as the roiling water. But he had no time to indulge his feelings. Splashing through the surf, he reached for his daughter.

She shrank back against the cold stone.

"Alicia. Let me get you out of here."

"You're not my father!" she wheezed, scooting farther out of reach. "My mama told me my father has red hair—like my grandma. But I saw the light on you when you came down the rope. You don't have red hair."

He gave a bark of a laugh. "I thought it would be a good idea to dye it brown to help me hide."

"Tiá Susana did that to me! She dyed my hair brown. To help me hide, too."

"So we both look different," he said as a wave crashed around his legs, reminding him that time was of the essence. "But when we get out of this hole, we can both dye it red again."

"Can we?"

"Yes. But we have to hurry. The water is coming up." This time when he moved toward her, she scooted awkwardly to the side of the ledge, and he was able to lift her down.

He allowed himself one quick hug before he untied her hands and feet. As soon as she was free, she pulled something soft and floppy from inside her dress. It was a doll.

"Take care of Maria," she said, thrusting the doll at him.

He nodded solemnly and tucked the doll inside his shirt as he used the extra rope to lengthen the cord he'd come down on.

After tying a loop around her waist, he instructed her to hold on, then called to Mariana, "Pull her up, then throw the rope back down."

As the child jerked upward, she gasped and clutched the lifeline.

"It's okay. Your mother is up there," he told her, standing below the rope in case she fell. But Mariana pulled the precious bundle upward with steady rhythm.

The water was getting deeper, and he lost his balance as another wave roared in and struck him in the midsection. Bracing his legs, he struggled to keep from being sucked toward the mouth of the cave and into the open water.

God, if Mariana didn't throw the rope back down soon, he was going to be battered against the rocks.

Finally, after what seemed like an eternity, the rope appeared again. Grasping the end, he looked up, wondering if he had the strength to make it.

But there was no choice. Either he pulled himself out of here, or he drowned like a rat in a sewer. And he was damned if he was going to let that happen. Damned if he was going to lose Mariana and Alicia now. He pulled himself into the shaft, then braced his back against the rock so he could rest every foot or so.

The hard surface scraped his back through his shirt, but he ignored the pain as he willed himself upward, the muscles of his arms and legs straining.

"Scott? Are you all right, Scott?" Mariana's frantic voice drifted down to him. He longed to reassure her, but he couldn't spare the energy, so he kept moving wearily upward, until he reached the top and flopped onto more rock, his chest swelling with relief—and the sweet knowledge that he'd conquered his fear for all time.

Mariana came down beside him, clasping him to her, rocking him in her arms.

"Scott, are you all right? Scott?"

"Fine," he said, gathering her close, holding on for dear life, absorbing the warmth of her into his body.

When he raised his head, he saw a pair of solemn green eyes staring at him from three feet away.

"Come here," he said, hearing the thickness in his voice as he held out his hand to his daughter. She came to him, and he wrapped her close, holding her and Mariana in a death grip. Her face was pressed against his chest, and he felt her shoulders shaking.

"It's over," he choked out. "It's finally over."

"You saved her," Mariana breathed.

"*We* saved her," he corrected her.

They stayed locked together for a long time, until it finally penetrated Scott's numb brain that he and Alicia were soaking wet and cold.

"We'd better get back," he said.

Mariana nodded, but made no move to turn him loose. Gently he eased away from her, then led the way back to the car.

"Are you really my father?" the little girl asked from the back seat.

"Yes," he said, his throat so tight he could barely speak.

"Did you come to stay with us?"

He shot Mariana a quick glance. "We'll have to see about that," he said.

BACK AT DOLORES'S HOUSE, Mariana bathed her daughter, listened to her prayers, then put her to bed, aware all the time that Scott was watching from the doorway—that he was feeling like an outsider.

"Is he going to live with us?" Alicia whispered again as she snuggled under the covers, casting a covert glance toward Scott.

"I don't know," Mariana answered, wishing with all her heart that she could say something more.

She stole a glance at him again and saw that he was still holding Alicia's doll, shifting it from hand to hand. After a moment's hesitation, she said, "Why don't you bring Maria here?"

He looked uncertain as he crossed the room, then hunkered

down beside the bed. Alicia reached out her arms, and he handed her the doll.

"Thank you," she whispered as she tucked Maria under the covers beside her. She looked at Scott again. "And thank you for getting her and me out of that dark...wet place."

"I'm glad I could," he answered thickly, his hand reaching out to stroke the child's hair.

She moved her hand against his fingers, then asked shyly. "Would you give me a good-night hug?"

"Yes." He leaned down, clasped her in his arms, and Mariana's eyes misted as she saw his fierce embrace.

In the cave, had he already formed a bond with his daughter? Was it strong enough to last?

"Tomorrow night, would you listen to my prayers?" the child asked.

"If you want me to."

"I do."

"Okay," he answered tentatively, and Mariana wanted to tell him it wasn't such a difficult duty.

She could see he wasn't sure how to end the conversation, so she leaned over and kissed her daughter before getting to her feet. He did the same.

"You'll both be here when I wake up?" Alicia asked.

"Yes," Mariana said, hoping it was true, hoping that the rest of it would be as easy as hearing a child's prayers.

When she and Scott reached the hallway, she took his hand and led him into the other bedroom. As soon as they were alone, she dropped her pose of confidence and lifted troubled eyes to him, needing to say the words that were tearing at her.

"Whatever you decided to do, I hope you can forgive me," she whispered.

"For what?" he asked.

"For what I did six years ago. And then today—for doubting you. For lashing out at you when you wanted to leave me here. I know you were only trying to protect me.

And…and if I had stayed here the way you wanted, Bernardo wouldn't have recognized me,'' she ended with a gulp.

He pulled her to him and held her tightly. ''I would have had to deal with Bernardo and the rest of them soon enough,'' he growled, then softened his voice ''And about the other part, I've already forgiven you. I hope you can do the same.''

''Oh, Scott. I understand why you've hated me all these years,'' she said in a low voice. ''I—I betrayed you.''

He pressed his fingers over her lips. ''No. You did what you thought would save my life. I understand that now. And you have to understand that I needed somebody to blame for the mess I'd gotten myself into. I never should have trusted Thompson in the first place. And I shouldn't have trusted Pepe, either. I figured all that out before we got to San Marcos.''

She tried to absorb his words. ''Then why…why didn't you want to make love with me on the plane? Was it because you were…worried about coming back to this country?''

''That was part of it.'' He cleared his throat. ''And I was worried I might let you down. I told myself I didn't deserve to take anything more from you—until I could make sure you and Alicia were safe.''

''You weren't taking anything I didn't want to give,'' she breathed.

''Yeah, well, I was trying to be honorable. I was just a little too late.''

''You were always honorable,'' she whispered. ''That was the reason I stayed with you at Chipotalli. I knew you weren't like Bernardo. I knew you wouldn't do anything I didn't want to do.''

''And I knew I could get you to want things you shouldn't be doing. I knew I was skating on pretty thin ice in that hotel room with you.'' He shook his head. ''I was a greedy kid who thought he could have his cake and eat it too. With you.

With my film career. I was in over my head with Thompson, and I didn't know it."

When she started to point out the flaws in his logic, he stopped her with his hand again. "Just give me your forgiveness for not being there when you needed me so badly, when you were running and hiding and trying to be the best mother you could. And...and let me be here for you now."

He looked toward the other bedroom where his daughter slept. "I've missed so much of Alicia's life. It's tearing me apart that I can never get those years back. But I can make a new start. I can be a father to her from now on. And a husband to you. Will you let me take the two of you home with me so we can be a family?"

She stared at him as if she's just been offered all the gold and silver on the earth.

"Say yes," he growled. "Because I love you and I don't want to waste any more time away from you."

"You love me?"

"Oh, yes."

Overwhelmed, she felt her vision mist. "Scott, I've loved you for so long."

"Then say yes. Say you'll marry me."

"Yes," she breathed, her heart bursting with joy. Then he claimed her mouth in a kiss that rippled with the hunger neither one of them could deny.

She kissed him back with the same fevered need, and when he finally lifted his mouth, they were both forced to drag in gulps of air.

Yet there was still one more thing she needed to say. "Scott, I...I can't give you any more children," she whispered, her forehead pressed against his shoulder.

He crooked his thumb under her chin and lifted her face to his. "If that's true, we have Alicia, and she's the only child we need." He stroked his fingers along her cheek. "But that country doctor who took care of you five years ago may have been wrong. He probably didn't know all the techniques modern medicine has to help a woman who wants a child. Probably some of the stuff they're doing in the U.S. now hadn't even been invented back then.''

She felt the world turn upside down. ''There could be a chance for me—for us to have another baby?'' she asked in a trembling voice, hardly able to believe that she would be granted this wish, too.

''A good chance.''

''Oh, Scott.''

He kept his eyes locked with hers. ''But whatever happens, I have you and Alicia.'' He turned toward the door. ''I want to tell her that. So she'll know—tonight.''

She followed him down the hall again into their daughter's room, to find the little girl's eyes wide open.

''You weren't asleep,'' Mariana said softly.

''I was thinking about you and my father.'' She looked shyly at Scott, then away.

''What were you thinking?'' he asked.

''That I wanted you to stay with us—so we won't have to keep hiding from the bad people all the time.''

He came down beside the bed, and Mariana joined him. ''You'll never have to hide from the bad people again,'' he said in a choked voice. ''And now that I know I have a little girl, I want the three of us to live together and be a family. Would you like to come live with me in the United States?''

''Yes,'' she said, then added in a rush. ''And go to Walt Disney World?''

''Alicia!'' Mariana admonished.

But Scott only laughed. ''That will be our first stop.''

''Really?''

''Really. And when you come to live at my house we can get a pet cat. I always wanted to have one.''

''A cat! I always wanted to have one, too!''

He grinned. ''Good. Make that two fluffy kittens.''

Alicia held out her arms to him, and he gathered her close, then reached for Mariana and included her in the embrace.

"Has your mother told you I make movies?" he asked the little girl.

"Yes."

"Well, I like to get the ending just right. So now we can make this story come out the way we want."

"What story?" Alicia asked.

"Our story. Alicia and Mariana and Scott."

His eyes were warm and confident as they met first Alicia's and then Mariana's. She felt a smile unfurl across her face. If any man could make the ending to the story come out the way she wanted it, Scott O'Donnell was the one.

And there's more 43 LIGHT STREET!

Turn the page for a bonus look at what's in store for you in the next "43 Light Street" book by Ruth Glick writing as Rebecca York, coming to you in September 2000.

AMANDA'S CHILD

Breathtaking romantic suspense only from Harlequin Intrigue!

Chapter One

Matthew Forester had done some things he wasn't proud of. Eavesdropping on a client wasn't one of them—until he'd tuned in the bellowing voice coming from Roy Logan's private office.

Matt had come from Baltimore to Logan's Wyoming ranch to install a state-of-the-art security system. A month ago, he'd wondered why a western cattleman needed such stringent protection. After twenty-four hours on the ranch, it was obvious why Logan lived in an armed camp.

If Matt had been asked to pick a few choice words to describe Logan, it would have been "millionaire son of a bitch." But not out loud, since he was always respectful of Randolph Security's clients.

He'd been looking forward to finishing the job and flying home, until Logan had demanded that he stay on to do an analysis of future security needs. After conferring with headquarters, he'd gnashed his teeth and told himself he could take another two weeks under siege.

But he didn't like the arrogant, barrel-chested Logan, didn't trust him farther than he could throw a yearling steer. And when he heard the name Amanda Barnwell mentioned in the same breath as Roy's recently deceased son, Colin, he froze in place.

An image of Amanda rose in his mind, complete with poetic words and phrases startlingly foreign to his usual form of expression. Eyes the fathomless blue of mountain lakes. Hair sparkling with sunshine. A body with generous curves she invariably hid under loose-fitting shirts. And a voice that felt like warm honey sliding over his skin. To his mind, she was the most appealing female he'd encountered in Crowfoot, Wyoming.

Crowfoot was hardly more than a wide place in the road, but he needed to escape from the claustrophobic atmosphere of the Logan Ranch by driving there when he could. And he'd had the good luck to run into Amanda several times. The first time had been at the post office, when she'd captured his attention as she accepted a couple of boxes of books from the plump little postmistress.

"That girl deserves better," Mrs. Hastings had said as she watched Amanda climb into her Jeep Cherokee. "She stayed at home to take care of her mom and dad when they got too old to do for themselves. Now they're gone, and she's past thirty, and too prickly with men to catch herself a husband."

"Past thirty? You're putting me on."

"No indeed." The denial had been the prelude to a fifteen-minute earful of fascinating tidbits about Amanda Barnwell—from her upset win in the Fourth of July horse race, to her quilting skills—showcased at the school fund-raiser last year. Matt emerged into the afternoon light wishing he could get to know the intriguing Miss Amanda a whole lot better.

The desire had strengthened after he'd wolfed down a couple of her chocolate brownies at the church bake sale. He'd toyed with the idea of asking her out to dinner. Then he'd reminded himself there was no way a ranch-raised girl would be attracted to a hard-bitten ex-spy. Besides, there was no future in the relationship, since he was leaving in a couple of weeks.

Matt's attention was snapped back into focus by Roy's raspy voice. Easing sideways against the wall, he saw the tip of a snakeskin boot and knew Roy was talking to his foreman, Al Hewitt, the weasel-faced little guy who did the boss's dirty work.

"She's carrying my boy Colin's child," Roy growled. "And I want that baby."

Carrying Colin's child? Matt's dark eyes narrowed. A woman like Amanda had been mixed up with Roy's lowlife son?

The notion was ludicrous, and Matt's muscles tensed as he pictured himself bursting into the office, taking Roy by the shirtfront and shaking some sense into him. But there was just enough rational thought left in his brain to keep him planted where he was.

"You can't just go snatching a baby away from its mother," Hewitt objected.

"Anyone can be bought. If I offer her enough money, she'll be glad to let me take the responsibility off her hands. What's she going to do with a kid anyway—a woman alone?"

The imperious question made Matt's large hands ball into fists at his sides.

"She don't need the money," Hewitt said abruptly. "Old man Barnwell left her with plenty of assets when he kicked the bucket."

"That kid is the only thing I have left of Colin. The way I see it, I'm entitled to my progeny."

"Roy, this is twentieth-century America, not the Old West. You can't just steal that gal's baby."

"Who's gonna stop me?" the Lord of Logan Ranch retorted. "Since her papa died, there's nobody around here I can't buy. I damn well own Crowfoot—the real estate and the local cops. They'll look the other way if she disappears. And maybe it won't come to that. Go out to her ranch and make her an offer she can't refuse."

"Are you sure Colin is the father?" Hewitt asked.

"Do you doubt my source of information?" Roy said.

"No."

Matt heard papers shuffling. "This is the preliminary report from the detective I hired. He's good. When he digs up a little more dirt, I can nail the bastards who killed Colin."

"We can avenge Colin. That's no problem," Hewitt agreed. "But the girl is another matter. I don't think she's gonna play ball with you. She's got more guts than you give her credit for."

"Listen, with her parents gone, she's just another unprotected female. If we can't buy her, we wait for the kid to be born, then arrange for her to have an accident. Anything it takes."

Matt's stomach muscles clenched as he tried to wrap his mind around what he was hearing—even from a man like Logan.

"If you lean on her too hard, she might just skip town."

"Oh yeah?" Roy's chair creaked, and Matt imagined him easing forward. "I think you'd better arrange to scoop her up and bring her out here where we can keep an eye on her."

There was a moment of silence behind the office door, then Hewitt cleared his throat. "Not a good idea. Not with that Matt Forester fellow around. The way I read him, he might not like to see you putting pressure on the girl."

"Tell him the deal is off and send him packing. And keep the little mother in one of the line cabins until he leaves."

Matt heard a chair scrape back, then the sound of someone dialing the phone.

"Give me some privacy, will you," Logan growled.

Without making a sound, Matt eased away from the office door, knowing that he had to get to Amanda Barnwell before Al Hewitt beat him to the punch.

If you enjoyed what you just read,
then we've got an offer you can't resist!

Take 2 bestselling love stories FREE!

Plus get a FREE surprise gift!

Mother's Day is Around the Corner...
Give the gift that celebrates Life and Love!

Show Mom you care by presenting her with a one-year subscription to:

HARLEQUIN
WORLD'S BEST
Romances

For only **$4.96**—
That's **75% off the cover price.**

This easy-to-carry, compact magazine delivers 4 exciting romance stories by some of the very best romance authors in the world.

Plus each issue features personal moments with the authors, author biographies, a crossword puzzle and more...

A one-year subscription includes 6 issues full of love, romance and excitement to warm the heart.

To send a gift subscription, write the recipient's name and address on the coupon below, enclose a check for $4.96 and mail it today. In a few weeks, we will send you an acknowledgment letter and a special postcard so you can notify this lucky person that a fabulous gift is on the way!

Yes! I would like to purchase a one-year gift subscription (that's 6 issues) of WORLD'S BEST ROMANCES, for only $4.96. I save over 75% off the cover price of $21.00.   MRGIFT00

This is a special gift for:

Name

Address   Apt#

City   State   Zip

From

Address   Apt#

City   State   Zip

Mail to: HARLEQUIN WORLD'S BEST ROMANCES
P.O. Box 37254, Boone, Iowa, 50037-0254 Offer valid in the U.S. only.

COMING NEXT MONTH

#561 HER PRIVATE BODYGUARD by Gayle Wilson
More Men of Mystery

New heiress Valerie Beaufort was forced to depend on Grey Sellers for
protection. She didn't want a bodyguard, especially one with smoky silver
eyes and a secret past he refused to reveal. But with danger stalking
Valerie, neither of them could deny the attraction they shared—and
Valerie couldn't resist the lure of a man of mystery....

#562 PROTECTING HIS OWN by Molly Rice

Forced to flee with her best friend's twin children, Katelynn Adams took
on a new identity and began a new life. Until Joe Riley arrived with the
news that Katelynn and the kids were no longer safe. Life on the run led
to shared dangers and shared passions, but if Joe was the twins' father,
would Katelynn lose her children...or gain a family?

#563 THE LONE WOLF'S CHILD by Patricia Rosemoor
Sons of Silver Springs

Chance Quarrels's return to Silver Springs brought back more than old
memories for Prudence Prescott. Someone was out to silence Chance,
and when physical intimidation didn't work, Prudence and her daughter
became the villain's pawns. Chance knew he had to save the only woman
he'd ever loved. What he didn't know was that he'd also be saving *his*
child.

#564 NO BRIDE BUT HIS by Carly Bishop
Lovers Under Cover

Detective Ann Calder found undercover cop JD Thorne wounded and
without memory. Hiding out as husband and wife, Ann could only hope
that JD's instincts of friend and foe were correct. Until JD could recall
who had attacked him and the crucial evidence he had found, he and Ann
weren't safe—and unless they could put some distance between them,
neither were their hearts.

Visit us at www.romance.net